A.D. STARRLING

IT ALL STARTED WITH A BITE

DIARY OF A RELUCTANT WEREWOLF

BOOK 1

COPYRIGHT

BOOKS BY A.D. STARRLING

SEVENTEEN NOVELS

Hunted

Warrior

Empire

Legacy

Origins

Destiny

SEVENTEEN SHORT STORIES

First Death

Dancing Blades

The Meeting

The Warrior Monk

The Hunger

The Bank Job

LEGION

Blood and Bones

Fire and Earth

Awakening

Forsaken

Hallowed Ground

Heir

Legion

WITCH QUEEN

The Darkest Night

Rites of Passage

Of Flames and Crows

Midnight Witch

A Fury of Shadows

Witch Queen

The Incubus and The Bodyguard

SEVENTEEN UNIVERSE

The Party

DIARY OF A RELUCTANT WEREWOLF

It All Started With A Bite

DIVISION EIGHT

Mission:Black

Mission: Armor

Mission:Anaconda

MISCELLANEOUS

Void - A Sci-fi Horror Short Story

The Other Side of the Wall - A Horror Short Story

DEAD MEN DON'T SNORE

Dear Diary,
My life has officially gone to hell.

Abigail West
(Soon to be very hairy.)

The first sign that my evening had gone sideways wasn't finding the body sprawled across the front steps of Parkside. It wasn't even my best friend Ellie projectile vomiting into Mrs. Chen's prized hydrangeas. No, the first sign would be when Bo, my normally friendly Husky, took one look at the unconscious man we'd decided to bring into our place and tried to climb the wall of our apartment.

I blamed the tequila for how long it took me to

realize this wasn't normal behavior for a dog who regularly tried to make friends with anything that had a pulse. But I digress.

We were currently ETA minus fifteen minutes before this entire situation turned into a shit show.

"Ellie?" I kept my voice low, partly because it was two a.m. in our quiet East Valley neighborhood and partly because loud noises tend to attract attention when you're standing over a body. "Please tell me you're seeing this too."

A wet retching sound was my only answer. I grimaced. The last round of shots had been a mistake, but Ellie had just lost her job at Mystical Moments and drowning her sorrows had seemed like a good idea at the time. Watching her decorate the shrubbery in front of Parkside with the contents of her stomach was making me reconsider this decision.

The man on our steps hadn't moved except to emit a thunderous snore. He wore what had probably been an expensive suit before someone had used it to mop up what looked like pizza sauce. At least, I hoped it was pizza sauce. The alternative wasn't something my slightly buzzed brain wanted to contemplate.

"This is fine," I muttered in a calm voice. "Everything is fine. I'll just call the cops."

Ellie emerged from the bushes, mascara streaked down her face and fuzzy pink earmuffs askew.

"What are you doing?" she asked, swaying slightly.

"Looking at a body." I indicated Exhibit A.

Ellie's eyes rounded. She let out a high-pitched shriek and jumped behind me.

"Is he—is he dead?!" She clutched my arm in a death grip.

"No. Can't you hear him snoring?"

"Oh." Ellie slowly let go and adjusted her earmuffs, embarrassed.

I reached for my cell.

"What are you doing?" Ellie said.

"Calling the cops."

"Do we really need to?" She squinted at the unconscious guy. "He's probably had too much to drink."

"He could be a serial killer," I said leadenly.

Ellie rolled her eyes and almost fell over. "Serial killers don't normally pass out in front of their intended victims' apartment, Abby. He might be drowning his sorrows, like us."

She had a point about serial killers. I was about to stress that she was the one drowning her sorrows when I recalled my recent breakup. My ex's face swam before my eyes, bringing with it the immediate urge to punch a wall.

Ellie hiccuped. "He looks comfy."

I sighed. "We can't just leave him here. Mrs. Chen will have a coronary if she finds him in the morning. Remember what happened to the college kid who passed out in her petunias?"

We shuddered. Our elderly neighbor might look harmless, but she wielded her garden shears like a ninja assassin. The college kid was lucky not to lose an ear.

"You'd better clean her hydrangeas before she sees them," I advised as I started dialing 911.

Ellie grabbed my arm with surprising strength for someone who was dead drunk.

"Let's just have him sleep it off upstairs. What's the worst that could happen?"

Famous last words.

I looked at the man, at my watch, and at my best friend's pleading face. The smart thing would be to stick to my original plan and call the cops. But I had a meeting with the auditors in the morning and the last thing I needed was to spend the night giving statements at the precinct.

"Fine," I agreed reluctantly. "But if he turns out to be a serial killer, I'm blaming you."

Moving an unconscious man to our apartment turned out to be about as much fun as doing my ex-boyfriend's taxes. Which, incidentally, was how I discovered Mark was cheating on me. Nothing says *I'm a total dickwad* quite like finding receipts for couples massages when you've never had a massage with the guy.

"On three," I grunted, trying to lift the stranger's shoulders while Ellie wobbled uncertainly near his feet. "One, two—"

"Wait." She swallowed hard, her face turning a shade of green that matched the shrubbery. "I think I'm going to be sick again."

Ten minutes and two more hurling incidents later, we finally managed to drag our unconscious guest into Parkside's art deco lobby. The ancient radiator hissed and popped ominously as we shuffled past it, casting strange shadows across the black-and-white tiled floor. I tried not to think about how many security cameras had just captured us hauling what looked like a dead body through the front door.

"You know, I still can't believe Mrs. Owens fired me," Ellie mumbled, her voice echoing slightly in the empty space.

I made sympathetic noises while mentally counting the ways her former boss had shown saintlike patience. Considering Ellie's talent for disaster, the owner of Mystical Moments deserved a medal for not firing her sooner.

"I mean, how was I supposed to know that crystal skull was actually an antique?" She lowered the unconscious guy's legs to the floor and adjusted her earmuffs with dignity despite the vomit on her sleeve. "It looked exactly like all the other decorative ones we sell."

I waited until she picked up the deadweight before maneuvering the body around a potted ficus that had witnessed far too many of our embarrassing late-night returns. "Maybe because it was in the locked display case marked *Not for Sale* in giant red letters?"

"But that kid was so convincing! He said it was for his mother's birthday." She dropped the man's feet with a meaty thunk. "And he had cash!"

The fact that a teenager was carrying around that kind of money should have been her first clue something wasn't right. But Ellie had been missing social cues since kindergarten and apparently over two decades of friendship hadn't improved her radar for suspicious situations.

A strange warmth emanated from our unconscious guest as we approached the elevator, like he was running a dangerous fever. I wasn't sure if it was my imagination, but his hair looked thicker.

"Did you notice how the lights always flicker at Mystical Moments when Mrs. Owens gets angry?" Ellie continued, oblivious to my slight unease. "And things fall off shelves for no reason? I swear that place is haunted."

I swallowed a curse as she bumped into a wall of brass mailboxes. "Look, I know you're convinced Amberford is secretly full of supernatural creatures, but you can't keep using that as an excuse every time you screw up. We're not in ninth grade anymore."

"There really was a ghost in our class, Abby." Ellie's expression turned stubborn. "It was Minty Mindy, that senior girl who got murdered by that caretaker behind the gym."

I grimaced. Mindy Parsons, a.k.a. Minty Mindy, had suffered an unfortunate fate some twenty years ago at the hands of Eddie Wilco. The school-caretaker-turned-serial-killer was still Amberford's most notorious criminal.

The elevator dinged, its doors creaking open with painful slowness. We dragged our increasingly warm passenger inside.

"I thought this job was going to be different," Ellie said mournfully, jabbing the button for the fourth floor. "I mean, I had business cards and everything."

She fumbled in her pocket and produced a shiny rectangle. "With glitter!"

The elevator groaned upward.

"Maybe this is a sign you should try something else," I suggested. "Something less risky."

"Like what?"

2

STRANGER DANGER (AND OTHER VALID REASONS TO PUNCH PEOPLE)

I GRAPPLED FOR IDEAS. "HOW ABOUT A JOB THAT MAKES it less likely for you to sell antiques to minors?"

The elevator opened on our floor.

I grabbed the man's shoulders and tried not to think too hard about how this probably counted as assault. Ellie lifted his feet and pondered her options out loud as we shuffled down the hallway.

"I liked that yoga class you took me to last week. The instructor said I had potential."

The instructor was being polite, but I didn't mention this to Ellie.

"A flower shop might be a good idea," I grunted as I hefted the man's increasingly heavy body. "You're great with plants."

The guy's suit was straining at the seams, like his muscles had gotten bigger. Which was impossible, obviously.

The sound of frantic barking greeted us as we approached our apartment, the corner unit on the fourth floor. Bo's deep voice echoed through the door in a way I'd never heard before.

"Hush, Bo!" I hissed. "You'll wake the whole building!"

The barking cut off abruptly. That should have been a clue that all was not well with this situation.

Bo had never listened to a command in his entire life.

I managed to fish my keys out without dropping our now-feverish guest. The door swung open to reveal my Husky standing in the middle of our living room, pupils dilated, hackles raised, and teeth bared. I froze.

In three years of owning Bo, I'd never seen him bare his teeth at anything, not even the vacuum cleaner he was convinced was his mortal enemy.

"What's wrong with him?" Ellie asked.

Bo took one look at our unconscious companion and backed away so fast he crashed into the coffee table. A high-pitched whine escaped his throat as he scrambled in clear panic, knocking over my carefully arranged stack of accounting textbooks in his attempt to get away.

"Bo?" I said worriedly. "It's okay."

My normally friendly goofball of a dog was now trying to climb the wall while making sounds I didn't even know dogs could make.

"Maybe he's drunk too?" Ellie suggested hopefully.

I shot her a look. "He's been home all night. Unless he got into a secret stash of doggy vodka I don't know about, this is definitely not normal behavior for Bo."

"Let's just get this guy inside before my arms fall off," Ellie groaned.

We managed to get the man inside our apartment and onto our sofa. His legs dangled over the armrest.

I hadn't realized how tall he was until we laid him out.

The overhead light gave me my first good look at his face.

"Oh." Ellie squinted. "He's kind of cute."

She wasn't wrong. Despite being passed out and drooling slightly, the guy was attractive in that possibly-murders-people-for-fun kind of way. His dark hair fell across his forehead rakishly, his cheekbones and jawline were chiseled like a minor Greek god's, and his lips were perfectly formed and the color of cherries.

I looked closer. Yup, definitely pizza sauce.

Ellie cocked her head. "Is it me, or does his face look kind of hairy?"

I stared. She was right. The guy was definitely sporting more facial hair than when we'd found him on the steps, like he'd grown a partial beard in the time it took us to get him upstairs. My gaze found his hands.

They were also hairy. And his nails had grown oddly long and sharp.

Bo let out another whimper from where he'd wedged himself behind my grandmother's antique sideboard. The sound sent a chill down my spine.

I slowly backed away from the sofa. "Maybe we should call the cops after all."

Several things happened at once.

The man's eyes snapped open, revealing pupils that looked unnaturally yellow in the light. Ellie screamed in surprise. Bo dove under the dining table.

Our guest sat up with surprising speed, grabbed my hand, and bit me.

"What the hell?!" I yanked my arm back, more shocked than hurt.

The man blinked at me owlishly. "Oh," he said in a surprisingly refined voice. "You're not a squirrel." He giggled.

I did the only sensible thing I could think of.

I punched him in the face.

He collapsed back onto the sofa with a strangled gurgle, out cold once more.

"Oh my God!" Ellie's hands flew to her mouth. "Did he just bite you?!" She rushed over, stumbling slightly.

I stared at my hand, my heart racing. Two neat puncture marks decorated my skin. They were already starting to bruise around the edges.

"Looks like it."

"We should call an ambulance!" Ellie fumbled for her phone, dropped it, and almost face-planted trying to retrieve it.

"How about you sit down before you hurt yourself?"

"But he bit you!"

"And I punched him. I'd say we're even." A wave of dizziness washed over me, making the room tilt sideways. Either I was drunker than I thought or our guest had rabies. Possibly both.

Bo poked his head out from under the dining table and whined. He hesitated before rising and trotting over, making those odd huffing noises that sounded disturbingly like he was trying to talk to me.

"I know." I ruffled his ears, trying to ignore my now-itchy hand. "This is definitely not how I planned to end my evening."

Bo sniffed my wound and curled his lip like he'd just caught a whiff of week-old garbage mixed with essence of skunk. Coming from a dog who regularly tried to eat his own vomit, this wasn't exactly reassuring.

The man on our sofa started snoring again.

"I really think we should get you to the ER," Ellie said, her voice small. She looked anxiously from my hand to the unconscious man, guilt clouding her baby-blue eyes. "What if he has rabies?"

"He's not a raccoon, Ellie." I didn't tell her that I'd had the rabies thought too.

"But—his face! And did you see his eyes?!"

I was too tired for this. My head was pounding and my hand felt like it was on fire. All I wanted was to crawl into bed and pretend this night never happened. Maybe I'd wake up tomorrow and discover this was all some tequila-induced nightmare.

"Look, it's late, we're both drunk, and I have that meeting with the auditors tomorrow." I gestured at our comatose guest. "He's not going anywhere." I paused and glanced at my still-trembling dog. "And if he tries anything, Bo will probably hide under my bed, but at least he'll bark really loud."

Bo gave me a look that suggested he'd do no such

thing. In fact, he seemed to be contemplating moving to another zip code altogether.

"What about your wound?" Ellie insisted.

I flexed my fingers. The bite marks were fading to a dull red, which seemed wrong somehow. "It barely broke the skin. I'll put some antiseptic on it."

Ellie didn't look convinced. "If you're sure."

"I'm sure." I wasn't, but that was tomorrow-Abby's problem.

I made sure Ellie was safely tucked in and had a bucket next to her bed before I retreated to my room. Bo gave the living area a wide berth and followed close on my heels, like he was afraid I'd leave him alone with our guest.

"Some guard dog you are," I muttered as I changed into my pajamas.

He huffed and burrowed under my covers, tail sticking out.

I crawled into bed, my hand still tingling. A strange thought came to me as I drifted off to sleep. I really hoped my health insurance covered bites from mysterious strangers.

I had no idea that by this time tomorrow, insurance would be the least of my problems.

3

THE HAIRY TRUTH

I woke up feeling like someone had stuffed my mouth with cotton wool and replaced my brain with an angry hamster on a wheel. The hamster was either rabid or high on something illegal.

A voice broke through the wheel's maddening squeaks.

"Oh shit! Oh shit! Oh shit!"

I groaned and pulled the pillow over my head. It seemed Ellie was having another crisis. Probably discovered she'd drunk-ordered more crystals online again.

"This is bad," the voice whined.

That didn't sound like Ellie.

I cracked open an eye. Sunlight stabbed my retinas like a vindictive ex with a grudge. Pain exploded inside my head.

I moaned and brought a hand up to shield my face, only to freeze.

My eyes snapped open. Bile burned the back of my throat.

"What the—?!" I bolted upright and stared at my hands, my heart racing.

They were covered in hair. So were my arms. And judging by the way my pajama top was straining, other parts of me had undergone some disturbing changes overnight as well.

A sob from the corner of my bedroom made me look up. Ellie sat curled in my reading chair, mascara still streaked down her face from last night. She was clutching a baseball bat to her chest like it was the last life preserver on a sinking ship.

Bo lay on his belly beside her, his paws over his face and his large eyes peeking at me worriedly between his toes.

"Oh man," the voice groaned. "Wait till the neighborhood woofs hear about this."

I was about to ask Ellie how she'd mastered ventriloquism when I realized she wasn't the one doing the talking. A lightheaded feeling swept over me as my gaze found Bo.

"Wait. Is that you?!"

Bo blinked. He sat up abruptly, jaw dropping open and head tilting to the side. "Whoa. You can hear me?!"

I swallowed hard, my pulse loud in my ears. "I'm still drunk," I mumbled to myself. "That's it. This is some kind of tequila-induced hallucination." My voice sounded hysterical even to my own ears.

"I wish." Bo fidgeted and peeked at me from under

his lashes. "I gotta say, you're taking this better than I expected."

I stared at him some more before deciding screaming was a good idea right about now.

Ellie cried harder as my shriek filled the room.

Bo winced and dropped to the floor again, paws on his ears.

"Abby," Ellie hiccuped between sobs. "I think—I think you need to look in a mirror!"

I ignored her and pointed at Bo. *My dog is talking!*

Ellie's confused gaze swung from me to Bo. "What?"

"That's not even the worst part," Bo huffed. "Wait till you see yourself."

"Why are you talking? Why is Ellie crying? *And why can I smell Mrs. Chen's coffee three floors down?!*"

I realized I was shouting and took a gulping breath.

Panicking was going to achieve nothing.

Ellie uncurled from the chair, took a hand mirror from my dressing table, and approached the bed, her knuckles white on the bat. She held out the mirror wordlessly.

I stared at it like it was a tax audit before taking it with trembling hands. I was pretty convinced I was not going to like what I was going to see. My eyes bulged when I caught my reflection.

It was ten times worse than I'd imagined.

"Argh!" The mirror slipped from my fingers and bounced on the bed.

"I tried to warn you about that guy." There was a sullen undertone to Bo's whine. "But nooo, you had to bring the werewolf inside our apartment."

I stopped arghing and dragged my gaze from the furry freak show that was my reflection to the Husky. "The what?!"

A loud groan from the living room made Bo and Ellie jump.

Bo glanced in that direction and gulped. "Sounds like the werewolf is up."

I listened with half an ear, still staring at my reflection in the mirror on the bed in horror. My cheeks sported an impressive coating of facial hair. My normally wavy brown locks had developed a definite wild quality. Even my neckline looked hairier.

That thought brought me up short.

I peeked inside my pajama top. This proved to be a bad idea.

"I have boob hair," I mumbled hoarsely. I looked at Ellie. "*I have boob hair!*" I yelled, stabbing an accusing finger at my chest.

Ellie hiccuped and wiped her nose, her grip relaxing slightly on the bat. "Waxing those is going to hurt."

"At least you don't have a tail." Bo's attempt at helpfulness needed work.

Another groan came from the living room. It was followed by a man's protest.

"Hey, could you keep it down? My head is killing me!"

Something snapped inside me. Maybe it was the facial hair. Maybe it was the talking dog. Maybe it was the fact that I could actually smell Mrs. Chen's coffee three floors down (Colombian dark roast with a hint of vanilla).

I yanked the sheets off my legs, sucked in air at the sight of my hairy toes, arghed some more, and stormed out of the room. I ignored Ellie's squeak of protest and Bo's "Oh boy" as they trailed reluctantly behind me.

Our guest was sitting up on the sofa, his head in his hands. He looked normal except for a weird yellow tinge to his eyes and what appeared to be the mother of all hangovers.

He spotted me and paled. "Oh no."

His expression of guilt confirmed my worst suspicions.

This asshole was the reason I'd woken up looking like Bigfoot's sister.

"Start talking," I snapped, advancing on him. "What did you do to me?!"

"I can explain." He gulped and raised his hands defensively. "It was an accident. I was high on werewolf nip and—"

I hit him again.

This time, he managed to stay conscious. "Ouch." He winced and swiveled his jaw with a couple of toe-curling pops. "I probably deserved that."

"Probably?!" I snarled. The word came out more growl than human speech. I blinked, momentarily shocked.

"You really pack a punch," he mumbled, still rubbing his chin. He flinched at the sound of my knuckles cracking. "Look, I'm really sorry I bit you. I'm Hugh, by the way." He brightened a little and offered his hand. "Hugh Hawthorne."

I slapped it away. "I don't care if you're the Hugh

with the claws from the movies!" I jabbed a furry finger at him. "Fix this, whatever the hell it—!"

I froze as his words finally sank in. The dots connected inside my head like death knells. I looked jerkily at my hand.

"It was the bite?!" I said hoarsely.

"Yeah," he said, contrite. "There's not a lot I can do to fix it." He swallowed at my glower. "But my older brother can probably help. Samuel is the alpha of our pack and our problem fixer, so I'm sure he'll—"

I held out a hand, stopping him mid-flow. I was pretty certain I'd heard him wrong.

"Could you repeat that?"

"My brother's the alpha of our pack. You know, like a wolf pack?" A nervous chuckle left him. "Because we're werewolves? Well, I am anyway and now apparently, so are you."

"Told you so," Bo muttered from behind the couch.

I stared blindly at Hugh's glassy smile. My chest tightened as my sick new reality began sinking in.

"Werewolves aren't real," I denied.

My life was complicated enough without me turning into a four-legged monster that howled at the moon and avoided silverware.

"Says the woman currently sporting more facial hair than a Viking," Hugh said.

I lunged for him. Ellie grabbed my arm.

"No more punching the werewolf." She waved the bat warningly at Hugh. "Even if he deserves it."

"He totally deserves it," Bo said indignantly. "Abby

looks terrible. I'm never going to live this down at the dog park."

The hamster wheel started squeaking in my head again.

Hugh's eyes bulged. "Your dog talks?!"

"Apparently that's a thing now," I managed between gritted teeth.

"Why do you keep saying Bo's talking?" Ellie said, puzzled.

Hugh and I stared at her.

"You can't hear him?" I asked.

"No." Ellie glanced suspiciously at Bo. "Is he really talking to you?"

"Yeah," I muttered.

"You should hear what Ellie says to her plants," Bo grumbled. "Also, she lied about that speeding ticket she got when she was driving your car last summer. She had her coochie waxed that day and was rushing home to ice it."

Hugh and I exchanged a look.

"Maybe your dog has werewolf blood in him?" he hazarded.

We studied Bo. He was attempting to discreetly lick his balls.

"Which part?" I said.

I realized I was getting chummy with the guy who'd turned me into a human Sasquatch and resumed scowling.

"Can we focus?" I gestured at my hairy self. "What exactly is happening to me? I mean, how can I become a werewolf overnight? I was a perfectly normal human yesterday!"

"Normal is questionable," Bo muttered.

I cut my eyes to the Husky. He gulped and avoided my stare.

I glowered at Hugh. "Start talking."

Hugh cleared his throat. "Well, when a werewolf bites someone—"

I showed him my fist. "If you finish that sentence with 'and that's how babies are made,' I swear to God I will punch you again."

"Right." Hugh scratched his cheek. "The short version is it's not actually that hard to turn a human into a werewolf by biting them. It depends on the cycle of the moon." He paused, like he was choosing his next words carefully. "The good news is, Samuel can help you control your transformation since he's an alpha. The, er, the bad news is—" He stopped, a sheen of sweat suddenly beading his forehead.

"What's the bad news?" I asked dangerously.

"You'll have to join our pack. That's kinda nonnegotiable." A brittle smile stretched Hugh's lips. "Also, the next full moon is in three days. That's when you'll shift fully for the first time."

I closed my eyes and counted to ten. It didn't help. I opened them again and glared at the asshole on the couch.

"Take me to your brother. Right now!"

"Don't you have a meeting with the auditors this morning?" Ellie said worriedly.

Acid reflux hit my chest hard. I'd forgotten about the damn auditors.

"Turning into a werewolf sounds like a legit excuse to call in sick," Ellie said.

"My boss will kill me if I do," I groaned. I cut my eyes to Hugh. "How long will it take for your brother to turn me back to normal?"

"I don't know." He flinched when I took a threatening step toward him. "Maybe an hour!" he warbled.

"We better get going then."

"You should wear some kind of disguise before you go anywhere." Ellie chewed her lip. "Halloween was a month ago."

I looked down at my pajamas and hairy everything.

"She's right," Hugh said. "You look pretty frightful, if I say so myself."

Bo nodded. "Ditto. I don't want this news out on tonight's social howl."

I scowled and stomped out of the living room, hairy toes and all.

"Don't forget to grab a hat!" Ellie called out after me.

"And maybe a paper bag for your face," Hugh added.

"Bro," Bo said.

I slammed my bedroom door so hard the walls shook.

4

THE HAWTHORNES

"This isn't working."

I frowned at my reflection in the rearview mirror as I drove us out of East Valley. Despite my best efforts with concealer, a beanie, and Ellie's largest scarf, I was still projecting strong Sasquatch vibes. Luckily, we'd managed to leave Parkside undetected by our neighbors, though Mrs. Chen's cat had taken one look at me through her window and fallen off its perch.

"You look fine," Hugh reassured from the backseat.

"You look like someone tried to groom an orangutan with a leaf blower," Bo commented bluntly from the passenger seat.

I shot the Husky a dark look. "Not helping." I paused. "How do you know about orangutans?"

"I watch the Discovery Channel when you guys aren't home," my dog said with zero compunction. "Also, Marshmallow told us he saw one at the zoo once. That trip scared the poop out of him."

"Marshmallow?"

"The Saint Bernard who lives on the next street over. Friendly guy, if a little overzealous when it comes to butt sniffing."

I fervently hoped werewolves didn't sniff each other's butts.

"At least your eyebrows look good," Ellie offered helpfully from beside Hugh.

I scowled. "That's because they've merged into a giant unibrow."

"That's the least of your problems," Bo said solemnly. "Wait till your tail starts growing."

I froze, horrified. That thought hadn't even crossed my mind.

"That's not going to happen, right?" I twisted to glare at Hugh. "Right?!"

"Um." Hugh suddenly became interested in the scenery outside the window. "Oh look, there's Hawthorne Manor." He pointed with a maniacal grin.

I followed his finger distractedly. An estate appeared at the top of a hill in Temple Heights, Amberford's historic district. The windows of a mansion sparkled faintly in the distance between the treetops.

I dragged my gaze from our destination and narrowed my eyes at Hugh. "Answer the question. Am I going to grow a tail?!"

"Only when you shift," Hugh admitted reluctantly. "But hey, it's a really nice tail," he added hastily as I ground my teeth. "It's super fluffy and shiny, if you use the right hair care products."

"You're not gonna use my dog shampoo, are you?" Bo said suspiciously.

"No!"

"Good." He sniffed. "I like that shampoo. It tastes like strawberries."

"I personally recommend Fur-Ever Fresh," Hugh declared magnanimously. "If you're having a bad fur day, there's no beating Moon Shine: Extra Glossy Coat."

Ellie took her phone out and started taking notes.

"Oh God." I pulled up at a traffic light and thumped my forehead against the steering wheel. The horn blared, making us all jump and drawing a stare from the guy in the pickup next to us.

His eyes bulged when he saw me.

I hunched down and slammed my foot on the gas when the light changed. The car jerked forward, throwing us all back into our seats. Bo whined in protest.

"Maybe we should let Hugh drive?" Ellie suggested in a small voice.

My knuckles whitened on the steering wheel. "No one drives Ethel but me."

"You named your car Ethel?" Hugh asked.

"You use a shampoo called Moon Shine," I shot back.

"Touché."

We entered Temple Heights. I could practically smell the trust funds in the air as I drove us past mansions that made my apartment building look like a garden shed. The Subaru chugged painfully up to the top of the hill.

I turned onto a private cul-de-sac that screamed old money and rolled Ethel to a stop in front of a pair of wrought-iron gates. My eyes found the statues atop the stone pillars bracing them.

They were wolves. Big, bad, dangerous-looking wolves. My gaze dropped.

"Whoa, look at the size of his—" Ellie started hoarsely.

"Holy ding-a-long!" Bo's jaw had sagged open.

I wrinkled my nose at the left wolf's impressive privates before addressing Hugh in the mirror. "Was someone trying to compensate for something?"

He shook his head with a sad expression. "I wish I could say yes, but that's an actual real-life representation of my great-great-grandpa Russell. Poor wolf died a terrible death."

Bo, Ellie, and I shared an uneasy glance. Bar a well-appointed silver bullet washed down with a wolfsbane tonic, I didn't know of any other way a werewolf could die.

"How did it happen?" I said cautiously.

"He got run over by a coven while chasing the newspaper truck. Dreadful thing." Hugh shuddered. "Those witches are a menace. Air traffic control means nothing to them on Sabbath night."

Ellie sucked in air.

I blinked. "Wait. Witches exist?!"

"Yeah," Hugh muttered. "Amberford's full of them."

"I knew it!" Ellie hissed with righteous triumph.

"He's right," Bo said. "Mrs. Chen is a witch. Her cat Mimi is her familiar."

"Mrs. Chen's a witch?!" I gasped.

Ellie clutched her chest. "Mrs.—Mrs. Chen?!" she spluttered. "Our Mrs. Chen? You mean, the little old lady in 1B with the beatific smile and the deadly garden shears?!"

"The very one," Bo huffed. "Saw her sneaking onto her broomstick in the rear garden once. She was wearing red bloomers." He sniffed. "I bet she was wild in her heyday."

I translated for Ellie, my eyes glazing over a little at the mental picture of our mostly harmless neighbor riding a broomstick while sporting red underwear.

The gates rolled open, distracting me from my mildly hysterical thoughts. Hugh stiffened in the back seat.

"Looks like they know we're here," the werewolf mumbled.

"Is it some kind of special power?" Ellie's eyes sparkled with the enthusiasm of someone who'd just discovered the dark side of her town and was fully committed to relishing it. "You know, like a wolfy sense?"

Hugh pointed. "There's a security camera on the gates."

Ellie visibly deflated.

We drove up a winding driveway lined with ancient oak trees. The trees thinned before giving way to extensive, immaculate Victorian gardens. I was wondering what it cost to maintain them when an imposing Gothic mansion came into view.

The walls were dark red brick and draped in places in climbing roses and ivy. The facade was a myriad of leaded-glass windows, decorative buttresses and corbels, and ornate stone carvings, most of them creepy-looking gargoyles. A steep pitched roof crowned the rambling structure, the gables decorated with intricate wooden trimmings and finials. Chimneys with decorative pots populated the roofline.

My gaze found a majestic central tower with a crenellated parapet.

It looked like the kind of place princesses went to die.

I experienced a sudden urge to run for the hills and wondered maniacally if this was a werewolf thing or an Abby thing.

"Nice place," Ellie said tentatively.

"For a horror movie," Bo muttered.

I was with Bo on this one.

"It's been in the family since Amberford was founded," Hugh said with a trace of pride.

I pulled into a circular, graveled forecourt and parked Ethel in front of a set of impressive stone steps leading to a covered portico with Gothic arches.

"Anything else I should know before we go in?"

I was trying not to let my nerves show. After all, I'd literally just driven us into a den of werewolves.

"Samuel can be a bit intense." Hugh scratched his cheek awkwardly. "His bark is worse than his bite. And Victoria is very particular about, well, everything."

"Who's Victoria?" I asked suspiciously.

The front door opened before he could answer. A middle-aged butler with a monocle, a mustache, and a lofty expression appeared.

"Master Hugh." Relief danced briefly across his austere face at the sight of Hugh exiting the Subaru. "I am so glad to see you. Your mother has been most concerned about your whereabouts—" He froze when I got out of the car. His eyes bulged. "Master Hugh?!" he gasped, composure crumbling.

"I can explain, Bernard," Hugh said warily.

The butler's horrified gaze swung from my face to the embarrassed-looking man beside me. He whirled around and vanished inside the mansion.

"You have a butler?" Ellie said, impressed.

"Bernard's family have been our butlers for as long as our pack has been in Amberford," Hugh said distractedly.

The sheen of sweat was back. The werewolf looked like he was getting ready to run for those hills.

"Bernard didn't look too happy to see us," I pointed out.

The sound of a commotion reached our ears. A horrified *"What?!"* echoed somewhere inside the mansion.

Hugh tensed. Ellie and Bo shuffled behind me.

Rapid footsteps approached.

A tall woman in her fifties with silver hair pulled up in a tight bun and an expensive tweed suit appeared, her clothes in mild disarray. She was clutching a white

Persian cat with sapphire eyes and a diamond-studded collar to her bosom.

Bernard followed, his monocle askew.

Bo started wagging his tail at the sight of the cat.

"What a pretty kitty," Ellie breathed.

The feline acknowledged the compliment with a slow blink and curled a lip at the rest of us in a distinctly judgmental way.

"Hugh Bartholomew Hawthorne," the woman hissed in an incensed voice, "what did you do?!"

5

WHEN FATE BITES BACK

HUGH BOLTED.

Or at least he tried to bolt.

Luckily, my new werewolf reflexes warned me he might pull a sudden disappearing act. My hand found the collar of his suit a fraction of a second before he started running. A choked sound left him as I yanked him close, his feet still cycling wildly on the gravel.

"Don't even think about it!" I hissed in his ear.

To my everlasting surprise, Hugh couldn't fight his way out of my grip. He finally gave up and went limp.

Ellie and Bo looked impressed.

I dimly recalled supernatural strength being a reported attribute of werewolves. I was discreetly checking my biceps to see if they looked like tree trunks when I became conscious of a burning gaze.

I could tell the woman scowling at us from the doorway of the mansion was Hugh's mother. She was projecting strong mother-disappointed-with-her-offspring vibes, a look I recognized, having been the

31

victim of it on many an occasion. I determined this must be Victoria.

"Mother, please don't have a meltdown—" Hugh started.

"Shut it, Hugh!" Victoria Hawthorne hugged the cat closer. The feline looked down at us with aristocratic disdain.

I was starting to regret not running for those hills when I had the chance.

"Look," Hugh tried again, his voice strained. "It's not as bad as—"

"It's pretty damning from where I'm standing," Victoria cut in icily. "That woman smells like a newly turned werewolf." She narrowed her eyes slightly. "Also, she looks like she got into a fight with a hair dryer and lost."

"We should get you that special shampoo soon," Ellie whispered anxiously.

I lowered my brows at Hugh's mother. "This is your son's fault, so how about you cut back on the attitude, lady?"

An incoherent sound left Hugh.

The temperature seemed to drop several degrees.

"I don't believe we've been properly introduced." Victoria's tone could have frozen Hell. "You are?"

"Abigail West." I jutted my chin, refusing to be cowed. "Everyone calls me Abby."

"How pedestrian," someone muttered.

Bo's ears shot up. I looked down.

The Persian cat's tail swished slowly. Its sapphire eyes studied me with an unsettling intelligence.

"Did that cat just talk?" I asked leadenly.

"The cat talks too?!" Ellie gasped.

Victoria ignored my best friend and studied me with a measured frown. "I guess the fact that you can hear Pearl means you really are a werewolf." Her tone had mollified a fraction.

"Pearl?"

The cat answered in her stead.

"Lady Veronica Pearl Whiskerton the Third," the feline said haughtily. "Though you may address me as Pearl, since we'll be pack mates soon." She paused and sneered. "Assuming you survive the next full moon, of course."

Bo stamped his paws. "I don't like her."

My eyes shrank to slits. "I know a good taxidermist. Want me to take you there, Veronica?"

Victoria drew a sharp breath. Pearl made an angry sound.

Victoria recovered her composure first and examined Bo with pursed lips. "Your dog talks?"

"Yeah. Hugh here thinks he might be part werewolf."

Hugh nodded.

Victoria digested this information with a cold look. She turned to Bernard. "Fetch Samuel."

The butler adjusted his monocle and vanished inside with impressive speed.

"We should continue this discussion somewhere more private," Victoria said tightly. She swept inside like a queen, Pearl peering around at us from her arms with a withering stare.

"Is the cat always this charming?" I muttered to Hugh as we followed.

"Pearl doesn't like anyone except Mother," Hugh said morosely. "And even that's debatable some days."

"She smells like entitlement and expensive cat food," Bo huffed.

We entered a grand entrance hall with a sweeping staircase and a crystal chandelier that probably cost more than my annual salary. Multiple sets of eyes watched our progress from the gilt-framed portraits lining the walls. All of them looked judgmental.

Hugh's face had taken on a sheen of pure dread again.

I tried to distract him by indicating the portraits. "Your ancestors?"

"Yeah." Hugh looked relieved at my attempt to break the nail-biting tension hanging over us. "The hairy ones were painted during the full moon."

I stared at a particularly shaggy gentleman in Victorian dress. "That explains a lot."

"Watch your mouth, young lady." Victoria appeared from a corridor to the right, her expression pinched. "That's my great-grandfather you're talking about."

I blinked. "Russell the newspaper truck chaser?" I whispered to Hugh out of the corner of my mouth.

"The very same."

"This way, please." Victoria gestured in the direction of what appeared to be a formal sitting room.

The sound of heavy footsteps overhead made us all pause. Hugh went pale.

"That would be Samuel," Victoria said with grim satisfaction.

The footsteps reached the top of the stairs. I looked up.

My breath caught.

Bo's ears flattened. Ellie whimpered. The pair of them scooted behind me and peered anxiously at the figure on the landing.

Power poured off the man in waves. Samuel Hawthorne wore a crisp white shirt and dark slacks that did little to hide his impressive build. His dark hair curled at his neckline and was slightly disheveled, like he'd run his hands through it in frustration. But it was his face that caught and held my attention—all sharp angles and brooding intensity, his eyes blazing like amber fire behind his tortoiseshell-framed glasses.

Those eyes locked onto mine. We both froze.

Something electric shot through me. My skin tingled and my pulse spiked, sending every hair on my body on end. Judging from the way his pupils flared, he was experiencing a similar reaction.

The world tilted sideways.

"What the hell?" I mumbled, grabbing the nearest solid object for support.

Unfortunately, that turned out to be Hugh.

"Careful." He steadied me and shot a nervous glance at his brother.

Samuel's gaze dropped to where Hugh was touching me. He lowered his brows.

Hugh let go hastily.

"What's happening?" I managed between clenched

teeth. My heart was pounding like crazy and my skin felt tight, like I was about to burst out of it.

"Abby?" Ellie's eyes were wide with apprehension.

Victoria was staring at me, slack-jawed and ashen faced. "Oh God."

Bo fidgeted nervously beside me. "I did not see that coming."

"What?!" I snapped, an edge of hysteria to my voice.

"I think you just bonded with the alpha of the pack," the Husky quavered, tail tucked firmly between his legs. He gulped. "You're now technically his loony."

"Luna," Hugh corrected automatically.

"Loony, luna, same thing."

Ellie's eyes rounded until they looked like they were about to fall out of her head. Victoria swayed and clutched the wall in an overly dramatic fashion. Even Pearl appeared lost for words.

The sound of my heartbeat filled my ears.

Things had just gone from weird to wackadoodle crazy.

Samuel scowled at his brother. "What the hell did you do, you dumb mutt?!"

His roar echoed across the foyer and jolted me back to my senses.

"It's not as bad as it looks," Hugh protested.

Samuel and I glared at him.

Samuel descended the stairs, his heated gaze finding my face again. "Start with why there's a newly turned werewolf in our home. One who appears to be my—" He stopped, jaw clenching.

"Mate?" Pearl had recovered. The cat smirked. "The woman who will bear your pups—"

"One more word out of you and I will confiscate the gourmet food you've been hiding all over the mansion," Samuel said in a dangerous voice.

The cat hissed.

I realized I was hyperventilating. *"Pups?!"*

6

WELCOME TO THE PACK (NO REFUNDS OFFERED)

"ABBY!" ELLIE GASPED SUDDENLY. "YOUR FACE!"

"What now?" I managed hoarsely, trying not to let panic get the better of me.

I realized everyone was staring at me with varying degrees of shock. Even Bo's jaw had dropped open.

I swallowed and crossed swiftly to a gilt-framed mirror on the wall, dreading whatever fresh horror awaited me. Relief made me weak-kneed when I saw my reflection.

The fur was gone. Well, most of it anyway. My face looked normal again, if slightly flushed and marked with a fading unibrow. Even my hair had settled down from its previous feral state.

"The mate bond must have stabilized your transformation," Hugh said, stunned.

His words sent a shiver down my spine.

Samuel reached the bottom of the steps and addressed me curtly. "Who's your friend?" He cut his eyes to Ellie. "She smells human."

I returned to Ellie's side and shifted protectively in front of her. "This is Ellie Martin."

Ellie swallowed convulsively, a rabbit in the headlights. She blew out a sigh when Samuel's gaze switched to Bo.

"Your dog seems to have special abilities," the alpha observed.

It was more a statement than a question.

"Yes," I admitted grudgingly. "Although I just found out about it myself."

"Hugh seems to think he's part werewolf," Victoria murmured.

Samuel examined Bo with a critical mien. "Which part?" He paused. "Also, he looks weak for being part werewolf."

Bo sat up straight. "And your cat's a snob mister, but you don't hear me complaining." His ears flattened at Samuel's deepening frown. He slinked behind me, tail between his legs.

A sound I'd never heard before worked its way up my throat. "How about you stop picking on my dog?"

Samuel's eyebrows shot up at the feral growl. Something that looked like admiration flitted in his gaze.

I was certain I was wrong.

This guy seemed too pigheaded to look favorably on anyone.

Victoria cleared her throat in the tense hush.

"Perhaps we should sit down." She led the way to the formal sitting room.

I hesitated before heading after her with the others,

Samuel bringing up the rear. His gaze scorched my nape.

The room was exactly what you'd expect from the mansion's exterior: antique furniture, Persian rugs, and oil paintings of people who looked like they'd rather be anywhere else. Kind of like how I felt right now.

Bo plopped down beside me, his body pressed against my leg. I wasn't sure if he was seeking reassurance or trying to reassure me.

Ellie looked uncertain as she perched on the edge of a chair, her initial enthusiasm at discovering Amberford had a supernatural side fading in the face of my new reality.

Samuel stood by the fireplace, his presence filling the space like a brewing storm. He hadn't stopped staring at me since we came downstairs, his amber eyes burning with an intensity that made my skin prickle.

"Now, how about we start with how my idiot brother managed to turn someone in the middle of downtown Amberford?" he asked in a carefully controlled voice.

"It wasn't downtown," Hugh protested where he'd taken refuge behind a sofa. "It was on Abby's doorstep." He scratched his cheek awkwardly. "More precisely, it was when she and Ellie took me up to their apartment so I could sleep off my hangover."

Samuel's face darkened. "Because that makes it so much better."

Hugh flinched.

Pearl's tail swished like a metronome of judgment from where she sat on a side table. "I suppose we should be grateful he didn't do it at the mall in front of everyone."

Victoria pinched the bridge of her nose. "Why did you bite her?"

Hugh squirmed. "I was high on werewolf nip and thought she was a squirrel."

You could have heard a pin drop in the deafening silence that followed.

My mouth pressed to a thin line. At least the guy was honest.

Samuel and Victoria stared wordlessly at Hugh, like they couldn't believe he was that dumb.

"You were what?" Victoria mumbled, pale-faced.

A muscle jumped in Samuel's jawline. "We should have sent him to rehab, like I'd suggested."

I was in agreement. Rehab sounded like a nice place for Hugh to keep out of trouble and not turn random strangers into werewolves. Shame they didn't decide to do it before he bit me.

Hugh opened his mouth to protest and closed it hastily at his brother's glower.

I raised my hand. "Excuse me. I know we're all disappointed in Hugh, but I have a burning question. Can I be turned back?"

The Hawthornes studied me like I'd grown a second head.

"No," Samuel finally said. "Once turned, you can never go back."

"Samuel is right," Victoria affirmed.

A bout of acid burned the back of my throat. I swallowed the urge to scream or punch something.

Deep down inside, I'd suspected that was the case, but it still stung to hear it.

"What about the bond thing?" I said sharply. "Can that be reversed?"

Victoria exchanged a guarded look with Samuel. "No. The mate bond is permanent." She hesitated. "The only thing that can break it is death."

Ellie sucked in air. Bo's ears flattened.

My hands curled into fists.

"Shouldn't I have been consulted before that kind of thing happened?" I asked in a dangerous voice.

"The mate bond isn't something you choose." Victoria frowned. "It's fate. Neither mate has any control over it."

I lowered my brows, fury a bitter taste on my tongue. "Fate needs better timing!" I snarled. "I like my life just the way it is. I don't need werewolves in it or a" —I cut my eyes to Samuel—"*mate*."

He narrowed his eyes.

"There's nothing you can do about it," Victoria said adamantly. "You'll just have to come to terms with your new life." She hesitated. "Ideally before your first shift on the next full moon."

I blinked, the rage draining out of me. I'd forgotten about the full moon situation.

"That's in three days, right?" Ellie quavered.

"Yes."

I realized the Hawthornes were avoiding my eyes. "What?"

Hugh gave in to my suspicious glare first.

"The first transformation can be, er, difficult," he admitted nervously.

My stomach clenched. I did not like the sound of that.

"Shut up, Hugh," Samuel snapped.

"She should know this, Samuel." Sympathy softened Victoria's face a little as she studied me. "The first transformation will feel like every bone and organ in your body is breaking simultaneously. It gets better after that."

My head started ringing.

Ellie reached over and took my hand, her own trembling.

I squeezed her fingers and swallowed hard. "What happens if I decide not to shift?"

Victoria's expression turned grave. "That's not an option. Fighting the change can drive a werewolf insane." She faltered. "Or kill them."

Bo made a distressed sound.

"There are ways to make the process easier," Samuel said. "Training is one of them."

I blinked. His voice had turned surprisingly gentle.

"What kind of training?" I said hesitantly.

"The kind that teaches you to control your new abilities. You need to learn how to manage your strength and your enhanced senses." His eyes darkened. "And your temper."

I squinted, my ire returning tenfold. "What's wrong with my temper?"

"You growled at me earlier," he pointed out.

"You insulted my dog."

"I merely made an observation."

"Yeah? Well, observe this." I showed him my middle finger.

Hugh choked on air. Ellie swallowed a snort. Bo grinned. Victoria sighed and muttered something under her breath.

"How uncouth," Pearl said haughtily.

"Bite me, Veronica," I snapped.

Samuel's lips twitched. "Case in point."

I opened my mouth to deliver another snappy retort when Victoria cut in smoothly.

"Samuel is not wrong. A luna's mood can affect the entire pack. That's why you'll need to be in control of your emotions at all times."

That made me pause. I chewed my lip. "Is a luna really that powerful?"

"Yes. She's the alpha's mate, after all." Victoria tapped a finger on her knee. "Since we're laying our cards on the table, we might as well broach the matter of your future responsibilities. Of course, I don't expect you to take over your duties straight away."

Her words derailed my train of thought. I stared. "My what now?"

"As luna, there are certain tasks you'll have to take care of." Victoria's expression grew calculating. "Tasks I have been in charge of until now."

This was all happening too fast for my liking. I also couldn't help but feel Victoria was about to dump a whole bunch of stuff I had zero inclination in doing on me.

"Like what?" I asked warily.

"Pack administration, social obligations, maintaining diplomatic relations with other supernatural entities," the Hawthorne matriarch recited like a laundry list.

I grimaced. "Other supernatural entities?"

"Witches, vampires, fae." Victoria waved dismissively. "The usual crowd."

"Oh." Ellie's eyes sparkled with renewed interest.

"Don't forget the gargoyles," Hugh added.

"We don't talk about the gargoyles," Victoria said sharply.

Samuel, Hugh, and Pearl exchanged a loaded look.

Evidently, the Hawthorne matriarch had issues with certain aspects of her supernatural life.

"Let me get this straight," I said carefully. "Not only am I stuck as a werewolf, but I'm also supposed to be some kind of supernatural socialite and pack leader?"

"While maintaining your cover in the human world, yes," Victoria said. She hesitated. "Speaking of which, what is it exactly you do?"

"I'm an accountant at Pennington & Graves." I looked at my watch and frowned. "Which reminds me, I have an important meeting in an hour, so how about we wrap this up for now?"

THE FINAL AUDIT (OR HOW TO LOSE A JOB IN ONE BITE)

AN HOUR LATER, I WAS STANDING IN RICHARD Pennington Jr.'s office, staring blindly at my boss while trying to shut my nose down against the overwhelming stench of his cologne. The scent was clearly trying to mask something. Probably fear mixed with a hefty dose of smug satisfaction.

"I'm what?"

"You're fired," Pennington said flatly. "The auditors wrote a damning report about our accounts. You didn't even turn up for the meeting." He fixed me with an accusing look.

I glanced beseechingly at the ceiling and bit back a scream.

Between the craziness that had been the last eight hours and this fresh hell, I wasn't sure which one I was most pissed about. There was no way I could explain to my boss the extenuating circumstances that had led to my absence.

Sorry, a werewolf bit me last night and I spent the morning growing fur wasn't exactly going to cut it.

"No one informed me the meeting time had changed," I said in a hard voice.

"Really?" Pennington leaned back in his chair and sneered. "My secretary tells me otherwise."

I looked to my right and spotted his secretary through the glass wall overlooking the open work area that occupied most of the floor space inside Pennington & Graves.

Tina Compton studied me with a faint smirk where she sat in her cubicle. Mark Little, my ex, was leaning over her pretending to show her something. I could tell they were both listening in on the conversation through the open door. I narrowed my eyes.

Tina was the one Mark had gotten couple massages with.

Pennington spoke again. "I'd love to hear why our most reliable accountant decided to skip a meeting with Audit or Die."

I shifted my frown at my boss. "Who?"

"The auditing firm operating out of that renovated Victorian building next to the park, in the business district."

I'd never heard of them before.

Pennington picked up a file from the stack on his desk and shoved it toward me, a muscle jumping in his jawline. "They were very thorough. Claimed our software was unreliable and our methods bordered on illegal."

I took the damning report and leafed through it, my hands shaking slightly with suppressed rage.

The injustice of it rankled.

I refrained from pointing out to my boss the number of times I had expressed my concerns about the new accounting suite that had been forced on us three years ago.

There was no point. I had been judged and found guilty in my absence.

I clenched my jaw.

It was obvious what was going on. I was being made to take the fall for the firm's failure at passing the auditors' inspection. And it seemed my ex and his new girlfriend had conspired with my boss to get me fired.

A knock on the door made us both look up. Mark stood in the doorway, Tina hovering behind him. They were both wearing expressions of fake sympathy that made my newly turned inner wolf want to pin them down and rip their throats out.

"Are you okay, Abby?" Mark said awkwardly.

A threatening sound rumbled through my chest before I could stop it.

Pennington startled. Even Mark took a step back.

"That was just my stomach," I said through gritted teeth.

Pennington squinted. "You sure? Your eyes look a bit strange."

I caught my reflection in the mirror above the fireplace in his office. I was looking distinctly feral.

I swallowed hard and fought back the urge to show

them exactly how strange I could look. The wild thing under my skin was itching to come out and play. It was fifty-fifty whether I was going to give in to her.

"I'm afraid I had no choice, Abigail," Pennington said curtly, clearly eager to end this meeting. "Your employment is terminated, effective immediately."

"But—"

"Please clear your desk." Pennington wasn't even looking at me anymore. "Security will escort you out."

I fisted my hands so hard I almost broke my nails.

"Fine," I ground out.

I shoved past Mark and Tina.

"Hey!" Tina protested.

"Let her be, Tina," Mark murmured.

I stopped, turned, and gave my boss, my ex, and Tina the middle finger.

Ted from security helped me pack my desk into a cardboard box. He looked uncomfortable as he escorted me through the premises, the other staff keeping their heads down and avoiding my eyes.

I wasn't especially close to any of them, but the lack of support still stung.

"For what it's worth," Ted said as we waited for the elevator, "I always thought you were the only one here who knew what they were doing."

My throat tightened.

"Thanks, Ted." I shifted the box in my arms. "By the way, you might want to check the cameras in the break room. Kevin from Accounts Receivable has been stealing people's lunches."

Ted's eyes widened. "Is that why my tuna sandwiches keep disappearing?!"

The elevator dinged. I nodded and stepped inside.

"That monster," Ted said hoarsely.

If only he knew about the real monsters in Amberford.

"Take care, Ted."

I walked out of the building and into the late morning sunshine, my career in shambles and my personal life heading for the supernatural dumpster.

I couldn't help but scream a little then.

The people walking by jumped and shot wary glances my way as they circled around me.

My phone buzzed. I moved the box to my hip and slipped my cell out of my pocket.

It was a text from Ellie. *How did it go?*

I pursed my lips and typed back. *Remember when you said being turned into a werewolf was a legit excuse to call in sick?*

Yeah?

It was a legit reason to get fired too.

A series of shocked emojis flashed across my screen.

OMG! Three dots appeared as she typed. *Don't do anything crazy.*

My best friend knew me well.

Too late. I already gave my former boss the finger.

Shit. Stay there. I'll bring ice cream.

I looked at my box of desk supplies and sighed before messaging back.

I have a better idea. How about we go check out that

new cafe you were telling me about? I need caffeine and sugar. Lots of it.

Sure. I'll be there in fifteen.

I was sitting on a bench opposite my former workplace looking at the sky and pondering how my life choices had led me to this moment when Ellie turned up with Bo on a leash. She was oblivious to the admiring glances she was drawing as she bounced along the sidewalk like a bunny.

My gaze dropped to Bo. "What's he doing here?"

"He looked bored," Ellie said.

"I was bored," Bo panted. "Also, I wanted to make sure you weren't planning any revenge murders. Though if you are, I know where to hide bodies."

I frowned. "Have you been watching the true crime channels?"

Bo wagged his tail. "They're fun. I didn't know humans could be so dastardly."

It was beginning to dawn on me that my dog might have a more extensive vocabulary than my best friend.

"What'd Bo say?" Ellie asked curiously.

"Nothing you want to know." I decided to change the subject before my dog could offer more criminal suggestions. "So where is this place?"

Ten minutes later, we were standing in front of Bean Me Up. The coffee shop occupied the ground floor of a converted Victorian townhouse in Sycamore Grove, Amberford's artistic district. Macramé plant holders and dream catchers decorated the bay windows. A hand-painted sign on the sidewalk promised *Ethically Sourced Coffee and Good Vibes.*

I squinted at the building. Something about it felt different from other coffee shops.

"There's a vampire at the counter," Bo said helpfully. "And I'm pretty sure that guy with the dreadlocks sitting by the window is a werewolf."

I grimaced. "So that's what those smells are."

8

COFFEE, CREAM, AND SUPERNATURAL MUFFINS

"WHAT SMELLS?" ELLIE SAID QUIZZICALLY.

"Bo says there's a vampire and a werewolf inside."

Ellie's eyes lit up. "Where?" She scanned the interior of the coffee shop eagerly.

"One of the baristas and dreadlocks by the window."

Ellie started looking like a kid of Christmas Day.

Bo fidgeted. "This is a bad idea. We can't let Ellie in there. She'll probably ask the vampire to bite her."

I pursed my lips. My dog had a point.

The bell above the café door jangled, distracting us.

I sighed. "Too late."

"Oh wow! You should see their muffins!" my best friend said excitedly from where she'd already stepped inside the door.

I looked at Bo. "What's the worst that could happen?"

"That's what you thought when you brought the

werewolf into our apartment last night," he said solemnly.

I wasn't sure how I felt about my dog giving me sass.

"By the way, aren't vampires supposed to be permanently allergic to daylight?" I asked as we headed for the door.

"They're allergic to sun beds, not daylight. Gives them a nasty rash."

I made a face. "So my entire childhood was a lie?"

"You shouldn't believe everything you watch on human TV."

The interior of Bean Me Up was all exposed brick, mismatched furniture, and more macramé. Crystals hung in the windows, casting rainbow patterns across recycled wood tables. The air smelled of coffee, incense, and something distinctly otherworldly.

"That's our vampire," Bo whispered as we joined the queue. He twitched his ears at one of the baristas. "He's not breathing. I mean, he's pretending to, but he's not. The girl next to him is a witch."

I studied the pale young man behind the counter. He had multiple piercings and a T-shirt that read *Peace, Love, and Hemoglobin.* The witch was wearing a top emblazoned with the words *Sticks Rule.*

I could feel a cool but subtle divide between the two supernatural camps.

"Do witches and vampires not get along?" I asked Bo in a low voice.

I realized my dog was staring at a couple by the window.

"What is it?" I said warily.

"I think they're ghouls," Bo said hesitantly. "The brain muffins are a dead giveaway."

I stared at the loved-up pair flirting and sharing heated glances. The baked goods they were consuming looked suspiciously pink and gooey.

"They can't be real brains, right?" I asked leadenly.

"Let's just say I wouldn't order the house special if I were you," Bo advised.

"This is so cool," Ellie enthused in a voice that could probably be heard in the next county. "Do you think they have supernatural drinks?"

I was about to tell her not to be silly when someone ahead in the queue ordered a Blood Orange Mocha, type O negative. My gaze found the menu board. It contained a list of beverages and food items with worrying names.

We reached the counter. The vampire barista's name tag read *Virgil*.

"Welcome to Bean Me Up," he said with a cheerful smile. "Today's special is our Moonshine Latte with extra hair of wolf."

I stared at his sparkling canines. "Just a regular coffee and a doughnut. Black, two sugars."

Ellie beamed. "I'll have a Witch's Brew Chai and a chocolate éclair."

Virgil flushed a little. I could tell Ellie was going to be popular in the supernatural world too. The barista's nostrils suddenly flared. He looked at me more carefully, his smile fading.

"You're newly turned," he said quietly.

Surprise shot through me. "How can you tell?"

Ellie was too busy examining pastries to hear our conversation.

Virgil's expression turned sympathetic. "You haven't learned how to mask your scent yet. You smell like stress and rage."

I died a little inside.

"Anything for the doggie?" Virgil asked with a friendly glance at Bo. "He can have a muffin, on the house."

Bo's tail thumped the floor. "Thanks, bro."

"No problem."

I blinked. "I, er, thought you'd be more surprised by the talking dog."

Virgil and the witch gave me strange looks.

"Most supernatural creatures can communicate with familiars." Virgil reached under the counter and produced what looked like a perfectly normal blueberry muffin. "Don't worry, no brains in this one."

Bo's tail wagging intensified.

I made a face. "He's not a familiar."

Virgil startled. "He's not?"

"No, he's just a regular dog."

"I might be part werewolf," Bo added helpfully around a mouthful of muffin.

"Which part?" the witch asked warily.

I could feel ears pricking around the coffee shop.

Bo became the subject of intense stares. Not that the glutton noticed.

Virgil suddenly leaned in and sniffed me. He stiffened. "Are you with the Hawthornes?"

I hesitated. "Why, do I smell like them too?"

"What's going on?" Ellie asked. She'd stopped examining the cakes and was looking at us curiously.

"Nothing," I said. It wasn't nothing, but I knew instinctively now was not a great time to go into details.

Virgil had almost looked scared for a moment.

The witch snorted. "Yeah, right. A newly turned werewolf belonging to the Hawthorne pack is nothing." She gave me a warning look. "Watch yourself. That family plays rough."

"Penny," Virgil warned in a low voice.

"What?" The witch shrugged. "Someone should warn her."

My phone chose that moment to buzz. I fished it out while Virgil and Penny prepared our drinks, still digesting the red flags they'd just mentioned.

It was a text from an unknown number.

I'll pick you up at 8. Wear something you don't mind getting dirty. S.

I wondered if it was too early to ask Virgil to pour whiskey into my coffee.

Another text came through.

Bring the dog. He needs to learn pack rules too. S.

"How does he even have my number?" I muttered.

"Who has your number?" Ellie asked, adding a worrying amount of sugar to the Witch's Brew Chai Penny had just handed her.

"Samuel. Apparently Bo has to come to tonight's training too."

Bo's ears flattened. "I decline."

"It wasn't a suggestion."

Penny was staring at me. "Samuel Hawthorne is texting you?" Her eyes rounded. "Wait. Are you his—?!"

"Here's your change," Virgil cut in smoothly, all but shoving the money at me.

I got the distinct impression he was trying to protect me from something. Or someone.

We found a quiet corner table. The ghoul couple had finished their suspicious muffins and left. Dreadlocks shot glances at us from his seat by the window.

"I don't understand." Ellie glanced at the supernatural clientele with a confused look. "Why does everyone get weird when they find out you're with the Hawthornes?"

"Because the Hawthornes are dangerous," the peace lily behind Ellie said.

I stared. Now I was hearing plants talk.

Ellie swallowed nervously. "Did that plant just talk?"

"It's Mrs. Chen," Bo said distractedly. He was staring at my doughnut and drooling a little.

I pulled my plate closer.

The peace lily leaves parted to reveal our neighbor, sans shears.

Mrs. Chen wrinkled her nose at me. "So that's what Mimi meant. You went and got yourself bitten by a Hawthorne, didn't you?"

I grimaced. Since the whole of Amberford's supernatural community seemed to know what happened last night, there was no point denying it.

"Kinda."

Mrs. Chen rose and joined us, a cup of ginseng tea and a basket in hand. The basket meowed when she put it on the floor.

Bo sniffed it. A black paw shot out and booped him on the nose.

"Mind your manners, mutt," Mimi warned as she emerged from the basket.

I gave Mrs. Chen a glassy look. "I can hear your cat talk."

"Why do I miss out on all the fun?" Ellie whined.

Mrs. Chen ignored her. "That's normal. You're a supernatural creature now, so you can communicate with familiars."

I wondered if Pearl was Victoria's familiar and put a hard stop to the thought. That was a dark and tortuous road best not traveled.

Ellie was studying Mrs. Chen with growing curiosity.

"How long have you been a witch?"

"Since I was born, so longer than you've been alive."

Ellie missed the sarcasm and brightened.

Mrs. Chen gave her a sharp look. "No, you can't just become one."

Ellie visibly deflated.

Mrs. Chen cut her eyes to me. "The Hawthornes are trouble." She sipped her tea and pretended not to see the perturbed look Ellie, Bo, and I exchanged. "That pack has been in Amberford since the town was founded. Did you know they own half the businesses here?"

"No, I didn't." I hesitated before carefully adding, "Is being rich their only crime?"

"It's not about the money. The rumor mill is rife with stories about them. Strange disappearances. Small mom-and-pop businesses going under." Mrs. Chen frowned. "Let's put it this way. No one messes with the Hawthornes. Not if they want to live to see another day."

My stomach sank.

It appeared I was now a member of a mafia werewolf pack.

Mimi jumped onto the table and fixed me with a piercing stare. "You're his luna, aren't you?"

Mrs. Chen spat out her tea.

I frowned at the cat. "How did you know that?"

"You smell different. Not just because you're newly turned." Mimi flicked her tail. "You have the same aura as Samuel Hawthorne. Like you're his mate."

I wasn't sure I liked the sound of that.

Mrs. Chen patted her mouth with a paper napkin. "This is worse than I thought," she muttered grimly.

Unease coiled through me. I'd never seen my neighbor so uneasy. Not even when she found the college kid in her petunias.

She met my wary gaze. "Abby, you are now the luna of the most influential werewolf pack on the East Coast."

My mouth went dry. "What?"

"The Hawthornes aren't just one of the powerful supernatural families in Amberford," Mrs. Chen explained. "Their reputation and authority reaches far afield."

"Isn't that a good thing?" Ellie glanced awkwardly from me to Mrs. Chen.

Our neighbor shook her head. "No. It means Abby now has a lot of enemies. People who will want to use her or hurt her. A luna can be a pack's strength, just as she can also be its weakness."

Bo whined and pressed against my leg. Ellie hunched her shoulders.

Heat flushed through my body. "I didn't ask for any of this."

Mrs. Chen watched me for a moment. "No one ever asks to be turned." She patted my hand. "But fate has a way of putting us exactly where we need to be, whether we like it or not." She hesitated. "Maybe this was always meant to be."

9

HOW TO TRAIN YOUR WEREWOLF

Eight hours later found me standing in my bedroom and staring at my closet.

I was trying to figure out what constituted appropriate attire for werewolf training.

"How about your old yoga pants?" Bo suggested from my bed. "You know, the ones with the hole in the—"

"I am not wearing those."

"You said Samuel told you to wear something you don't mind getting dirty."

"That doesn't mean I have to look like I rolled in it first."

This was my third outfit change. Not that I was trying to impress anyone. I just didn't want to look completely incompetent on my first day as a supernatural creature.

"I may be overthinking this," Bo huffed, watching me swap shirts again, "but you seem to be paying more attention to your appearance than you did on your last three dates."

I flinched. I'd taken Ellie's stupid advice to get over Mark and briefly signed up to a dating app.

"Those weren't dates. They were mistakes."

"Like the guy who collected ceramic chickens?" Bo said innocently.

"We agreed never to speak of him again."

My phone buzzed. It was another text from Samuel. **_I'm outside._**

I checked my watch. 7:55 p.m.

"He's early," I muttered.

"Alphas probably don't do fashionably late," Bo commented, climbing off the bed with obvious reluctance. "Unlike some people I could name."

Luckily, Ellie wasn't in the room. Not that it would have mattered anyway, seeing as she couldn't understand my dog.

I grabbed my house keys and gave myself one last look in the mirror. I'd settled on black leggings and a fitted long-sleeve top that wouldn't get in the way. My hair was pulled back in a sensible ponytail.

I pursed my lips. I looked ready for a workout, not a supernatural training session.

The sound of an engine idling reached my ears as I exited my room. Even from four floors up, I could tell it was something expensive.

"That's a Bentley," Bo said, his nose pressed against the sitting room window. "Very alpha-ish."

I rolled my eyes. "Since when are you a car expert?"

"Discovery Channel did a series on luxury vehicles." He paused. "It must be new. I can smell the leather seats from here."

I realized that I could too.

These enhanced senses were going to take some getting used to.

Ellie popped her head out of the kitchen. "You leaving?" She had flour on her nose and smelled of sugar.

I grimaced. "Are you stress baking again?"

"Yes." Ellie's mouth pressed to a thin line. "Who can blame me after what Mrs. Chen told us this afternoon?"

I sighed. "I'm sure she was exaggerating. Also, you know I need to watch my calories."

"Not anymore you don't," Bo said.

I stared at him.

"Are you saying werewolves don't get fat?"

"Yes," Bo said, tail thumping the floor. "High metabolic rate and all that."

I brightened a little. The fact that I wouldn't put weight on was the only silver lining to my day so far.

"Not to mention the constant humping," Bo added.

"You're ruining the moment."

We said goodbye to Ellie and headed for the elevator.

"You ready?" I asked Bo as the doors creaked closed.

"Not really." His tail drooped. "Do I really have to come?"

"Yes. Samuel said you need to adapt to the pack."

He gave me puppy eyes. "My favorite show is on tonight."

I grimaced. "The one about serial killers?"

"No, the one about wolves in Yellowstone." Bo huffed at my expression. "Fine. But if he tries to make me do tricks, I'm filing a complaint with the ASPCA."

We found Samuel leaning against his car, arms crossed and expression unreadable behind his glasses. The street lights caught the amber in his eyes, making them gleam like a predator's.

My pulse quickened as the connection between us hummed to life.

"You're late," he said.

I checked my watch. "It's 8:01."

"It's 8:02, actually." His gaze swept over me. "At least you dressed appropriately."

"If you only knew how many outfits she tried on—*ow!*"

I'd stepped on Bo's tail.

Samuel's lips twitched. "Get in. Both of you."

Bo brightened. "I call shotgun."

"You're in the back," Samuel and I said in unison.

We looked at each other, startled.

Bo huffed and climbed into the rear seat. "This is discrimination against canines. Also, the two of you had better not canoodle while I'm in the car."

"No one is canoodling," I said firmly, sliding into the passenger seat.

Samuel's scent filled my nostrils as he got behind the wheel. It was something wild and masculine that made my inner wolf sit up and take notice.

"Where are we going?" I asked, desperate to focus on anything else.

"Somewhere private."

"That's not ominous at all," Bo observed from the back.

Samuel's mouth curved slightly. I could tell Bo was growing on him.

"There's a preserve outside town where the pack trains. It's protected by wards that keep humans away."

"Wards?" I raised an eyebrow. "Like magic?"

"Yes. The local coven maintains them for us."

I recalled Mrs. Chen's words about the Hawthornes owning half of Amberford.

"Do witches usually help werewolves?" I asked in a casual voice.

The way he glanced at me indicated he'd not missed my wary undertone.

"They do when it's mutually beneficial." His expression grew thoughtful, suggesting there was more to that story.

We drove in silence for a while, the lights of the city giving way to darker roads that wound upward into the forested mountains around Amberford. I became more and more aware of Samuel as his car ate away the miles.

Every breath he took. Every slight movement of his hands on the wheel. Every rustle of his slacks over his muscular thighs as he worked the gas and brake.

My nails sank into my palms.

I had never been so conscious of any human being in my entire life.

Of course, Samuel wasn't a human being.

I rolled down the window to cool my flushed face, convinced the mate bond was going to drive me crazy before the first full moon.

"You hot?" Samuel asked with a faint frown.

"Kinda."

His frown deepened. "It's probably to do with you having just turned."

I decided not to deny his assumption.

"So what exactly are those pack protocols we need to learn?"

"They are rules that keep order in the family," Samuel replied. "And ways of behaving that maintain hierarchy."

"Like rolling over and showing your belly?" Bo asked suspiciously.

"Among other things."

"I knew it!" Bo's tail thumped an annoyed beat against the leather seat. "This is totally going to involve tricks."

"It's not tricks," Samuel said with a sigh. "It's survival. A pack without order is dangerous to itself and others."

Something in his voice made me stare at him. "You sound like you're speaking from experience."

His jaw tightened. "Let's just say I learned the hard way what happens when wolves don't respect the hierarchy."

The Bentley turned onto a dirt road that led deep into the woods. I picked out details in the darkness I wouldn't have before, including eyes gleaming in the shadows. I suppressed a shiver.

"The wards start here," Samuel said. "You'll learn to feel them eventually."

He was right. Something buzzed against my skin for a moment, like static electricity but warmer.

"That feels tingly," Bo said. "Like that time I stuck my nose in an electric socket."

I twisted to stare at him. "Wait. Was that when our TV went out and blew all the fuses in the building?!"

"I was young and curious," Bo admitted without an iota of shame.

Samuel chuckled. I looked at him.

He shrugged. "It's funny."

The car emerged on the edge of a hilly clearing bathed in starlight. Samuel pulled to a stop under a sycamore tree and killed the engine.

"We're here."

I stepped out and looked around warily, my breath misting in front of my face. The space was roughly the size of a football stadium and ringed by oak trees, the heavy branches leaning inward to create a natural arena.

It smelled different here, like the whole place was charged with something old and wild.

"This is where the pack trains?"

"Among other things." Samuel shrugged off his jacket, revealing a fitted black T-shirt underneath. "It's also where we gather for full moon runs." He went to the back of the car and got a duffel bag out of the trunk.

I eyed it warily. "Do these runs involve hunting and killing prey by any chance?"

Samuel shot an amused look my way. "Yes to the hunting, no to the killing. Most packs stopped doing that decades ago."

I swallowed a sigh, relieved I was not going to accidentally rip Thumper's or Bambi's throats out. Another concern came to mind.

"How excruciating is my first transformation going to be?"

Samuel didn't sugarcoat his answer and I was strangely glad for that.

"It's pretty bad," he said curtly. "But I will help you as best as I can."

I swallowed. "Promise?"

I should have hated the vulnerability in my voice. But I found I didn't mind this man seeing me at my weakest.

Samuel stilled, his eyes flaring.

Both he and I sensed the slight shift in our bond. Like neither of us was fighting it that hard anymore.

"I promise," he said solemnly.

The air thickened between us. We took a step toward one another.

Bo licked his chops noisily. "Sooo, I get that you two are having some kind of moment, but I'm still here."

Samuel looked at the ground and muttered something under his breath. I sighed.

The Hawthorne alpha's expression turned serious once more.

"First things first. Your wolf? She's right there, under your skin. You need to learn to work with her, not against her."

The creature that had been prowling inside me all day stirred at his words. I nodded nervously.

Samuel's smile was like a punch to my gut.

"Good. I'm going to teach you how to control your strength."

10

SUPERSTRENGTH AND OTHER SURPRISES

SAMUEL GUIDED US ALONG THE EDGE OF THE CLEARING until he spotted what he wanted. He stopped and pointed.

"Pick up that branch."

He was indicating a fallen bough as thick as my arm.

I walked over and picked it up. It felt surprisingly light.

"Now break it," Samuel ordered.

"I can't just—" I started. The branch snapped like a toothpick in my hands. My mouth went dry. "Oh."

"That's why young werewolves undergo training as soon as they can walk," Samuel explained. "Better than them accidentally breaking something expensive. Or someone."

"Like Mark," Bo suggested helpfully.

"No mauling humans," Samuel said sharply. "It's our most important rule."

"Even if they deserve it?" I hazarded.

"Even then." Samuel wrinkled his brow. "Who's Mark?"

"My ex." I grimaced. "He and his new girlfriend got me fired from my job today. To be fair, my boss was also gunning for my blood."

Samuel blinked. "You got fired from Pennington & Graves?"

"The auditors weren't happy with the firm's performance. I was the sacrificial scapegoat." I waved the broken branch. "So how do I do this?"

Samuel hesitated, like he wanted to ask more questions.

"Control comes from focus and intent," he finally said. He picked up another branch. "Watch me."

He applied exactly enough pressure to crack the wood without shattering it.

"Your turn," he said.

I tried to copy him with my next branch. It disintegrated.

"Again," Samuel ordered. "And while you practice, let's discuss pack hierarchy."

"Oh boy," Bo muttered.

Samuel ignored my dog's sass. "The alpha's word is law. Always."

"What about the luna?" Bo asked innocently.

"The luna has significant influence too," Samuel admitted grudgingly.

An impish impulse had the next words out of my mouth before I could help myself. "Over the alpha?"

Bo looked impressed at my boldness.

"Over the pack." Samuel's eyes gleamed. "And over the alpha, when she chooses to exercise it."

The intensity in his gaze sent heat crawling up my neck. I broke eye contact first and went hunting for more boughs, knowing I was being chicken and not caring.

Three more branches met explosive ends before I started to get a feel for it. It was like learning to use a muscle I didn't know I had.

"Better," Samuel said when I finally managed to crack a branch cleanly. "Now do it ten more times."

By the eighth attempt, I was consistently breaking the branches with controlled pressure. It felt like something had clicked inside me. Like my human mind and new wolf instincts were beginning to sync.

Samuel's eyebrows rose slightly as he watched me fracture my tenth branch. "You know, you're learning this stuff faster than I expected."

"Is that good or bad?"

"It's unusual." He studied me thoughtfully. "Most newly turned wolves take weeks to develop this level of control. You've done it in under an hour."

"Maybe I'm just naturally talented," I hazarded.

"Abby is the smartest cookie I know," Bo huffed proudly.

"The other cookie you know isn't exactly smart," Samuel pointed out.

"Touché," Bo admitted grudgingly.

I was glad Ellie hadn't insisted on coming with us. But I also couldn't help but agree. I'd known Ellie since kindergarten and she was never the sharpest tool in the box to begin with.

"Next lesson," Samuel said. "Catching without crushing."

I wrinkled my nose. "What I am catching?"

He reached inside the duffel bag and removed a Tupperware.

"Oh." Bo brightened, his tail wagging. "Are we having snacks?"

"No." Samuel removed an egg from the container and tossed it at me.

I caught it instinctively. It pulverized in my grip. "Damn."

"I don't think you were meant to do that," Bo said unhelpfully while Samuel passed me some hand wipes.

"Let's try again," Samuel murmured.

Five minutes and fifteen eggs later, I caught my first intact egg.

Samuel's eyes widened a little. "Not bad." He recovered his composure. "Next pack rule. Showing respect to pack elders."

Bo stamped his forepaws with an indignant look. "If you say we have to roll over, I quit."

This coming from the dog who habitually exposed his stomach to complete strangers for gratuitous belly rubs.

Samuel sighed. "You don't have to roll over. You just need to be polite and courteous." He paused. "Speaking of which, you might want to reconsider your attitude toward Pearl."

Bo sniffed. "Your cat is a snob."

"He's not wrong," I said.

"She's not my cat. She's my mother's cat." Samuel rubbed the back of his neck awkwardly. "Look, Pearl has been in the family forever. She's like an heirloom no one wants. She was around when our pack first moved here."

Bo and I traded a cautious look. Amberford was several centuries old.

"Is she immortal?" I said warily.

"We don't know what she is, frankly. But no alpha has ever dared remove her from the pack."

"I reckon she was embalmed," Bo offered. "Like a mummy."

"He watches the Discovery Channel," I explained at Samuel's leaden expression.

"Anyway, everyone in the pack respects Pearl. And Victoria doesn't take kindly to disrespect either." Samuel picked up a tennis ball next. "Let's try something faster. Head over to the other side of the clearing."

I did as I was told. "Here?" I called out a moment later from across the way.

The ball came at me like a bullet. I snatched it out of the air, surprising myself.

"Again," Samuel said.

His throws got increasingly challenging, his arcs growing wider and his speed accelerating as he tested my reflexes.

I caught them all, some by the skin of my teeth.

"This is weird," Bo commented uneasily after my twelfth perfect catch. "Even for a werewolf."

Samuel's expression had grown brooding. He reached into his bag and pulled out a lacrosse ball.

"Last exercise," he said. "I don't want you to catch this one. I just want you to jump and stop it." He paused at my confused look. "Imagine creating a wall of compressed, moving air in front of your hand as you leap," he explained. "You want to time it perfectly so it meets the ball at the correct velocity. Focus all your senses on this."

What he was describing didn't sound within the realm of normal physics. I said as much.

Samuel shook his head. "Trust me, it's possible," he said confidently. "Even Hugh can do it."

I made a face. "That's not helping."

He smiled faintly. "It's unlikely you'll manage it the first time, but you'll get there eventually."

I hesitated before reluctantly agreeing to give it a try.

"Ready?" Samuel said.

I cracked my neck and shook out my limbs. "I'm ready."

He drew his arm back and threw the ball without so much as a warning. It whistled high through the air, so fast I would have missed its trajectory had I blinked.

Time seemed to slow as it curved toward my position.

I focused all my senses just like he'd told me to. My breath caught.

The air was suddenly sharper.

I could see every speck of dirt, every minuscule

droplet of water, every infinitesimal blade of grass being carried by the breeze.

Muscles bunched as I crouched, my gaze locked on the rotating ball, its every revolution crisp and clear. I jumped when my inner wolf told me to, hand shooting out and fingers clawing slightly to trap the wind.

The ball stopped dead an inch from my palm, the thump it made echoing across the clearing like a gun shot.

I landed lightly on the ground and caught the ball without even looking. I stared at it, my heart racing and my blood singing with elation.

"I did it!" I looked up with a grin.

Samuel had gone very still on the other side of the clearing. Even Bo looked stunned, jaw agog beside him.

My smile faded at their stares. It dawned on me that I'd just done something that shouldn't be technically possible for someone who'd been a normal human twenty-four hours ago. Elation gave way to apprehension.

"It was probably beginner's luck, right?" I said nervously.

Samuel and Bo exchanged a look.

The Hawthorne alpha frowned. "There's only one way to find out."

Five minutes and several ball throws later, we concluded it was not beginner's luck.

"Could Abby be a super werewolf?" Bo asked in an awed voice as I crossed the clearing to join them.

"Super how?" Samuel said guardedly.

Bo fidgeted. "You know, superstrong, superfast,

super—snarky? Is there such a thing in werewolf world?"

"No." Samuel studied me with a frown when I reached them. "How about we stop here for the night?"

I swallowed, unsure if it was disappointment or annoyance I was feeling. I'd executed his every instruction just like he'd told me to and yet I couldn't help but feel like I'd done something terrible.

Samuel's face softened at my expression. "You didn't do anything wrong, Abby." His fingers brushed mine as he took the ball back, causing the mate bond to hum between us. "It's just—I've never seen or heard of a newly turned human adapting to their inner wolf this fast. It's almost like you were meant to be a werewolf."

Mrs. Chen's chilling words came to me in that moment. From the nervous look Bo gave me, he was recalling the same.

Samuel ran a hand through his hair. "I need to talk to Victoria and our pack about this." His eyes darkened a little as he watched me. "Maybe someone knows something I don't."

The trip back to Parkside was taken up with him telling me and Bo the rest of the Hawthorne pack rules. He took out his cell after he pulled up outside our apartment building and started typing.

"I'm sending you an address." His fingers moved rapidly on the digital keyboard. "Be there at nine a.m. sharp tomorrow."

My phone pinged. I looked at the text he'd just sent me.

It was in downtown Amberford.

"Where is this?" I said warily.

"It's the headquarters of Hawthorne & Associates, our family firm. We're always in need of a good accountant."

"Oh." My chest tightened as I stared at him. "You're offering me a job?"

He hesitated, a strange look flitting in his gaze. "Yes."

11

WELCOME TO THE FIRM (TERMS AND CONDITIONS APPLY)

THE VICTORIAN BUILDING NEXT TO THE PARK IN THE business district looked exactly like what you'd expect from a place in Amberford's most expensive real estate: all red brick, ornate cornices, sparkling windows, and gleaming fixtures. You could almost smell the money in the air.

A large brass nameplate beside the impressive front doors read *Hawthorne & Associates: Financial Services* in elegant script.

What the nameplate didn't mention was the smaller firm operating from inside it. The one with the innocuous sign reading *Audit or Die* just beneath it.

I stood on the sidewalk, staring at that sign while my blood pressure steadily rose.

"What's the matter?" Bo asked warily.

"That's the firm that audited my old work place," I ground out.

"Oh," Bo murmured awkwardly. He scratched his

ear. "I guess that explains why Samuel looked weird when you mentioned you'd been fired."

I scowled. It also explained the guilty expression he'd sported as he'd driven off hastily last night, like the hounds of Hell were on his wolfy tail.

A stylish woman in a designer suit gave Bo a strange look as she passed us. Not because he was talking, but because he was wearing a service dog vest.

"I still can't believe you made me put this on," Bo grumbled.

"Would you rather wait in the car? Or better still, spend a day with a stress-baking Ellie?"

"No!" Bo protested quickly. "She's trying new recipes today. I don't wanna be poisoned." His tail drooped. "Still, this vest itches."

"Consider it training."

The woman reached the doors just as they opened from inside. A tall man with multiple piercings, vivid purple hair, and an expensive suit held it for her.

"Morning, Dave," she greeted.

Dave nodded. "Morning, Janet."

"You off to see a client?"

"Yeah. Count de Ville. He's claiming fang replacement expenses. Fifth time this month." Dave grimaced. "Watch out for Kevin. He's on a rampage about someone stealing his lunch again."

"That werewolf is an idiot," Janet said succinctly. She vanished inside the building.

Dave glanced at me and Bo curiously as he headed down the road.

"Didn't you work with a guy named Kevin?" Bo said.

Motion in an upper window caught my eye before I could answer. The morning sun danced off something beyond the glass. I squinted.

Whatever it was vanished from view.

Bo's ears flattened. "Were those tentacles?"

I chewed my lip. So I wasn't the only one who'd seen the tentacles. "It must be our imagination." I took a deep breath, straightened my shoulders, and headed for the doors. "Okay. Let's do this."

Bo didn't look convinced by my battle cry.

The inside of the building was all marble, potted plants, and strange smells. A security desk that looked like Fort Knox loomed at the far end of the lobby. A guard who could have doubled as a linebacker and a petite, mousy brunette sat behind it.

My steps echoed on the floor as I closed the distance to them, Bo's nails clicking along in tandem. I was wearing my best suit and heels and had definitely not spent the better part of an hour changing outfits this morning or putting on a thin veneer of makeup that made me look like I was naturally pretty without trying.

The guard gave me a once-over as I approached, like I'd committed a crime by just walking into the building. I got a whiff of a faint sulfurous smell and was wondering who he reminded me of when his expression cooled.

"Dogs aren't allowed in here."

"He's rude," Bo huffed.

The guard blinked. "He's a familiar?" The sulfur aroma got stronger. "He doesn't smell like one."

The receptionist was talking patiently to someone on the phone. "No, sir, we don't provide pet insurance for krakens. We don't deal in any pet insurance whatsoever. We're a financial firm."

I looked at Bo, certain I'd heard wrong.

He did a version of a doggy shrug. "Krakens are real. They said so on the Discovery Channel."

I squinted. "Which Discovery Channel are you watching?"

"The supernatural one. It's on channel 999."

The guard was leveling a wary stare at Bo's vest. "What services does he offer?"

"Sass and free belly rubs," I said a smidgen darkly.

Bo grinned, tail thumping the floor.

The receptionist's face had tightened. "I don't care if your Uncle Norman thinks we provide pet insurance, sir. We do not." A vein began throbbing in her temple.

The guard looked worried all of a sudden. "Hmm, Charlene, how about you calm down?"

Charlene ignored him. Her knuckles whitened on the phone handle and her expression turned glassy.

The guard dove under the desk and came up with what looked like industrial-grade ear protection.

"Here!" He tossed two sets of noise-canceling headphones at Bo and me. "Put these on! Now!" he said urgently.

I caught them reflexively, confused until I saw the way Charlene's eyes were glowing with an otherworldly light.

Bo ducked behind me.

I stared in horrified fascination as the receptionist's hair unwound itself from her top knot and began to lengthen, the tips turning silver as they levitated around her face.

"Sir," Charlene ground into the receiver, her voice taking on an echoing quality that made the hairs on my neck rise. "For the last time, we do not—"

Her mouth split to gargantuan proportions.

"Put your headphones on!" the guard yelled, already wearing his own pair.

I slipped my headphones on and barely got Bo's on him before Charlene lost it completely.

Her shriek shattered every piece of glass in the lobby. The security desk cracked down the middle. Three ceramic planters exploded, showering dirt across the marble floor. Even with the ear protection, the sound made my teeth vibrate and Bo whimper.

The echoes finally died down. The security guard removed his headphones, his expression weary. I hesitated before slowly taking mine and Bo's off.

Charlene looked mortified.

"I am so sorry," she said in a normal voice. She hung up the phone. "That's the fifth time this week someone's called about kraken insurance." Her hair was coiling back into a bun and her eyes had stopped glowing.

"It's probably just a prank, Charlene." The guard picked up another phone and dialed a number. "Hi, Janet? Yeah, we need someone from Risk Assessment down here. Charlene had another moment." He paused.

"No, no windows this time, just the glassware, some planters, and the desk. Thanks."

Bo was staring wide-eyed at Charlene. "This is my first time seeing a real-life banshee."

"Banshees exist?" I asked warily.

"It's about time you came to terms with your supernatural life," he huffed.

Charlene pretended she hadn't heard any of this, cleared her throat, and pasted a professional smile across her face. "How may I help you?"

"I'm Abigail West. I'm here to see Samuel Haw—"

A sudden change came over Charlene and the guard.

They stared at me with dawning awe and respect.

I looked over my shoulder just in case someone else had walked into the building. Like Pearl or Victoria.

Charlene beamed. "You are the new Hawthorne luna. Everyone is excited to meet you."

The guard nodded shyly.

I wrinkled my brow. "Samuel told you guys about me?"

"Hugh Hawthorne did," the guard said.

My mouth pressed to a thin line. Figures.

Bo looked at me. "Your future brother-in-law is a liability."

"I'm Charlene Armstrong, reception and front desk security," Charlene said. "I'm a banshee."

"I'm Fred," the guard said with a friendly nod. "I'm half demon."

That explained the brimstone smell.

I was surprised that I was not more surprised by

this. Maybe I was coming to terms with my weird new reality after all. Or maybe my sanity had fled the building.

I hesitated as I studied Fred. "Any relation to Ted, the security guy at Pennington & Graves?"

Fred blinked. "Good guess. He's my cousin."

Of course he was. "Is Ted also a—?"

"Nope, he's totally human," Fred said cheerfully.

Charlene handed me a security pass. "Mr. Hawthorne is expecting you. Take the express elevator to the fifth floor."

I stared at the pass. It already had my photo on it.

I sighed and headed in the direction Charlene had indicated with Bo, the receptionist's and the guard's stares boring into my neck.

"Bo?"

"Yeah?"

"Demons are real?"

"Yeah."

I grimaced. "How?"

"Ouija boards and summoning circles, mostly," Bo replied. "Humans do the craziest things."

The express elevator was hidden behind a panel of Brazilian rosewood. I accessed it with the pass and stared at the flashy interior.

It was all chrome and gold.

The mirrors made me uncomfortably aware of how nervous I looked all of a sudden.

"You smell like daffodils and stress," Bo commented as it rose smoothly.

"Thanks for that insight."

He perked up. "Want to rub my belly?"

"No."

The doors opened on the fifth floor. We stepped out of the elevator, stopped, and stared.

The scene in front of us could only be described as organized chaos.

The stylish woman in the designer suit we'd seen outside the building was cursing and chasing what appeared to be floating papers down a corridor, her polished look a thing of the past and her eyes glowing yellow. A man who looked suspiciously like Kevin from my old job was arguing with someone I couldn't see inside a break room. The carriage of a vintage typewriter moved ponderously on a desk in the open office ahead, keys click-clacking slowly under the hands of a pale figure with sharp canines, a suit that looked like it belonged in a museum, and a two-finger typist attitude. A woman with a pointy hat scowled and muttered under her breath while she color-coded a file with vicious swipes of her highlighters, a slick broomstick that looked like it could break the speed of sound floating next to her. A guy with horns and smoke curling out of his nostrils was rearranging the tiny fire extinguishers on his desk while he spoke with someone on the phone, reptilian tail swinging slowly where it poked out of his trousers.

"This place is a supernatural zoo," I said leadenly.

"Better get used to it," Bo contributed unhelpfully.

"Welcome to Hawthorne & Associates," someone drawled to my right.

I turned to find Hugh looking surprisingly professional in a suit.

"You work here?" I asked incredulously.

"Yeah." He grinned. "When I'm not high on werewolf nip."

A cold voice reached us then.

"I thought I told you not to come in today."

Hugh stiffened and stared past my shoulder, his smile fading.

SPECIAL INVESTIGATIONS, THE WEREWOLF WAY

I turned at the sound of Samuel's voice and nearly swallowed my tongue.

The man had been handsome as sin in casual clothes last night. In a perfectly tailored charcoal suit and silver tie, he was devastating in an ovaries-exploding kinda way. Even his work glasses looked more expensive than my monthly rent.

"You're drooling," Bo observed in a low undertone.

I closed my mouth. "I'm not."

Samuel's lips twitched as he approached us, like he could hear every word. He probably could, what with being a werewolf. His expression cooled as he turned his gaze on his brother.

"I believe I was clear about you taking the day off."

"I just wanted to welcome Abby to the firm." Hugh's voice had turned decidedly sullen.

"You've done that. Now leave."

"But—" Hugh fell silent at Samuel's frown.

Samuel sighed. "Look, Mother and I are still

deciding what to do with you, so how about you lie low for a while?" His gaze held a measure of tired resignation.

Hugh swallowed. "Alright." He slinked toward the elevator.

I reminded myself that I shouldn't feel terrible for the guy since he was the reason I was in this mess in the first place.

Samuel waited until Hugh was gone before addressing me. "My office is this way." He glanced at Bo's service vest and looked like he was biting back a smile.

I followed him past the open office, conscious of the stares following our progress. The guy with the horns accidentally set some of his paperwork on fire and cursed as he fumbled for an extinguisher.

"Is it always like this here?" I asked warily.

"This is a quiet day." Samuel led me down a corridor lined with meeting rooms and opened a door marked *CEO* at the end. "Usually there's at least one explosion before lunch."

His office was exactly what you'd expect from a high-end corporate type: all dark wood, expensive leather, and rich furnishings. My gaze moved from the floor-to-ceiling windows offering a view of the park to the wall of security monitors showing various areas of the building.

I was about to comment that this seemed a bit excessive when it dawned on me that this was a business belonging to one of the most powerful families in Amberford.

The Hawthornes probably had as many enemies as I'd had hot dinners.

Samuel indicated a Chesterfield sofa next to the fireplace before heading for the newfangled coffee machine on a sideboard.

"Drink?"

"Coffee, black." I hesitated. "Two sugars."

He saw Bo eyeing a selection of fresh muffins and tossed him one.

"Thanks, bro."

"Don't call me 'bro.'"

Bo was too busy snarfing his muffin to answer him.

"By the way, he doesn't need to wear that service vest," Samuel said. "Pets are allowed in the building."

A shining light of adoration gleamed in Bo's eyes. He wriggled out of the vest in a flash and rolled unashamedly around on the floor until he clocked my frown and Samuel's mildly disapproving look.

To my surprise, the werewolf took his coffee with a hefty amount of cream and four sugars. He brought my drink over and sat on the chair opposite.

I pinned him with a hard stare. "How about you tell me why Audit or Die is part of your business?"

Samuel had the grace to look uncomfortable behind his glasses. "It's the human front of Hawthorne & Associates. We only deal in supernatural affairs under our real name."

My fingers clenched on my porcelain cup. "Were your auditors the ones who recommended I get fired?"

"No." Samuel sighed and ran a hand through his hair. "I spoke to Dave last night, after you told me what happened. He said your reports were the only ones that made any sense."

I recalled the man with the piercings and purple hair we'd bumped into outside.

Samuel hesitated. "The rest of your firm's accounting practices were highly questionable."

My irritation drained away. "I can't deny that." I took a sip of my coffee and played with the handle of my cup before looking at him from under my lashes. "Did you offer me a job out of pity?"

Samuel's expression turned serious. "No. I offered you a job because we need someone with your skills." His gaze turned a little heated, making the mate bond spark between us. "I would be lying if I said the fact that you're my luna didn't influence my decision one iota. But I'm also running a business. I wouldn't jeopardize this firm's future just for your sake."

My breath caught. Though his words were cool and practical, his face was anything but. I crossed my legs nervously and shivered as his eyes focused on the shape of my calves.

Noisy panting had us both turning.

Bo was sitting on his rump grinning at us knowingly.

"He's far too sassy for his own good," Samuel said thinly.

"I have to live with him twenty-four seven," I muttered.

"I didn't say anything," Bo protested.

"You didn't have to." I finished my drink, put the cup down with a decisive clunk, and studied Samuel with a faint frown. "What does Hawthorne & Associates do?"

For once, he looked relieved at the question.

"We are a full-service financial firm serving the supernatural community in Amberford and several of the neighboring towns," he explained. "We deal with everything from cursed object insurance to vampire investment portfolios. We also handle more delicate matters. Ones that are never made public."

My wolfy sense tingled. "Define delicate."

Samuel leaned his elbows on his knees, his face growing focused. "We investigate supernatural fraud and track down stolen magical items. Managing territorial disputes between different species also falls under our remit."

I recalled what Mrs. Chen had said concerning the strange tales circulating about the Hawthornes and wondered if their secret activities were feeding the rumor mill.

I hesitated before asking him about it.

Samuel grimaced. "Your neighbor told you that?"

"She was just trying to help," I protested.

"I thought I smelled a witch in your building when I came to pick you up last night." Samuel rubbed the back of his neck. "Yes, those rumors concern our undercover work. We can't exactly shout it from the rooftop that many of the people who've suddenly disappeared from Amberford are criminals currently sitting in Darkside Prison."

Darkside Prison was a huge correctional facility in the mountains between Amberford and the next town.

I raised an eyebrow. "Even those small mom-and-pop businesses she mentioned that went under?"

Samuel's mouth pressed to a thin line. "They are the worst. You have no idea how many gun-toting and knife-wielding moms and pops I've had to face over the years."

Surprise shot through me. "You get down and dirty with the business?"

I realized how the words sounded the moment they left my mouth. I pinched my lips closed. Heat crawled up my neck as Samuel's curved in a wicked smile.

Bo was wheezing.

"Sometimes," Samuel drawled. "When it's an important assignment or the suspect is known to be especially dangerous."

I waited until my face cooled down before asking the most salient question of the morning. "What exactly would my role be in your firm?"

OFFICE POLITICS, MONSTER STYLE

"I WANT YOU TO JOIN OUR SPECIAL INVESTIGATIONS Unit." Samuel ignored my startled look. "Your accounting background makes you perfect for following paper trails and your new abilities will give you an edge in the field."

Except from finding out where Bo liked to hide my shoes and where Ellie habitually lost stuff, I'd never investigated anything in my life. I told him as much.

His smile did weird things to my pulse and had my inner wolf sitting to attention. "It's okay. We'll show you the ropes."

I swallowed at the idea of him showing me any kind of rope.

A knock came at the door.

"Come in," Samuel called out.

It was the stylish woman in the designer suit. She blew a strand of disheveled hair out of her face and gave me a curious glance before addressing Samuel.

"We're ready for the meeting."

"Thanks." Samuel made the introductions. "Abby, this is Janet Pearsons from HR. Janet, this is Abigail West, our newest employee." He paused and glanced at Bo. "This is her Husky, Bo. I imagine he'll be accompanying her most days, so it would be best if you included him in the paperwork."

Bo perked up. "Do I get a pass too?"

"No."

Bo's ears dropped.

We followed Samuel and Janet to a noisy conference room. The brouhaha inside died when we entered. Bo and I became the focus of curious looks as I took the seat Samuel indicated. Janet sat next to us.

"Everyone, this is Abigail West," the Hawthorne alpha said in a businesslike voice. "She's joining our firm as of today."

"So it's true." The woman with the pointy hat and highlighters studied me with an intense stare. "She's your luna."

Samuel narrowed his eyes. "Who told you that?"

"Hugh," Pointy Hat said with a shrug. "He told everyone in the building. Besides, we can smell your mate bond from a mile away."

I chewed my lip. The mate bond was becoming an embarrassing problem.

"Who's the canine?" the guy with the horns and reptilian tail asked curiously.

"This is Bo, Abby's dog." Samuel frowned. "Please refrain from looking at him like he's lunch."

He was addressing the pale man with sharp canines and the suit that smelled faintly of mothballs.

"I do not know what you mean, Samuel," the vampire drawled in an aristocratic voice that wouldn't have been out of place several centuries ago.

"I can tell you're trying to figure out his blood type," Samuel retorted coldly.

Bo slinked quietly behind my chair and peeked out nervously at the Nosferatu wannabe.

Janet gave me a reassuring smile. "It's okay. Barnabas knows where to draw the line."

"Yeah, right over the jugular," Pointy Hat scoffed.

Samuel's frown deepened. The room fell silent.

He began making introductions. "Abby, this is Barnabas Bludworth. He's our Head of Finance & Investments."

The vampire nodded regally. "You can address me as Barney, fair lady."

Samuel's expression grew pinched. "Dorothy Dupree is our Chief Compliance Officer." He indicated Pointy Hat. "You'll be working with her and Gavin Burlington, our Risk Assessment lead."

The guy with the horns nodded shyly. "Hi."

"You can call me Didi," Dorothy declared magnanimously.

Janet leaned sideways. "If she ever invites you to look at her private jar collection, run for the hills," she hissed into my ear.

"Why?" I whispered back.

"That's how she lured several of our clients before she turned them into frogs and put them in said jars," Janet said darkly. "That witch makes me stress howl at least once a lunar cycle."

My soon-to-be coworkers were not inspiring much confidence.

"And Gavin?" I eyed the faint trail of fumes curling out of the corners of Gavin's mouth.

"A nice if fire-prone dragon newt." Janet hesitated. "If your office supplies go AWOL, check his drawers. He's a compulsive hoarder."

Bo slowly wagged his tail. "I think I'm going to like working here."

"Eating all the muffins in the building doesn't count as work," I muttered.

Samuel continued the introductions.

"Over here, we have Mindy Parsons." He paused, his tone turning sharp again. "Mindy, I'm pretty sure I told you to make yourself visible for our biweekly meetings."

My pulse quickened.

A ghostly figure was flickering into view in what I'd taken to be an empty chair. It was a teenage girl with a militant expression, a school uniform, and a knife sticking out of her neck.

"Minty Mindy," I mumbled hoarsely.

Mindy grimaced. "FYI, I hate that nickname."

Bo fidgeted nervously and looked up at me. "Ellie is going to have a cow when you tell her ghosts exist."

"Mindy got murdered by a school-caretaker-turned-serial-killer when he found her rearranging the work tools in his murder shed," Janet revealed in a low voice. "Her organizational skills are why we hired her."

I was still reeling from the fact that the real reason behind Mindy's demise was because she'd had OCD and that my best friend had been right about ghosts all along, when a purple tentacle shot out from behind the large potted cactus near the window.

I froze. Bo's tail went south.

A human hand appeared and yanked the tentacle back.

"Nigel, we know you're behind there," Samuel said dully. "We just saw you."

Silence emanated from the cactus.

"No, you did not," a small voice quavered.

"It's okay, Nigel," Janet said soothingly. "There's no need to be afraid. Abby doesn't bite." She paused. "Yet."

The others made encouraging noises while I debated whether to take this as an insult.

Bo gulped. "What kind of supernatural creature is Nigel?"

I had a sneaky suspicion I knew the answer to my dog's question.

"He's the Thing in the Closet," Janet replied. She waggled her eyebrows at our expressions. "You know, *the* Thing in the Closet?"

"You mean, the boogeyman?" I asked carefully, just to be sure.

"Exactly." Janet looked awkward. "Except ours is a scaredy-cat."

"I changed my mind," Bo declared. "This place is full of weirdos."

I had to concur.

Mindy crossed her arms and heaved a sigh that was one hundred percent bored teenager. "Can we get on with this meeting? I have some copy machines to go haunt on the third floor."

Samuel cleared his throat. "Right. First order of business. We have a new case that requires immediate attention." He slid a file across the table toward Didi. "A cursed artifact was stolen from a witch's shop two days ago."

Didi took the folder and leafed through the contents, Gavin peering over her shoulder.

The witch frowned. "Someone stole something from Mystical Moments?" She looked at Samuel like he'd grown a second head. "That's one of the oldest magical establishments in Amberford. How could someone steal something from there? It's got first-rate security."

My stomach dropped. I had a horrible feeling where this was heading.

"I should clarify," Samuel said with a grimace. "It wasn't so much stolen as it was manipulated out of the hands of a gullible employee."

Bo put his paw over his eyes, clearly on the same wavelength.

Samuel shot a puzzled look our way before continuing. "The item in question is a crystal skull. It was disguised as a cheap decoration and locked up in a display cabinet."

Barney paled, which was saying something for a vampire. "Wait. You don't mean *that* crystal skull, do you?!"

Samuel nodded grimly. "The very one."

Didi's gaze swung between them. "What crystal skull?"

"It's an object of considerable power belonging to an old vampire family that liked to dabble in the dark arts." Samuel's expression hardened. "According to legend, the curse can control supernatural creatures in some way or another."

A chill ran down my spine as a deathly silence befell the room.

Controlling supernatural creatures sounded like the kind of crazy power a madman would be after.

The tension in the room broke when Gavin accidentally set the corner of his notepad on fire. He mumbled an apology and patted it out with practiced ease.

"How was the object stolen?" Janet asked curiously.

Didi's expression turned scathing as she continued reading. "According to this, the idiot employee sold it to a teenager while the owner stepped out to deal with an emergency."

Bo peeked at me worriedly from between his toes.

I could feel a sheen of sweat building on my forehead.

Samuel frowned at me. "Are you okay?"

"Yeah," Mindy muttered. "You don't look so good."

I closed my eyes and counted to ten. When I opened them, everyone was staring. There were no two ways around this. I was going to have to confess.

"My, er, best friend Ellie was the idiot employee who sold that skull," I admitted in a small voice. "In her defense, she had no idea it was a cursed artifact."

Samuel stared. "Ellie works at Mystical Moments?"

It was hard to tell if his tone held horror or disgust.

"She used to. The owner fired her after that incident."

Samuel rubbed his temples. It was a moment before he spoke.

"We believe the teenager in question was working for someone else. Someone who knew exactly what the artifact was."

Didi drummed her fingers on the table. "That thing might be on its way to a private auction house by now."

"No." Samuel's pupils flashed amber behind his glasses. "It's still in Amberford. Clarissa Owens, the owner of the shop, put a tracking spell on it. Although something is interfering with her ability to pinpoint its exact location, she's convinced it hasn't left town."

My stomach sank. Not only did my best friend accidentally sell a magical artifact, she might have put the entire Amberford supernatural community I now belonged to in mortal danger.

"So we need to track down this skull before it falls into the wrong hands?" I asked stiffly.

A tentacle emerged from behind the cactus. "Um, technically it's already in the wrong hands."

"Thank you, Nigel," Samuel muttered.

Bo and I jumped when a horrifying screech echoed from the depths of the building and rattled the windows. I clutched my chest.

It sounded like Charlene.

"Uh-oh," Janet said, pale-faced. "That was a DEFCON 3 warning."

Samuel muttered something under his breath and began rubbing his temples harder.

Didi licked her lips. "We still had her on DEFCON 3?"

Mindy flickered and faded. "I'm outta here. Catch me up later!"

The potted cactus near the window suddenly looked lonely, the boogeyman having also made himself scarce.

"What are you talking about?" I said once my heartbeat had slowed down.

The sound of heels clicking on the hardwood floor outside interrupted us. Samuel and my new coworkers visibly tensed, their unblinking stares following the approaching footsteps through the wall. Bo shuffled behind my chair.

A familiar figure opened the conference room door and swept inside in a cloud of respectability and *Chanel No. 5*, a white cat perched regally in her arms.

"There you all are," Victoria said. She was tucking away two sets of matching rose-gold noise-canceling headphones into her handbag. "And DEFCON 3, really?" she told Samuel sourly. "There are better ways to make use of your receptionist."

Pearl sneered.

The temperature dropped by several degrees. Hawthorne & Associates's top management looked about as pleased at seeing the pack matriarch as they would an inquisition.

"Why exactly are you here, Mother?" Samuel asked coolly.

"To take care of our new luna's induction into supernatural society." Victoria scanned my outfit and frowned. "You were right, Pearl. We can't have her running around in off-the-rack suits." She checked her watch while Pearl swished her tail with a smug expression. "Come along, Abigail. We're going shopping."

"What?" I blinked. "But—I'm in the middle of work!"

"I'm sure Hawthorne & Associates won't mind if its CEO's luna took a leave of absence for pack reasons." Victoria gave the room and Samuel a small smile edged with pure steel.

Samuel opened his mouth to protest.

His employees gazed at him beseechingly.

He hesitated before giving me an apologetic glance. "You should go with her," he said reluctantly. "Dorothy will catch you up on the case."

Traitor.

SHOPPING WITH WOLVES (AND ONE JUDGMENTAL CAT)

VICTORIA PULLED UP OUTSIDE A PRIVATE BOUTIQUE IN downtown Amberford and parked her Mercedes smoothly in a spot reserved for the clientele. I stared warily at the stylish frontage.

It looked like it catered exclusively to people who wiped their noses with hundred-dollar bills.

"Are you sure about this?" I said nervously. "I feel like my credit card might spontaneously combust just from being in the vicinity of this place."

"Don't be ridiculous," Victoria said briskly. "The pack pays for luna-related expenses."

I stared. This was my first time hearing this.

"Including designer clothes?" I asked suspiciously.

"Especially designer clothes." Victoria frowned. "You represent the Hawthorne pack. You need to look the part, not just at work but in day-to-day life and at social engagements."

I was beginning to think this sounded like a good deal bar the social engagement aspect until Pearl spoke.

"We can't have you looking like you're of common stock," the cat said disdainfully from the back seat.

Bo, who'd been forced to ride in the rear with her, made gagging noises.

I narrowed my eyes at Pearl in the mirror. "That taxidermy place isn't far from here."

The cat hissed. Victoria sighed.

We got out of the car and crossed the sidewalk. A discreet sign above the boutique's door intimated that its name was Moonlight Couture. A bell tinkled when we entered. I was hit by the smell of blank checks and what I was beginning to recognize as the distinctive bouquet of the supernatural.

I looked around nervously.

The place reminded me of the cover of a home interior magazine. The kind featuring a snake milker who hit it big and was now living the millionaire life somewhere exotic.

A willowy blonde with a scent similar to Mrs. Chen and Didi materialized from between racks of clothing that probably cost more than my annual salary. Her expression brightened.

"Victoria." She came over and air-kissed the Hawthorne matriarch's cheeks. "And Pearl, darling. How divine to see you both." She pecked the cat on the head.

Bo and I both curled our lips.

Her gaze landed on me and widened slightly. Even Bo got a once-over.

"Claudette, this is Abigail West." Victoria hesitated for a fraction of a second. "She's Samuel's mate."

Claudette's perfectly shaped eyebrows shot up. "The new luna?" She studied me more carefully. "I heard the rumor. How interesting." She paused. "And not at all what I envisaged for your son."

I narrowed my eyes slightly.

Claudette shot a puzzled glance at Victoria. "Wasn't there talk between your pack and the Luptons about an engage—?"

"Abby needs a complete wardrobe," Victoria interrupted hastily, "including shift-friendly pieces. She will require business outfits, evening wear, formal daywear for social functions, and casual wear."

I blinked, certain I'd just heard a distinct death flag. I decided to file this away for further investigation and focused on what I'd just heard.

"Shift-friendly?"

"Clothes that transform with you," Victoria explained. "Unless you want to keep destroying your wardrobe every full moon."

I blinked. "That's possible?"

"With the right enchantments, yes." Claudette was circling me like a well-dressed shark. "I must say, you have excellent bone structure. The clothes in my boutique will hang beautifully on you once we get you out of these"—she waved a derogatory hand—"department store pieces."

I looked down at my suit, which I'd thought was perfectly nice until about thirty seconds ago. "This is my best suit."

I lifted my head and faced a trio of pitying stares, Pearl's the worst of them.

"Now then," Claudette clapped her hands. "Let's start with casual and business wear. You'll need at least five suits for the office to begin with. We'll move on to formal day wear for pack functions and evening wear afterward. Girls, take her measurements."

A couple of shop assistants who looked like they belonged on the catwalk appeared out of nowhere. They took my elbows and ignored my protests as they ushered me toward a back room.

Victoria nodded approvingly and followed. "Oh and she needs something suitable for tonight's family dinner."

"A family dinner?" Claudette pressed her fingers to her mouth excitedly. "How lovely!"

I choked on air. "What family dinner?"

"You will be meeting the rest of the pack ahead of tomorrow night's run."

The reminder that I was T-minus thirty-six hours until I underwent my first full transformation resulted in a sharp bout of indigestion.

Victoria's surprise revelation about the family dinner was still sinking in when I was escorted into the boutique workshop. One of the assistants leaned in and inhaled discreetly as she guided me to stand on a low platform.

"Did she just sniff me?" I whispered to Bo.

"Yeah." He wrinkled his nose. "She and her friend are fae. Probably curious about your *Eau de Luna*."

That explained the assistants' stunning looks.

The next hour was a blur of pins, measuring tapes,

and increasingly expensive fabric as Claudette and her assistants brought out the shop's repertoire.

"Arms out," one of the assistants ordered.

"Higher," the other one said.

"Straighten your shoulders," Claudette snapped.

I swallowed an "Argh!" of protest.

Bo, Pearl, and Victoria were not helping where they sat on a velvet chaise offering a running commentary.

"That one makes her look like an angry banana," Bo said as I modeled suit number three.

"It's an improvement on the previous suit," Pearl contributed. "She looked like a tax collector."

"At least she doesn't look like something the cat dragged in anymore," Victoria mused. "No offense, Pearl."

"None taken, Victoria."

I gritted my teeth.

Just when I began considering running for the hills, Claudette emerged from the back room with what looked like a small fortune in silk. "Try this. It's for tonight's function."

I stared. The one-piece pantsuit was charcoal gray with subtle silver threading that caught the light. The fabric felt like water against my skin when I put it on, the neckline revealing the right amount of cleavage to be alluring rather than red-light-district raunchy.

"Now that's alpha mate material!" Bo panted.

Even Pearl looked impressed. "It'll do."

Victoria nodded. "That's perfect for tonight's dinner."

My stomach clenched. "About this dinner. I'm not sure I'm ready to meet the entire pack yet."

"Nonsense." Victoria waved away my protest. "They are dying to see who their luna is. Besides, Samuel will be there."

That was what worried me the most.

The mate bond had been difficult enough to handle last night and in his office that morning. How was I supposed to maintain my composure through an entire family dinner?

"Speaking of Samuel," Victoria said carefully. "Have you two discussed your sleeping arrangements yet?"

My eyes bulged. "Our *what*?!"

"Traditionally, the luna lives with the alpha," Victoria said like she was commenting on the weather. "And they share the same bed."

I scowled and straightened to my full height. "We are not having this conversation!"

Bo's tail wagged hopefully. "Can I have your room when you move out?"

"No one is moving anywhere!" I snarled.

"Actually," Pearl drawled, "the pack might have something to say about that."

I turned to Victoria. "Is she serious?"

The Hawthorne matriarch suddenly became interested in a rack of evening wear.

"Victoria?" I asked in a dangerous voice.

"Let's try on some cocktail dresses," Victoria said brightly. "You'll need them for pack social functions."

I looked at my reflection and wondered how I had gone from normal accountant to supernatural socialite in less than a day. Two hours and numerous shopping bags later, including a visit to a shoe store that specialized in shift-friendly footwear, Victoria dropped me back at Hawthorne & Associates.

"Don't be late tonight," she said as I climbed out. "Seven o'clock sharp."

"Sure," I muttered wearily.

"And bring the dog," Pearl warned from the back seat. "I chose that bow tie for him. He'd better be wearing it when he turns up."

"I will." Bo wagged his tail hesitantly. "I like the bow tie."

"Good," Pearl said, surprising us even more than when she'd picked out the accessory.

Had I been less tired, I would have been more concerned about my innocent Husky becoming friends with Satan's feline spawn.

Janet was waiting in reception when we entered the building.

"Ready for your orientation?" She clocked my leaden expression and gave me a sympathetic smile while Charlene and Fred pretended not to eavesdrop. "I see you're suffering side effects from your shopping session with Victoria. Don't worry, this is mostly paperwork and a tour." She paused. "Though there are a few, shall we say, unique aspects to working here that I'll need to point out."

The next hour was a whirlwind of forms, security protocols, and increasingly bizarre workplace guidelines.

"No blood drinking in the break room," Janet read from the employee handbook.

I realized she was directing a narrow-eyed stare at Barney.

The vampire looked up from his ancient typewriter. "What?" he said with an innocent shrug.

From Janet's expression, Barney broke that rule regularly.

Janet sniffed and continued reading. "No setting fire to the filing cabinets." This time, she side-eyed Gavin hard.

"It's not like I do it on purpose," the dragon newt protested, accidentally knocking over his collection of fire extinguishers.

"No turning anyone into frogs," Janet stated firmly, staring Dorothy right in the eye.

The witch uncapped a highlighter with a deadly sound and an even deadlier smile.

"And absolutely no unauthorized exorcisms," Janet finished. "Mindy gets very touchy about that."

The copy machine near the window made a threatening sound.

By the time the werewolf completed the tour of the other floors and finished introducing me to the supernatural staff making up the departments headed by Samuel's top management, a headache was hammering at my temples. I returned to the fifth floor to find Didi gathering her things.

"You leaving already?" I glanced at the clock on the wall.

It was only four p.m.

"I have a dental appointment," Didi said briskly. "Gavin is technically in his hibernation period right now, so he's gone home early. Be here at eight tomorrow. We're visiting Mystical Moments first thing."

I nodded, vaguely wondering how I was going to face Mrs. Owens after everything that had happened.

Didi paused, her bag on her shoulder and her broomstick hovering impatiently beside her. She studied Bo warily.

"Will he be coming with us?"

I looked at Bo.

"If you leave me at home, I'll chew your brand-new shoes," my dog threatened.

"He's coming with us," I sighed.

15

PACK DINNER AND OTHER FORMS OF TORTURE

THE SUBARU'S ENGINE PROTESTED AS IT CREPT UP THE hill toward Temple Heights. At this rate, I doubted I was going to get to the Hawthorne mansion in time for the dreaded family dinner.

"We would have been okay if you hadn't spent half an hour trying to console Ellie," Bo said sullenly from the passenger seat.

"We couldn't just leave her like that."

Ellie's day hadn't gone well. Not only had her new recipes been a complete disaster, she'd accidentally deleted her resume when she was applying for new jobs.

We'd come home and found her sobbing on the living room sofa, her hair caked in flour and eggs and her eyes puffed up like she'd had some kind of allergic reaction. I'd managed to get her into the bath before jumping into the shower and changing.

To my surprise, my best friend hadn't insisted on tagging along for the family dinner. I wasn't sure if this was because she was worn out or because she had an inkling it might be about as much fun as having a date with a serial killer.

The Subaru finally made it to the cul-de-sac. I used the remote control Victoria had given me to open the gates and headed up the driveway.

The Hawthorne mansion looked even more imposing at night. Light shone from the windows and smoke curled from several chimneys, the scent of burning logs sharp and crisp in the cold evening air.

I pulled into the circular driveway at precisely 6:59 p.m.

"Your heart's going crazy," Bo observed from the passenger seat. "You should calm down before you have a coronary."

"I am calm," I lied.

Bo adjusted his bow tie with a paw. "I can smell the acid reflux on your breath."

A figure emerged onto the portico before I could come up with a suitable retort. I stared, my heart going crazy for a whole other reason.

Samuel looked stunningly charismatic in a dark evening suit that hugged his powerful frame and left little to my fevered imagination. He'd slicked his hair a little and was wearing his tortoiseshell-framed glasses.

The sight of him made my inner wolf sit up and beg.

He came down the steps as I climbed out of the car.

"You're right on—"

Samuel froze, his eyes widening. His gaze swept over me in a way that made the mate bond sing, the amber fire that flashed in his pupils and the scent suddenly coming off him telling me he liked what he saw.

I swallowed and resisted the urge to fan my face.

"You look beautiful."

I blinked, surprised at the raw honesty in his expression and his voice. "So do you."

He smiled. "I would rather be called handsome."

My inner wolf went *Woof!*

Samuel's gaze dropped to Bo. His expression turned amused. "Nice bow tie."

"Pearl picked it for me," Bo preened.

Samuel blinked. His startled gaze switched to me. "She did?"

"Victoria practically fell off her chaise longue."

A concerning grinding sound came from Ethel's engine as the Subaru cooled. Samuel inspected the vehicle with a faint frown.

"Please tell me that's not your regular transportation."

"Ethel is perfectly reliable," I said defensively.

"You named your car Ethel?"

I lowered my brows.

Samuel sighed and rubbed the back of his neck. "We need to get you something more appropriate for a luna."

"But I like my car," I said mutinously.

"Your car sounds like it's about to die," Samuel said sharply. "At least let me find you something you can make a quick getaway in if you need to."

I narrowed my eyes. "Why would I need to make a quick getaway?"

"Your new job might land you in situations where that might become a priority." He made a face. "Also, you're about to have dinner with a pack of werewolves who are dying to meet their new luna. Some of them can be…persistent. And by that, I mean you might experience the sudden urge to make yourself scarce mid-dinner."

Great. I wasn't even through the front door and I already wanted to leave.

Samuel clocked my expression and escorted Bo and me into the mansion before I could change my mind. Bernard materialized out of nowhere and took my coat.

"The pack is gathering in the formal dining room," the butler said with a dignified nod. "Welcome home, Miss West."

I wasn't sure how to respond to that. From the way Bo suddenly pressed against my leg, he wasn't certain what to make of it either.

We followed Samuel down a corridor lined with more portraits of judgmental Hawthornes. The sound of voices and laughter reached us as we approached what had to be the dining room. My pulse quickened.

"Ready?" Samuel asked quietly.

"No."

His lips twitched. "They don't bite."

"Technically, your brother already did," I pointed out.

Samuel's expression darkened a little. "Hugh won't be joining us tonight."

I stared, surprised. "Victoria grounded him?"

"Something like that." He opened the double doors.

The dining room was as opulent as the rest of the mansion. I looked past the decorative wood paneling, crystal chandeliers, and the large windows overlooking the rear gardens to a long table dominating the polished parquet floor. It was already set for dinner with gleaming cutlery, glassware, and china that probably cost more than my apartment.

About twenty people were standing around talking, many with drinks in hand. Kids ran around the room playing. A teenage girl who looked like she would rather be anywhere but here sat next to the fireplace reading a book.

They all turned to stare as we entered.

Samuel waited until the brouhaha settled down before he spoke. "Everyone, this is Abigail West, our new luna." He glanced at Bo. "And this is her Husky, Bo. He's now an honorary pack member."

A heavy silence followed. Bo gulped and slinked behind me.

A tall woman with pretty features and dark hair finally stepped forward. "About time this pack got a luna." She offered me her hand with a friendly smile. "I'm Caroline Walsh, pack enforcer."

I relaxed a little and shook it, noting her firm grip and wondering what an enforcer did. "Nice to meet you. I'm Abby."

"This is my partner, Kent. He's also an enforcer."

Caroline indicated the bear of a man who'd appeared at her shoulder.

I stared. Kent's muscles had muscles.

"Welcome to the pack," he rumbled.

It dawned on me that enforcers probably meant pack security of some sort.

Caroline jerked her head at the reading girl by the fire. "The brat over there ignoring everyone is our daughter, Amanda."

Amanda apparently pretended not to hear her, licked a finger, and carefully turned a page.

"And this is our son, James."

A boy with bright eyes and sharp canines appeared in front of Caroline. He beamed at me. "You smell like Uncle Samuel."

Heat warmed my cheeks. Luckily, Samuel had drifted off to talk to a family member. Others came forward to introduce themselves.

"Don't mind the teeth, dear," an elderly werewolf said cheerfully through her dentures. She tugged me close with bone-breaking strength and kissed my cheek. "Silver bullets are hell on dental work."

"Aunt Lucille used to be a pack enforcer during Victoria's days as the alpha's mate," Caroline explained in a low voice at my expression. "She took a couple of shots when someone attempted to eliminate Samuel's father."

I swallowed hard. Assassination attempts had not been on the agenda of things Samuel had said might happen to me. I was wondering why I hadn't heard anything about Victoria's husband when an elderly gentleman in tweed introduced himself as Uncle Frederick and peered at me curiously through thick glasses.

"Do you like bugs?"

I blinked at the unexpected question. "Not especially."

Uncle Frederick deflated. "Oh. I was going to show you my collection."

I saw the encouraging looks the other pack members were giving me.

"I like butterflies," I volunteered hesitantly.

Uncle Frederick perked up. "Splendid!"

Though I tried my best, I couldn't remember half the names of the pack members who greeted me next.

"Don't worry," Caroline reassured. "You'll soon get to know them by their scent."

That statement warranted a drink. I eyed the wine bottle on the table with a calculating look. A heavy sigh distracted me.

"It's been so long since we've had a luna," an elderly woman named Margaret confided. She hesitated and shot an awkward look at me. "In all honesty, we expected Samuel would end up with one of the Lupton girls—"

"Margaret," someone cut in sharply. "We agreed not to talk about that."

I turned.

Victoria had appeared with Pearl. The Hawthorne matriarch wore a beautiful cocktail dress that matched the diamond-encrusted ribbon around the cat's neck.

"Hi," Bo panted at Pearl.

The cat jumped out of Victoria's arms and swished her tail in acknowledgment before bumping noses gently with the Husky.

Someone gasped and dropped a glass. The rest of the Hawthornes gaped, equally shocked.

"What?" Pearl said irritably at their stares.

"That's a first," Caroline said, deadpan. "I was expecting you to shred him to pieces."

Pearl sniffed haughtily. "The mutt is under my protection." She placed a proprietary paw on Bo's flank in a way that made my hackles rise a little.

My fool of a dog grinned and wagged his tail. "I am?"

"Yes."

The tail wagging intensified. "Wanna come over to my place for playtime?"

"Does Abby serve caviar?"

"No."

"Then, no."

I decided to bring the conversation back on track. "Who are the Luptons?"

Victoria exchanged a guarded look with Caroline and a few of the elderly Hawthornes. "Now might not be the best time to—"

"Now's the perfect time," I interrupted coolly.

Victoria sighed at my frown. "Pack alphas rarely meet their fated mates. Hence why packs usually arrange marriages between their children." She faltered. "You're the first luna we've had in three generations, Abby. The last one was my mother."

Surprise jolted me at this. I hadn't realized lunas were so uncommon.

"The Luptons are an old pack from Connecticut," Caroline explained cagily. "There were discussions about whether one of their daughters would be a good fit for Samuel."

"Discussions which are now irrelevant." Samuel appeared beside me, his expression tight. He passed me a glass of wine and pressed a possessive hand to the small of my back.

His touch ignited my skin and made my breath catch.

Caroline noted my reaction and gave me a shrewd smile.

Kent spoke. "There's something I've been wondering about." The werewolf enforcer was studying me with a focused look. "Does anyone else think Abby's scent is unusual?"

"I do," Aunt Lucille said promptly.

Uncle Frederick and Margaret nodded in agreement.

"Excuse me, Abby." Caroline leaned in and took a careful sniff of my neck before I could react. Surprise widened her eyes as she straightened. "You're right."

I became the subject of a battery of intense stares.

"What's different about my scent?" I asked warily.

"It's stronger and wilder than it should be for a newly turned werewolf." Samuel wrinkled his brow. "Even more so than it was yesterday."

"And sweeter too." Victoria was observing me with

an odd expression. "My mother was a luna and she did not smell like you."

"Is it my shampoo?" I grimaced at their leaden looks. "Okay, not my shampoo, then."

"Maybe it's related to your super-werewolf abilities," Bo suggested.

Caroline stared. "What super-werewolf abilities?"

"Dinner is served," Bernard announced from the doorway before I could respond.

A bevy of uniformed staff filed into the room with serving carts exuding a host of delicious smells. My stomach grumbled. I blushed.

Samuel smiled and offered me his arm. "Shall we?"

The mate bond sparked as I took it.

"This is going better than I expected," Bo whispered as we headed for the table. "Although I'm still worried about the way your heart is behaving."

I decided not to address that statement. And he was right. So far, the Hawthornes hadn't turned out to be the meddlesome busybodies Samuel and Victoria had intimated they were.

Maybe tonight's dinner wouldn't be as bad as I feared.

16

WITCHES AND MISSING SKULLS

DIDI'S BMW PURRED ALONG PROVIDENCE ROW AS WE headed away from downtown Amberford. I shifted uncomfortably in the passenger seat and did my best to ignore the headache squeezing my skull. It wasn't just my hangover that was getting to me.

My skin felt too tight for my body, my jaw ached from trying to stop what I suspected were fangs from sprouting from my gums, and my hair was threatening to go Shania-wild again.

The full moon was tonight and my inner wolf was evidently more than ready to greet the world.

"It's the worst before your first shift," Didi said, noting my discomfort. "Though I must admit, you're handling it better than most natural werewolves."

I thought back to the tense expressions I'd seen at the office that morning. Even Gavin had commented on how agitated the werewolves in Compliance had been.

"Speaking of handling things well," the dragon newt

said behind me, "how did the pack dinner go yesterday?"

I squinted at him in the rearview mirror.

"How do you know about the pack dinner?"

"Charlene tattled," Didi said. "Hugh told her before he left the office yesterday." She rolled her eyes at my indignant look. "You might as well make your peace with it. Nothing is sacred at Hawthorne & Associates."

I pursed my lips.

The witch was right. I couldn't spend the rest of my days being constantly surprised at what was considered normal behavior in the supernatural community, even if said behavior was wholly inappropriate in the human world.

My headache worsened as I relived the first half of last night's dinner conversation. None of the Hawthornes could explain why I was adapting so quickly to being a werewolf or why I'd demonstrated abilities during my training with Samuel that should have been impossible for someone so newly turned.

Didi's voice interrupted my troubled thoughts.

"Well?" the witch said with unabashed curiosity. "How *did* the dinner go?"

"The food was great and no one died," I said flatly.

Didi's mouth pressed to a thin line. "We don't want cryptic, Abby. We want details."

"I got a whole chicken to myself," Bo volunteered cheerfully from the back seat. "And Abby got drunk, although I'm not sure if it was the alcohol, Samuel's pheromones, or the persistent questions about their mating habits."

Gavin sucked in air, his expression one of shocked delight.

Didi smirked. "So the pack wants you and the alpha to do the dirty—?"

"How about we not go there?" I interrupted coolly.

Heat crawled up my neck as I remembered the latter half of the dinner.

Having lulled me into a sense of false security, the pack members had turned merciless over dessert and coffee. I still wasn't sure which had been worse: the questions about my prior relationships and sex life, their comments on Samuel's stamina, or their bold ideas on the exact sleeping arrangements of their alpha and his new luna, including how many times we should mate a week.

Bar giving me tired looks that said they'd warned me about this, Samuel and Victoria had been of zero help.

As for the mate bond, it had practically sung a hallelujah every time Samuel had looked at me or his hand had brushed mine during dinner. His scent had nearly driven me to distraction, to the point I had drunk far more than I would normally have under the circumstances.

Since he hadn't had anything to drink, Samuel had dropped me and Bo back home and had promised to get Ethel over to the office sometime today.

I had a dim memory of making a fool of myself in his car on the drive to Parkside. From the way Bo was smirking at me this morning, I suspected the memory was accurate.

Luckily, I hadn't seen Samuel that morning to confirm this.

"I heard Pearl actually acknowledged your dog's existence," Didi said. "That's practically a miracle in itself."

"Who told you that?"

"Caroline. We're friends."

I scowled. So she really didn't need the details about the dinner.

"Pearl's not that bad once you get to know her," Bo protested.

We stared at him.

"What?" He thumped his tail irritably against the door.

Luckily, we pulled up outside Mystical Moments. The shop looked exactly as I remembered it, sitting between a bookstore and a beauty salon in Sycamore Grove: all crystal displays, glowing objects, and dream catchers in the windows. A Closed sign hung on the door.

I could see movement inside.

"How about we wrap up this interview in time for lunch?" Didi said briskly as she gathered her files. "Stake My Shake is having a crab special today."

Gavin brightened. "I like their crab special."

I swallowed a sigh. It was becoming clear the employees of Hawthorne & Associates prioritized gossip and food above all else. I exited the car with the witch and the dragon newt and did my best to ignore the irresistible siren call of the impending full moon as we crossed the sidewalk.

Didi rapped sharply on the shop's front door.

Footsteps approached a moment later. A middle-aged woman with graying blonde hair and sharp green eyes appeared behind the glass. She frowned at the sight of Didi.

"We're closed for business today."

"We're from Hawthorne & Associates." Didi flashed her ID card.

Mrs. Owens stiffened. A bell jangled as she unlocked the door and hastily ushered us inside. Her gaze found me. She froze.

"Abby?!"

"Hi, Mrs. Owens."

This was going to take some explaining.

The witch stared. "What are you doing here?"

"I work for Hawthorne & Associates," I said awkwardly.

Didi, Gavin, and Bo watched our exchange with a mixture of curiosity and secondhand embarrassment.

The way Mrs. Owens stiffened told me she'd just gotten a whiff of my scent. Her tone cooled. "You're the new Hawthorne luna."

"Yeah."

Mrs. Owens hesitated. "So, it's true? You really got bitten by Hugh Hawthorne?"

I scratched my cheek self-consciously. "We, er, found him out cold on the front steps of our apartment building three nights ago. Ellie suggested we bring him inside so he could sleep off his hangover."

Mrs. Owens frowned. "That girl has zero common sense."

"To be fair, we were both drunk."

Bo sniffed the air curiously. "This place reminds me of Mrs. Chen's apartment."

There was definitely something otherworldly about the shop's atmosphere now that I knew what to look for, besides the fact that its owner was a witch.

"Wait." I stared at Bo. "You've been inside Mrs. Chen's apartment?"

Bo swished his tail. "Yeah. She makes a mean steak sandwich."

"Your dog talks?" Mrs. Owens asked leadenly.

"It's a long story." I was beginning to realize Bo had a much better handle on the supernatural community than I did.

Mrs. Owens led us inside the shop. "About Ellie." She glanced at me over her shoulder. "It wasn't just the skull incident that made me fire her. She doesn't know this, but she recently sold a human customer a love potion that was actually a foot treatment for pixies."

My stomach dropped. "What?!"

"Wow," Didi muttered. "Your best friend sounds like she should come with a warning label."

"Luckily, there were no casualties." Mrs. Owens sighed. "Though the customer did spend a week in the hospital with an interesting rash."

Didi cleared her throat in the uncomfortable silence. "How about we get down to business? We would like information on the crystal skull that was taken from your shop."

Mrs. Owens's face tightened. "Follow me. We'll talk on the way."

She confirmed the story she'd told Samuel as she guided us through to the back. She'd found the crystal skull on her doorstep one night ten years ago. It wasn't until she did some research that she realized it was a cursed artifact of considerable power.

"I knew some members of the Amberford Alliance would salivate at the prospect of getting their hands on the thing, so I decided to hide it in plain sight. I bought a bunch of other crystal skulls that looked identical to it and put them all over my shop."

No wonder Ellie hadn't known it was special.

"What's the Amberford Alliance?" I asked.

Mrs. Owens and Didi gave me a blank look.

"I keep forgetting you're new to this," Didi said. "It's the council of supernatural leaders. They meet once a month at the Chamber of Commerce. Samuel and Victoria are members."

Bo gulped nervously as we passed shelves crammed with crystals, herbs, and what looked suspiciously like actual shrunken heads. A door marked *Staff Only* opened into a small office.

"I have the security footage from that day, though the quality isn't great." Mrs. Owens indicated a computer that looked like it belonged in a museum. "I've already put out feelers to my contacts in Amberford. So far, no one has heard of anybody trying to purchase a crystal skull."

Gavin sat at the desk and brought up the security footage for that day. Didi and I leaned over his shoulder while Bo poked his head under Gavin's arm.

A grainy video showed Ellie behind the counter,

looking bored. A teenager in a hoodie entered the shop.

We watched as he nonchalantly looked around Mystical Moments.

"Samuel mentioned you'd stepped out of the shop to deal with an emergency. What was the emergency?" I asked curiously

"The salon owner next door messaged to tell me my car alarm was going off. I park in a private lot around the corner from here."

The kid stopped in front of a display cabinet. It had a sign on the glass saying *Not for Sale*.

I frowned. "Was your car alarm going off?"

"Yes. Someone had broken into it."

"Let me guess," Didi said sourly. "Nothing was missing?"

"Bingo."

Didi, Gavin, and I exchanged a guarded glance.

Samuel was right. Whoever was behind the missing skull had planned the job meticulously.

The kid pointed at something inside the cabinet.

Ellie frowned slightly and shook her head. The kid said something, his shoulders visibly drooping. He removed a wallet from his jeans and showed Ellie a wad of bills.

My best friend hesitated before reluctantly grabbing a key from behind the counter and going over to the display cabinet.

"Is she normally this gullible?" Didi asked.

"Yes," Mrs. Owens and I murmured in unison.

I got my first look at the crystal skull as Ellie

removed it from the display case. It glittered ominously as it caught the light, the empty eyes radiating a chill that was almost palpable.

Ellie was oblivious to it as she carefully wrapped the artifact and put it in a bag. The kid paid her and turned to exit the shop.

My pulse spiked. "Stop there! Gavin, can you zoom in on his clothes?"

The dragon newt clicked a few keys. The image enlarged.

My breath caught. The hoodie label was partially visible.

"That's from Moonlight Couture," I said. "Victoria took me there yesterday."

Didi and Gavin exchanged a surprised look.

Mrs. Owens frowned. "That's not the kind of place teenagers usually shop."

"He was walking around with a whole wad of money." Gavin scratched the back of his head. "Maybe he's just a rich kid who got bored and fancied a crystal skull?"

"Can you play the footage again?" I asked. "I want to confirm something."

Gavin obliged.

My scalp prickled as we watched the replay. "He made sure the cameras didn't capture his face."

"Definitely not an amateur then," Didi said coldly.

I nodded. "We should pay a visit to Moonlight Couture."

17

THE WEREWOLF AND THE BOOGEYMAN

CLAUDETTE LOOKED UP FROM THE CASH REGISTER WHEN we entered her shop twenty minutes later. Her eyebrows rose.

"Back so soon?" Her gaze danced approvingly over my outfit before landing on Didi and Gavin. Her eyes lost some of their shine as she scanned their attire. "And with friends, no less."

"Don't take it personally," I muttered at Didi's and Gavin's expressions.

Didi recovered her composure and pulled out her badge. "We're here on official Hawthorne & Associates business."

"When do I get a badge?" Bo panted hopefully.

"When you can pay the rent," I muttered.

"Ah." Claudette sobered. "How can I be of assistance?"

I looked around the shop and spotted what I was looking for. "That hoodie." I pointed to a garment identical to the one the kid had worn in the security footage from Mystical Moments. "I take it it's from your current season?"

"Of course," Claudette said with mild affront. "Our stock is always in season."

"Great, this makes it easy," Didi said curtly. "We need to know who bought it and when."

Claudette's eyes rounded. "What?!" she squeaked.

One of her assistants poked her head out of the workshop.

"Everything okay, ma'am?" the fae asked in a musical voice.

She floated into view, her movements ethereal. The shiny earrings dangling from her ears swung with her every graceful step.

Gavin's gaze locked on the jewelry. His horns popped out.

"The person we're looking for was wearing that hoodie," I explained distractedly.

A thin trail of smoke started curling from Gavin's nostrils.

"Don't you dare set anything on fire!" Didi hissed to the dragon newt in a threatening undertone. "The markup on these clothes is ridiculous enough without adding fire damage!"

Gavin listened with half an ear, his expression glazed.

"What's the matter with him?!" I whispered to Didi.

"Dragon newts love shiny things," the witch said in a disgusted voice. "It's their hoarding instinct at work."

An excited dragon newt was the last thing we needed right now.

Gavin decided to participate in the investigation.

"We'd also like to check your security cameras," he said, panting in a disturbing way.

Gone was the sweet and shy dragon newt I'd met yesterday.

"Should I go fetch a pail of water?" Bo contributed unhelpfully.

My hangover headache started to get worse.

"Ah, Lana," Claudette said with the glassy expression of someone determined to ignore the conversation taking place under her nose. "Can you help me go through our sales records?"

The fae met Gavin's rapt stare. She smiled and bobbed her head in a greeting. The movement made her earrings sparkle alluringly.

Gavin's tail popped out. Didi stepped on it.

Ten minutes later, Lana found the relevant receipts. There were fifty of them.

The Amberford supernatural community was way more affluent than I'd thought they were.

"Maybe we should split this up." I wrinkled my brow. "It'll take a forever to look through the security footage for all those dates."

"Are you looking for a particular purchase?" Lana asked curiously.

Didi and I shared a hesitant glance.

I shrugged. "No harm in showing them."

Didi brought up a segment of the security footage from Mystical Moments on her phone.

"That customer bought that particular hoodie three

weeks ago," Lana said promptly. "I remember because he paid in cash."

The hairs rose on the back of my neck. Either our suspect was loaded or he didn't want any traces left that could help track him down.

"Let's take a look at that security footage," Didi said grimly.

Claudette led us to a back office. Unlike the vintage aesthetic of the shop floor, this room was all modern chrome and glass. Multiple screens showed different angles of the boutique.

Moonlight Couture took its security seriously.

"Let me pull up the archives." Lana sat at a sleek chair and started working on a computer, her fingers dancing lightly over the keyboard.

My wolf stirred restlessly under my skin as we crowded around the monitor. The moon's pull was getting stronger by the hour, making my bones ache and my senses keener. I could smell something sweet and sparkly coming off the fae, like honeysuckle and starlight.

I shifted uncomfortably.

Didi shot a frown my way. "You okay?"

"Yeah," I lied.

"Found it," Lana announced a couple of minutes later.

The footage showed a tall man in an expensive suit examining the hoodie. We stared.

Didi lowered her brows. "He's not our kid."

I squinted. "Actually, I'm pretty sure that's our guy. Same gait. Same telltale hand gestures."

Gavin nodded.

"But he's taller," Didi protested. "And older."

"He could be a mimic," Bo huffed.

We looked at him.

Claudette blinked. "He's right."

Even Lana looked impressed at my dog's suggestion.

I raised a hand like I was back in fourth grade. "What's a mimic?"

"A doppelgänger." Gavin was back in control of his senses and looked embarrassed at his recent ungentlemanly display. "They're also called changelings. They can evolve in any supernatural race."

Didi narrowed her eyes at the man on the screen. "And they can take on the appearance of anyone they see."

I digested this information with remarkable self-possession and came to the conclusion that the supernatural world was a scary-ass place.

Gavin stiffened. "There! We can see a close-up of his face in that view."

Lana froze the shot of the stranger at the till.

We studied the man. He had coarse features with a cruel mouth and thick eyebrows that almost met in the middle of his forehead.

"He looks like a werewolf on a bad hair day," Bo said. He glanced at me. "Kinda like you that first morning after you turned."

I pressed my lips together.

"Can you send that to the head of the IT department at Hawthorne & Associates?" Didi asked

Claudette. She wrote down the email address on a notepad.

"Sure."

"Thank you. We appreciate your help."

"No problem," Claudette said graciously. She accompanied us to the front door. "By the way, how did the family dinner go yesterday?"

I tensed at her curious stare. "It was alright."

Claudette's expression turned sympathetic at the obvious lie. "Let me guess. The pack insisted on giving their opinions on how you and Samuel should consummate your union?"

I couldn't help but groan at the flashback.

Didi voted for lunch before we returned to the office.

Stake My Shake wasn't far from the Amberford police station. The diner looked like any other '50s-style establishment, complete with chrome fixtures and red vinyl booths. The only hint that something was different was the neon sign in the window that flickered between Stake My Shake and Milk My Shake depending on whether you had supernatural blood or not.

To my surprise, it wasn't just the staff and the general clientele that gave off distinct otherworldly smells. Several cops eating inside did too.

I tried not to stare at table six as we were led to a booth.

"Those officers are from the supernatural task force," Didi explained.

The handsome, muscular guy who appeared to be

in charge of the group sighed as one of his dragon newt colleagues singed the burger he was eating.

"What exactly does a supernatural task force do?" I asked carefully.

"They handle nonhuman community crimes and infractions," Gavin explained.

I arched an eyebrow. "Like?"

"Like that time a troll tried to set up residence under the Third Street bridge," Gavin said.

"Or when someone reported a dragon newt doing loops around the water tower." Didi shot Gavin a pointed look.

He flushed. "That was one time! And I'd just discovered energy drinks."

I recalled the Third Bridge underpass being closed for a couple of weeks last summer. "That was a troll?"

"Yeah."

Bo and I traded a troubled look.

"Aren't trolls giant monsters that eat people?" I asked uneasily.

"And dogs?" Bo quavered.

"You guys are thinking of orcs," Didi said dismissively. "They don't exist."

Bo and I both breathed a sigh of relief. That was one less terrifying creature to strike off our list of monsters we never wanted to meet.

"Trolls are harmless," Gavin explained. "They're big softies actually. And vegetarian. They can even grow mushrooms on their own—"

Our waitress appeared. She was a perky blonde

with slightly pointed ears who introduced herself as Sunshine.

"Let me guess," I whispered while Sunshine cooed over what a pretty boy Bo was. "Fairy?"

"Pixie," Didi corrected. "You can tell by the wing shimmer."

I squinted but couldn't see any wings.

"They're glamoured," Gavin said. "Health code regulations for catering businesses."

Sunshine recommended the dragon-friendly crab special with extra hot sauce and something called Moonshine Milkshakes. Bo perked up at the mention of the shakes.

"What's in them?" I asked warily.

"Nothing illegal." Sunshine beamed. "Just a little fairy dust for extra zing. Your dog will love it."

A thought occurred to me as we waited for our food.

"Does turning a human into a werewolf count as a crime?"

Didi exchanged a cautious look with Gavin. "Technically, yes."

"But no one is gonna go after the Hawthornes," Gavin said hastily at my expression. "Besides, the penalty Samuel and Victoria impose on their pack members for breaking supernatural laws is often harsher than what local enforcement would do."

I started feeling a little sorry for Hugh. But only a little.

Lunch was an enjoyable affair despite Gavin accidentally setting his napkin on fire halfway through the meal and me canceling Bo's order of a Moonshine Milkshake when we saw a guy at the counter start floating after one sip of his.

My dog burped and licked his chops as we exited the diner. "What's on the agenda for the afternoon?"

Didi checked her watch. "We should pay Nigel a visit. He's probably seen the video footage from Moonlight Couture by now."

Bo's ears drooped a little. "That sounds about as much fun as going to the vet."

I grimaced. "You mean the boogeyman is our head of IT?"

"He's a nice guy," Gavin said as we climbed into Didi's BMW. "Amazing with technology despite his terrifying appearance." The dragon newt paused. "Also, he radiates light when he's excited, so try not to, er, stimulate him too much."

The prospect of stimulating a boogeyman was right there at the very bottom of the list of things I wouldn't be caught dead doing.

The moon's influence was even stronger when we reached the office. We passed several restless werewolves in the lobby and in the elevator. Bo whined softly and pressed against my leg at the hints of amber in their eyes.

Even Janet looked tense as she chatted with a translucent Mindy by the copy machine when we emerged on the fifth floor, her foot tapping a nervous beat on the floor.

Didi led us down a corridor I hadn't noticed yesterday and stopped at a door marked *IT Department*.

"Isn't this a janitor's closet?" I said warily.

"It is," Didi said breezily. "Nigel likes confined spaces. Says they make him feel secure."

I was wondering whether that was why boogeymen liked to lurk under beds and inside wardrobes when the witch issued a terse warning.

"Remember," Didi said, "no sudden movements. He scares easily. And whatever you do, don't mention his tentacles."

"Don't move, don't talk," Bo mumbled. "Gotcha."

She knocked. A muffled voice answered. "Come in."

Didi opened the door. The narrow office space beyond was dark except for the glow of multiple monitors. A figure hunched in the shadows.

My gaze rose. Bo stared, equally transfixed.

The shadowy figure's head brushed the ceiling.

I caught a glimpse of purple fur, tentacles, multiple eyes, and a bevy of mouths with sharp teeth before the shadows shrank and took on the shape of a slender human.

"Holy tenta—!" Bo gasped. I muzzled him with my hand.

"Hi, Nigel," Gavin greeted cheerfully.

"We need your help with that footage we had forwarded to you from Moonlight Couture," Didi said briskly.

"Oh. I was wondering what that was about."

I blinked, still reliving that split second of bladder-loosening horror at Nigel's true form. His voice was surprisingly sweet.

He moved in the gloom. There was a click. A light came on.

I stared at a quiet-looking young man with glasses.

"He-hello," Nigel stammered nervously. A tiny tentacle sprouted from his left ear and waved. He grabbed it and pushed it back inside his body.

"Er, hi."

Bo wagged his tail hesitantly. "You smell like grape soda."

Nigel blinked. "Thank you. I think?"

WHEN THE MOON CALLS

"Hmm." Nigel adjusted his glasses and stared at the enhanced version of the Moonlight Couture footage he'd just brought up on the screen. "I think I've seen this guy before."

I exchanged a startled look with Didi and Gavin.

"You have?" the witch said.

"Give me a minute."

Multiple screens flickered around us as Nigel began working several keyboards at once, his glasses reflecting the displays' glow. A couple of tentacles emerged from his sleeves and tried to help. He tucked them away absentmindedly.

My skin itched. The moon's pull was getting stronger by the hour, making everything starker, brighter, and more intense. Even the hum of the computers seemed amplified in the enclosed space that was the boogeyman's office.

"That's strange." Nigel was frowning at one of the

screens. "It's taking a while to run him through facial recognition."

"We think he might be a mimic," Gavin said helpfully.

Nigel almost fell off his chair. "That's it!" He brightened—literally—and immediately dimmed his glow when we squinted. "Sorry."

"Do you think you can track him down?" Didi asked while I was still blinking the black spots out of my eyes.

"Maybe." More windows opened across Nigel's screens. "I've been building a database of suspicious individuals and strange activities involving supernatural establishments in Amberford and the neighboring towns. I should be able to pinpoint similarities if this guy's modus operandi stayed the same."

I was impressed. The boogeyman really was great at his job.

We watched as images and text scrolled past for several minutes.

Nigel suddenly stiffened. "There!" Dozens of glowing tentacles emerged all at once in his excitement and pointed at a screen. "His real name is Clayton Wheeler. He's officially registered as a werewolf. He's been flagged multiple times for suspected criminal activities."

I frowned. Though they were of different heights and ages, the men in the frames all walked and moved the same way.

I wondered which one was the real Clayton Wheeler.

"What kind of criminal activities?" Didi asked in a steely voice.

Nigel checked his database. "Assault and theft." He paused. "Oh. There was an incident last year involving a cursed object at an antique store in the next town. The charges were dropped due to lack of evidence."

My pulse quickened.

Didi narrowed her eyes. "Sounds like our guy."

"We should check the shops around Mystical Moments," Gavin suggested. "See if anyone saw Wheeler or noticed anything unusual in the days leading up to the theft."

We said goodbye to Nigel and returned to Sycamore Grove in Didi's car. It didn't take long to find our first clue.

The beauty salon next to Mystical Moments was run by Madame Rosa, a witch who specialized in magical makeovers. The bell above the door tinkled cheerfully when we entered the premises.

We introduced ourselves and showed her the pictures Nigel had printed of our suspect, including the screenshot from Moonlight Couture's security footage.

"Oh, that guy." Madame Rosa nodded at Wheeler's photo from Claudette's shop, her fingers busy enchanting gray hairs into gold. "Yup, I saw him alright. He was in a dark blue Lexus SUV that was parked around the corner five days straight last week."

Her customer sneezed. All her hair turned green.

We stared.

"She looks like that frog I caught once," Bo whispered.

I remembered the frog in question. Ellie had not been impressed.

Madame Rosa sighed. "Mrs. Emerson, did you have chrysanthemum tea this morning?"

Mrs. Emerson flinched guilty.

Madama Rosa's expression grew pinched. "You know chrysanthemum tea and my transformation magic don't mix well."

Bo and I watched with mounting dread as other parts of Mrs. Emerson started turning green. She began gurgling.

"And by don't mix well, I mean it can lead to a serious allergic reaction," Madame Rosa grumbled. She turned and shouted at one of her assistants. "Jane, bring the detox potion, *now!*" She glanced at Mrs. Emerson's swelling face. "And the funnel!" she added grimly.

Bo shot behind my legs.

I licked my lips nervously. "Shouldn't we call 911?"

"911 can't help with magical incidents," Didi said in an unconcerned tone.

"Also, the supernatural emergency line is 666," Gavin added helpfully.

Madame Rosa shoved a pipe into her client's throat and poured a gloopy blue liquid down it from the glass bottle her assistant passed to her. Mrs. Emerson's bloated form deflated like a balloon and her hair and skin slowly resumed their normal color. She hiccuped and groaned.

I blew out a sigh.

"What just happened is right up there on my list of constipation cures," Bo muttered.

Madame Rosa cut her eyes to my dog before addressing her assistant. "How about you take Mrs. Emerson for a lie down?"

Mrs. Emerson stumbled a little under the support of the witch's assistant as she was gently guided to a rest lounge, her passage garnering concerned looks from the salon's clientele as well as disapproving stares that said she should have known better.

"Now, where were we?" Madame Rosa said briskly.

"Did you notice anything unusual about the SUV?" Didi asked.

"Besides the fact that it seemed to change shade depending on the angle?" Madame Rosa snorted. "I've been in this business thirty years. I know a glamour when I see one."

My stomach sank. "How about the license plate?"

"Honey, I can't remember what I had for breakfast yesterday." Madame Rosa paused. "But the dwarf who owns the liquor store opposite might have caught something on his security camera."

I realized the witch was watching me with a shrewd stare.

"So you're the new luna everyone's been talking about?"

I grimaced. This fame business was starting to get old.

"Dwarf?" I asked Didi and Gavin when we exited the beauty salon.

"They're an endangered species," Didi said.

"Reproductive problems," Gavin explained at my look.

"You mean infertility?" I hazarded as we crossed the road.

"Like they can't tell who's a lady dwarf and who isn't, what with the beard and everything," Didi replied. "Leads to all kinds of brawls. It's the reason they're constantly grumpy."

I was certain they were making this stuff up until we entered the liquor store and I saw the bearded dwarf perched on a high stool behind the counter. Grumpy was a mild word to describe his countenance.

"He looks like he eats small children for breakfast," Bo commented.

I hushed my dog while Didi spoke to Grumpy.

"Security cameras?" he grunted at her request. "In the back." He squinted menacingly. "You better not touch anything else."

The footage room was barely bigger than a closet and reeked of smelly socks. Gavin narrowly missed setting fire to a cobweb and earned a death glare from Didi.

It didn't take us long to find the SUV in the security footage. We could just make out a partial plate number.

Didi called Nigel on the way back to the office.

"I know someone at the DMV who owes me a favor," Nigel said. "When I say 'someone' I mean a gremlin, and when I say 'favor' I mean he lost a bet involving Windows 95 and a flying toaster." He chuckled in a way that I found strangely endearing.

My life was full of weirdos and I was getting used to their weirdness.

The full moon meant Hawthorne & Associates stopped work early so their werewolf employees could get ready for their pack run. Charlene gave me a message about my car being in the parking lot behind the building when we entered the lobby and passed me an envelope with the words *Abby's car key* on it in elegant cursive.

"From Samuel," the banshee said.

Even the guy's handwriting was sexy.

Didi and Gavin made reassuring noises about my first transformation as they said goodbye, which only served to make me more nervous.

I frowned as I made my way to the parking lot. Bar a text message telling me when he'd pick me up tonight and the envelope, I hadn't heard from Samuel all day.

I stopped and looked around. My Subaru was nowhere in sight.

Bo padded over to a brand-new, gleaming, midnight-blue BMW. "I can smell Samuel's scent on this."

I joined him. He was right.

Suspicion roused its ugly head. I emptied the envelope. It contained a key with a BMW logo and a curt note that said, *The Subaru has gone to a better place. Use the new car.*

"That wolf had better give Ethel back," I growled.

Bo looked at me warily. "Your knuckles are growing hairy."

I reeled in my inner wolf and briefly debated

storming back into Hawthorne & Associates and demanding where Samuel was. I decided I was too darn tired, got inside the BMW, and drove it gingerly all the way home.

By the time I reached Parkside, my bones were aching and my wolf was practically clawing to get out.

"I sure as hell hope every full moon isn't like this," I muttered as we rode the elevator.

Bo remained unusually quiet beside me.

We found Ellie in the kitchen, surrounded by what looked like every baking implement we owned. The counters were covered in cooling racks laden with protein bars, muffins, and what appeared to be an attempt at raw meat treats.

"Ellie?" I stared at the mess. "What are you—?"

"I looked up what werewolves might need after transforming," she babbled. "I got you some Gatorade. And protein shakes. Oh, and I found this website about post-transformation care—"

"Ellie." I caught her flapping, flour-covered hands. "I'll be fine."

My best friend looked like a deer caught in headlights. I could tell the guilt of being partly responsible for what I was going to go through tonight was getting to her.

"It wasn't your fault."

Tears bloomed in her eyes at my words. She started bawling.

I sighed and hugged her, flour and all. Bo whined.

"Look, Samuel's gonna be there," I reminded them,

trying to sound more confident than I felt. "And the rest of the pack."

"That's what worries me," Ellie muttered in my shoulder. "You'll be on your own."

Bo started howling.

These two were not helping.

I stayed with them a few more minutes before heading for the shower, hoping the hot water might ease some of the tension in my muscles. It didn't. If anything, being alone with my thoughts made everything worse.

The fears I'd harbored about becoming a werewolf bubbled to the forefront of my consciousness like a nasty bout of indigestion.

What if I hurt someone one day? What if I bit Ellie or Bo in a moon-induced frenzy? What if I could never turn back into a hum—

A sound at the bathroom door interrupted my spiral of panic.

"Your heart's going crazy again," Bo said anxiously through the door. "I can hear it from here."

I wrapped myself in a towel and froze at the glint of amber in my eyes when I saw my reflection in the cabinet mirror. I swallowed and opened the door.

"I'm fine."

Though Bo's ears flattened at my sight, he didn't back away.

"I'd feel better if I could come with you," he quavered.

I realized he was trembling and ruffled his head.

"Even Pearl doesn't go on pack runs."

Probably because she might accidentally get eaten, but I refrained from voicing that thought.

I'd already laid out the clothes Victoria had insisted on buying specifically for shifting on my bed that morning: soft pants and a top made of some kind of magical fabric that was supposed to transform with me. I got dressed and checked my watch.

It was six-thirty p.m.

The doorbell rang at exactly seven. My pulse spiked where I sat waiting with Ellie and Bo in the living room. I took a deep breath and went to answer the door, the pair of them trailing behind me like they were going to a funeral.

Samuel stood in the hallway, looking tall and brooding in dark clothing that hugged his physique. His eyes already held more than a hint of amber and the power rolling off him made my skin tingle.

"Ready?" he asked quietly.

I nodded and grabbed the bag of goodies Ellie had packed for me. My best friend and my dog watched us leave wordlessly.

19

HOW TO WOLF (A BEGINNER'S GUIDE)

THE DRIVE TO THE PRESERVE WAS MOSTLY SILENT. I could feel my wolf getting closer to the surface with every mile, like she was pressing against my skin from the inside and dying to get out. Everything around me felt heightened: smells, sounds, even the texture of the leather seat beneath me.

As for Samuel's scent, it filled the car and swamped my senses, the untamed undertone making my wolf want to roll over and show her belly. Or possibly jump him. I wasn't entirely sure which and that was terrifying in itself.

"Not feeling like groping my thigh tonight?" he teased with a smile.

I groaned. "I'm trying to forget I did that."

He chuckled. "I never said you couldn't."

I knew he was trying to lighten the mood. Still, I didn't miss the sexual tension that sparked between us.

I suddenly remembered that I was still upset with this guy.

"Where's Ethel?" I said coolly.

"Somewhere she can rest her weary wheels." Samuel sighed at my expression. "She's in our garage at the mansion."

He turned the Bentley onto the dirt road leading to the training ground. Metal glinted faintly between the trees as we approached the clearing where Samuel had trained me. There were already cars parked in the lot ahead. My supernatural hearing picked up voices and laughter drifting through the woods, along with a distant noise that sounded suspiciously like howling.

Samuel killed the engine and turned to look at me.

"Whatever happens tonight, remember that I'm here. That we're all here for you." His quiet voice filled the space between us. "Trust your instincts, Abby. Your inner wolf knows what to do."

I met his gaze and saw my own apprehension reflected there, along with something else. Something that made the mate bond sing between us.

Pale light filtered through the treetops. The moon was rising.

We got out of the car and joined the Hawthorne pack.

The clearing felt different tonight. The air buzzed with electric tension and the ancient oaks cast strange shadows across faces that were already starting to show signs of their wolves.

"Hi, Abby," Caroline greeted cheerfully. She was helping Amanda out of her jacket while James bounced around them with barely contained excitement.

Kent herded some wayward kids back to the pack.

"The first shift is always memorable." Aunt Lucille gave me a gentle pat on my back that almost broke a rib. Her dentures glinted in the night as she beamed. "I remember mine like it was yesterday. Took out three fence posts and someone's prized hydrangeas."

Hopefully not Mrs. Chen's, I found myself thinking slightly hysterically.

"You still do that, Lucille," Uncle Frederick reminded his cousin with a sigh.

Victoria approached, looking regal in a charcoal-gray pantsuit. Her expression was a mix of concern and something I couldn't quite read.

"How are you feeling?"

"Like I want to find Hugh and punch him again," I said bluntly.

Victoria's face softened a little. Several pack members chuckled. Even Samuel smiled.

"Speaking of Hugh, where is he?" I looked around curiously.

"He went on ahead," Victoria said, indicating the looming mountains. She paused, her eyes glinting amber. "It's almost time."

An uncanny stillness came over the Hawthornes as they looked up at the sky. The silence that fell over the clearing and the woods made my heartbeat speed up and sent a shiver of fear and anticipation down my spine.

The moon finally crept over the tallest peak and sent dazzling light washing across the clearing.

All my hairs rose on end as the supernatural glow washed over me.

The first twinge hit me like a punch to the gut. My breath caught on a gasp of pure agony as something grabbed all my internal organs and gave them a sharp twist. The pain was unlike anything I'd ever experienced.

It felt like everything in my body was trying to break and re-form at once.

I was barely aware of falling to my knees as I began screaming, the sound that escaped me so feral it sounded like a beast was trying to tear its way out from my very innards.

I heard voices dimly through the blood rushing inside my skull. Victoria was calling my name and telling me not to fight what was happening to me. Caroline and Kent were ordering the younger pack members to stand back.

A presence loomed close to me. One whose scent focused my scattered senses.

"Breathe," Samuel said. "Breathe, Abby." His hands cupped my face, strong and hot. "Look at me!"

His face blurred in front of me. I blinked and willed myself to focus on his amber gaze through my tears. Even through the haze of agony, it dawned on me once again how beautiful his eyes were.

Great. Trust me to focus on that while I was literally being torn apart from the inside. I cursed my inner wolf as another wave of excruciating pain washed through me and robbed me of breath.

"This part will hurt." His expression grew determined. "But I think I can help make it easier."

Before I could ask how, his lips found mine.

I froze even in the throes of the most savage agony I had ever endured in my life.

The kiss was gentle at first, his mouth exploring mine like he was testing the resilience of my lips. It deepened as the mate bond flared between us. Heat flooded my body, the fire filling my veins different from the burning torment of my transformation. My wolf surged forward with a joy and hunger that momentarily overwhelmed the debilitating pain threatening to drown me.

I found myself clinging shamelessly to Samuel, my nails lengthening and digging into his powerful shoulders as I molded myself to his body, seeking his heat just as he sought mine.

When Samuel pulled back, his eyes were fully wolf.

"Let go," he whispered against my lips. "Let your wolf loose, Abby."

I did. And it was easier than I could have imagined.

The last thing I saw before my vision shifted to that of my wolf's was Samuel's expression changing from concern to wide-eyed shock as my fur began to emerge under the moonlight.

Victoria's gasp cut through the night air. "It can't be!"

I was too busy marveling at my new senses to process her tone.

Everything around me was sharper, more clear, more vibrant than ever before.

The scents surrounding me painted vivid pictures in my mind, just as my new vision and nose did. Earth and greenery. Water gurgling in distant brooks. The wild tang of my pack and the fear of prey hiding in the woods.

Even the moonlight felt different on my fur.

Fur that was apparently causing quite a stir among the Hawthornes.

"After all these years," Aunt Lucille breathed.

"But—I thought they were just urban legends!" Caroline mumbled.

I turned my head, trying to see what had everyone so worked up. My wolf moved with surprising grace at my command, like I'd been born to this form.

I froze.

I was white from head to toe. A pure, dazzling white and not at all like the mousy brown of the first morning after I'd turned.

Even my tail gleamed blindingly in the moonlight.

A low growl rumbled through the clearing. I looked around to find a massive black wolf where Samuel had been standing. His amber eyes locked onto mine with an intensity that made my fur stand on end.

More wolves emerged around us as the pack transformed. They spread out in a loose circle, all of them staring. Yet I did not feel in the least bit threatened.

"Why—why am I white?!" I said, my heart racing.

My words came out a questioning whine instead.

We can only communicate with our thoughts in this form.

Samuel's voice rang clearly inside my skull. His wolf moved closer, his head lowering to touch his nose to mine. The mate bond exploded between us, no longer just a hum but a full-blown orchestra with cymbals and flutes.

I gulped, momentarily distracted from the white wolf issue. *Wow.*

He grinned. *Yeah.*

Well, this explains a few things. Victoria watched me with piercing eyes, the Hawthorne matriarch regal even in her silver-gray wolf form. *And complicates matters.*

I was about to ask what exactly it complicated when Samuel's wolf nudged me gently.

Let's run.

20

NO BUTT SNIFFING ALLOWED

MY LEGS MOVED BEFORE I COULD THINK ABOUT IT. I shot forward, relishing the way my new body responded instinctively to my command. Samuel loped beside me, matching my pace as we headed for the tree line. The rest of the pack followed, their excited howls filling the night.

I thought turning into a wolf would freak me out. Yet I couldn't think of a more thrilling moment than the one I was experiencing right now. Running as a wolf was nothing like running as a human. It was freedom. It was joy. It was—

Oh my God, is that a rabbit?!

I skidded to a halt in a shower of dirt.

Yes. Samuel stopped beside me, his breath misting in the cold night air.

I groaned. My wolf really wanted to chase that rabbit.

Samuel's amused huff beside me suggested he knew exactly what I was thinking.

I shook my head and told myself to focus. I was a sophisticated supernatural being, not some common—

Another rabbit darted across our path. My wolf's instincts took over.

What happened next was not my finest moment as the new luna of the Hawthorne pack. I'm pretty sure even Samuel's wolf snickered.

I shot after the rabbit like a furry bullet and ended up skidding in packed dirt and sliding on my belly as I failed to control my supernatural speed. I jumped up, found my balance, and barely touched the ground as I weaved between trees and leapt over fallen logs.

To my surprise, I wasn't just fast. I was ridiculously fast.

Samuel's surprised yelp echoed behind me as he and the rest of the pack gave chase.

I left them in the dust. Right now, my wolf was in charge of our body and I was just a passenger riding along.

The rabbit darted left. I followed, my wolf responding with impossible grace.

The rabbit zigged. I zagged. It jumped. I lunged.

The thrill of the chase made my senses buzz with delight.

It felt like we'd been doing this our whole life.

The hunt ended when the creature dove into its burrow. I skidded to a stop, panting happily despite my failure to pin it down.

I stamped my paws. *That was amazing!*

You're a natural. Samuel's wolf emerged from the

trees, the rest of the pack following. His voice held a tone of pride and his eyes shone brightly in the night.

I spotted Hugh among the pack behind him, his dark wolf a fraction smaller than his older brother's. He came over to greet me.

Hi.

I huffed an acknowledgment and stiffened when he sneaked behind me. A growl worked up my throat.

Sniff my butt and I will tear your throat out.

Hugh's wolf rolled his eyes at the threat and moved away.

Caroline's thoughts reached me then. *No newly turned wolf should be able to move like that.* Her russet-colored wolf studied me with sharp eyes.

Kent's hulking brown wolf watched me just as cautiously.

I understood their wariness. As pack enforcers, they were probably assessing whether I was a threat.

James's smaller gray form bounced toward me excitedly, oblivious to his parents' concerns.

That was so cool! Can you teach me to run that fast?!

Even Amanda came closer, her wolf's eyes shining with awe.

More of the pack's thoughts crowded my mind as they gathered around me, a jumble of excitement and confusion that made my wolf's ears flatten for a second.

Enough. Samuel's commanding tone cut through the mental chatter, silencing them. His wolf moved to stand shoulder to shoulder beside me. *We'll talk later. For now, let's hunt.*

We started running, the pack spreading out in formation like a well-oiled machine. I found myself falling naturally into step beside Samuel, our movements fluid as we moved through the preserve like shadows.

In the two hours that followed, the Hawthorne pack showed me how to track scents, check territorial boundaries, and hunt prey without killing them. My wolf learned quickly, like she already knew all this from memory.

A herd of deer watched us warily from a ridge when we stopped to drink at a brook on the edge of the moonlit forest. I gazed up at the starry sky and closed my eyes, savoring the night air.

Crisp with the dazzling smells of winter, it carried untold stories of the woods on the wind that soared through the treetops. The call of an owl. The bark of a fox. Herbivores rustling in the undergrowth as they came out of their burrows to look for food.

This is what it means to be a pack. Samuel's wolf pressed his flank against mine. *To move as one. To know our lands. To run together. It means trust and loyalty. Family and belonging.*

I looked into his mesmerizing amber gaze and felt something I had never experienced before. He huffed when he sensed my feelings and licked my face tenderly.

We returned to the clearing when the moon reached its zenith.

Shifting back to my human form wasn't anywhere

as challenging as transforming into a wolf had been. Not being naked was an added bonus.

To my surprise, the Hawthornes brought out a veritable feast and we sat on blankets on the grass having a picnic under the stars. Ellie's baked goods were a hit and Hugh practically had half my Gatorade to himself.

It wasn't until we were getting ready to leave that Victoria's expression turned serious.

"The Council of Elders is going to want to meet Abby."

The rest of the Hawthornes exchanged strained glances. A low growl rumbled through Samuel's chest. Even Hugh looked annoyed.

"Don't give me that look," Victoria told her sons sharply. "You know what being a luna means, let alone one who also happens to be a white wolf."

I frowned. "Okay, what exactly is the deal with white wolves? And who is this Council of Elders?"

"White wolves are incredibly rare." Victoria hesitated. "Doubly so for white lunas."

I scratched the back of my head. "So I'm some kind of unicorn werewolf?"

Aunt Lucille chortled. Several pack members grinned.

They sobered at Victoria's stare.

"Please." Hugh wrinkled his nose. "Those bastard unicorns can't even begin compare to a werewolf."

I was about to question the existence of unicorns when I saw that Hugh meant what he'd just said. I filed this in my things-to-freak-about-later mental folder.

"White werewolves are born leaders," Victoria explained. "They are natural alphas with abilities far beyond normal werewolves, including the power to control multiple packs." She hesitated. "The last recorded white wolf was my great-great-grandmother. She was a luna who united not just all the packs in New England during the Shadow War, but also convinced other supernatural clans to work with the werewolves."

My scalp prickled as the ramifications of what she'd just said sank in. That explained a few things. Why I was adapting so fast to being a werewolf. Why I'd managed to outrun even experienced pack members after my very first transformation tonight. Why I was, as Samuel had essentially described, a natural at this.

Caroline's gaze turned calculating. "The question is, why did a white wolf manifest in Abby? She wasn't even born a werewolf."

Uncle Frederick squinted at me. "Any chance one of your distant relatives was a werewolf?"

"Nope," I replied succinctly. "So, the Council of Elders? Who are they?"

Samuel's face darkened. "A bunch of old busybodies who should keep their noses out of everyone's business." He paused. "No offense, Mother."

"Still, there's no avoiding them," Victoria said curtly. "We may be a group of middle-aged women, but our words are often treated as law in the supernatural community." She pinned me with a pointed look. "I shall make the arrangements and contact you."

I had a nasty feeling my life was about to get even more complicated than it was.

Samuel was still frowning by the time we pulled up outside Parkside. Movement at the living room window of my apartment had us both looking up.

Ellie and Bo had their faces squished against the glass.

Samuel relaxed, his expression growing amused. "They look like they've been there a while."

From the condensation steaming up the window, I had to agree.

"So what did you think of your first pack run?"

I turned to see him watching me closely, his amber gaze behind his glasses carrying a heat that made my insides tingle.

"Bar Hugh trying to sniff my butt, I thought it was pretty damn cool."

His mouth curved into a smile that made me blink.

"I'm glad," he drawled.

My wolf acted before I could stop her.

Samuel's breath caught when I leaned across the console and kissed him. He froze for a heartbeat. Then he was moving, his hands finding my face and his body gravitating instinctively toward me.

He deepened the kiss with a groan that made my toes curl.

By the time he pulled back, my heart was racing, my blood was on fire, and I was biting down the urge to rip his clothes off and have my wicked way with him, witnesses be damned. Judging from the way he was looking at me and his chest was heaving, he was entertaining similar thoughts.

I swallowed hard and reached for the door handle. "I should go."

Samuel recovered his composure. "I'll bring lunch tomorrow for everyone." A low chuckle escaped him as I darted out of the car. "It seems my luna is a chicken, so I'll make sure to get some."

His laughter followed me as I made a run for the lobby, my face hot.

NOT JUST ANOTHER DAY AT THE OFFICE

CHARLENE BEAMED AT ME WHEN I WALKED INTO Hawthorne & Associates the next morning with Bo.

"Congratulations on not eating anyone."

I grimaced. "Thanks. I think."

Samuel had told me I would feel the full moon's influence for a while yet. Although my skin still felt tight and my bones ached, it wasn't nearly as bad as yesterday.

The banshee's smile faltered slightly. "You did resist eating things, right? I mean, living things?"

"If you mean did I kill Thumper or Bambi, the answer is no. I only chased them."

"Oh." Charlene looked embarrassed. "Of course."

"I did murder a steak sandwich afterward though."

Bo flicked his tail accusingly. "I knew I could smell steak on your breath!"

I'd been forced to spend a good hour last night recounting how my first pack run had gone to my dog and my best friend. Though I'd been careful to omit the gory details of my actual transformation, Bo's wary look told me he'd guessed it hadn't been a walk in the park.

"By the way, Caroline and Aunt Lucille want to know the recipe for those protein bars and muffins you made," I'd told Ellie.

She'd blinked. "They do?"

"Yeah."

"Maybe I should open a bakery." Her face had brightened. "A bakery for werewolves."

I'd been tempted to remind my best friend that there seemed to be plenty of those in Amberford but hadn't had the courage to shatter her dreams.

Fred emerged from the back room. His eyes widened at the sight of me. "Oh, hey Abby." He faltered, his expression turning hopeful. "Can I get your autograph?"

I stared. "Why?"

Fred's brimstone smell got stronger. "Because you're a white wolf, of course!"

Charlene nodded enthusiastically and shyly pushed a notepad and a pen my way. I looked from it to them.

"How did you guys find out?" I asked suspiciously.

"The pixie who delivers our morning papers told us," Fred said. "Her cousins were in the forest last night. It's all over town."

I groaned. That explained the occasional faint light trails I'd spotted in the trees last night.

"Ted is never gonna believe this," Fred added enthusiastically as I reluctantly signed the notepad.

"Ted knows about the supernatural world in Amberford?" I asked carefully.

"My mom accidentally transformed into her demon at a family dinner once," Fred said. "Almost gave Uncle Herbert a heart attack. Everyone else was cool with it."

No wonder Ted looked like he could deal with anything a Pennington & Graves employee could throw at him.

A piercing shriek suddenly echoed through the building, making us all jump and sending Bo diving between my legs. Though nowhere near as bad as Charlene's screech, the sound still felt like it was drilling into my skull.

My newly enhanced hearing was not helping.

The sound died down. I lowered my hands from my ears.

"What the hell was that?!"

Bo emerged from where he'd stuck his head between my knees. "It sounded like an angry ghost."

Charlene chewed her lip. "That's because it was an angry ghost."

"Someone probably used the magic photocopier without Mindy's permission," Fred said worriedly.

Another shriek rattled the windows.

"You'd better go up there and see what's going on," Fred told me.

He and Charlene watched me expectantly.

I made a face. "Aren't you supposed to be security?"

"This isn't a security matter," Fred glossed over.

Charlene nodded. "It's a higher-up matter."

"I just started working here two days ago," I pointed out. "I'm as low-down as you get."

Fred and Charlene exchanged a glance.

"Ain't no one higher up than the Hawthorne luna," Fred declared confidently.

"You should give up," Bo told me.

The lobby doors opened before I could come up with a suitable riposte.

A man in an expensive suit walked in. He had the same nose and chin as Kevin from my old workplace. His eyes widened a little when he saw me, his pupils holding a faint ember glow.

Even without the glow, I could tell he was a werewolf from his scent.

"Hi, there. We didn't get to meet yesterday." He crossed the floor and offered his hand. "I'm Kevin Mullen, Head of Marketing."

"Abby West." I shook his hand cautiously. "Any relation to Kevin from Pennington & Graves by any chance?"

The guy blinked. "Yeah, he's my second cousin." He gave me a puzzled look. "How did you know?"

I was wondering whether the other Kevin was also a werewolf when another shriek shook the building.

"Gotta run." I made for the express elevator with Bo.

"You might want to take the stairs," Charlene warned.

I stopped and turned. "Why?"

Charlene fidgeted. "Nigel had a moment in it

yesterday, after you left. The clean-up crew isn't here yet."

"Great," Kevin muttered.

"Let me guess," I said warily. "Someone surprised Nigel?"

Charlene grimaced. "Their phone did. Dave downloaded Beethoven's Fifth Symphony as his new ringtone. It went off between the third and fourth floor."

I digested this for a moment. "Is Dave okay?"

"He's taking the morning off."

I trudged toward the stairwell with Bo.

"Your third day at the office isn't exactly going well either, huh?" Bo said sympathetically.

"I get the feeling it's going to be like this every day," I muttered.

"Good thing you fancy the owner."

I decided not to respond to my dog's taunt. Luckily for me, my new werewolf stamina meant I wasn't a breathless hot mess by the time we reached the fifth floor.

The scene that greeted us was not that dissimilar to my first morning.

Papers flew through the air like confetti at a particularly violent party. The lights were flickering alarmingly and the glassware in the office area was vibrating at a frequency that set my teeth on edge and made Bo's ears flatten.

The main difference was Mindy. She was hovering near the ceiling in the open office area, her school uniform rippling with spectral energy and the knife in her neck glowing ominously.

"That ghost has lost it," Bo observed warily.

I spotted Nigel behind the water cooler. The boogeyman was trying his best to calm the angry specter, a purple tentacle waving tentatively in the air.

"Now, now, Mindy. I'm sure whoever did this is very sorry—"

"Sorry isn't good enough!" Mindy growled, her ghostly form flickering like she'd stuck her fingers in an electric socket. "Do you people know how long it took me to organize the paper trays by color and supernatural species?!"

"Wow." Bo glanced at me. "And I thought your OCD tendencies were bad."

Mindy's glowing eyes found us.

I nudged my dog into silence before he became the accidental victim of supernatural office violence. Gavin appeared at my right elbow with a cup of coffee.

"Organizing by supernatural species?" I asked the dragon newt while one of Nigel's tentacles materialized and quickly retreated at Mindy's glare.

"It's a pretty neat filing system once you get used to it."

Janet emerged from her office, her eyes still holding an ember glow and her hair somewhat wild. She looked like she'd barely slept last night.

"How about you people pipe down?" she said irritably. "The guys on the fourth floor keep messaging me about the noise."

Mindy scowled. "They're probably the ones who messed up the copy machine in the first place."

"For Christ's sake, Mindy, it's not the end of the world!" Janet snapped.

Mindy made an indignant sound.

I studied the shadows under Janet's eyes and wondered if she was suffering from post-full-moon blues. Ellie had warned me about it last night, after reading up on the phenomenon on a supernatural blog. I hadn't believed her until I messaged Caroline this morning and she confirmed it was actually a thing.

"Not the end of the world?" Mindy had drawn herself to her full spectral height, which wasn't that tall considering she'd been five-foot-three while still alive. *"Not the end of the world?!"*

The windows trembled.

"Uh-oh," Gavin muttered as the ghost started turning an alarming shade of red. "She's repeating herself. That's never a good sign."

Neither was a scarlet ghost.

"Someone used the werewolf paper for vampire forms!" Mindy was bellowing across the way. *"The werewolf paper, Janet!* It's cream colored! Everyone knows vampire documentation requires pure white paper!"

She threw some more files in the air for effect.

A paper landed on Barney's desk.

He ignored it and carried on typing with nerve-racking slowness. The vampire sensed our stares and looked up.

"What?"

"Know anything about this paper situation, Barnabas?" Janet asked in the tone of someone who was wishing she'd never gotten out of bed that morning.

"I do not," Barney replied coldly. "I'm not the only vampire in the building." He sniffed. "Also, everyone knows I don't dabble in newfangled technology."

That explained the typewriter.

"He's got a point," Mindy said grudgingly.

"He has two in his mouth," Bo said helpfully.

I hushed him.

A tentacle gestured hesitantly from behind the water cooler. "I can help you reorganize the copy machine."

Mindy sniffed. "Thanks, Nigel. I'd really like that."

Nigel's tentacle blushed and brightened.

I stared before leaning sideways and hissing to Gavin out of the corner of my mouth. "Does Nigel have a thing for Mindy?"

"Yup. Three years and still going strong. We have a betting pool on how many more years it will take before he asks her out."

I was wondering where a ghost and boogeyman would go on their first date when Didi stuck her head out of the break room. She brightened when she saw me.

"Oh good, you're here. We need to have a meeting about—" The witch spotted the paperwork strewn across the office. Her mouth pressed to a flat line. "Those had better not be my compliance reports."

Mindy ducked inside the copy machine.

STAKEOUT PLANNING

DIDI SLAMMED A FILE ONTO THE CONFERENCE ROOM table, making Nigel jump and accidentally manifest several tentacles.

"Sorry," he mumbled, quickly tucking them away.

The boogeyman looked like this was the last place he wanted to be. I didn't blame him. It wasn't even ten a.m. and I was more than ready to call it a day.

"Nigel's contact at the DMV came through." Didi opened the file and spread the contents on the table, her expression grimmer than usual. "Wheeler has multiple vehicles registered under different identities."

I pulled some of the documents and photographs over. "How many?"

"Seven." Didi lowered her brows. "All expensive models."

"Why the hell would someone need seven cars?" I muttered.

"Maybe he uses one for every day of the week?" Gavin suggested distractedly. He was busy rearranging his fire extinguishers in size order on the conference table. He looked up at the sudden silence and grimaced at Didi's scowl. "Sorry."

"Crime sure pays, huh?" Bo had peeked his head above the table and was staring at the pictures.

"The question is, where's he getting the money from?" Didi said.

"What do you mean?" I asked.

Nigel cleared his throat nervously. "I found a whole host of employment details for Wheeler under his various identities, but none of them were real."

"I guess we won't know the answer to any of our questions until we talk to him." I frowned. "Any idea where he might be hanging out these days?"

"There was a recent sighting in the Crossroads," Nigel said. "One of his vehicles is registered to an address there."

"The Crossroads?" The name was unfamiliar to me.

"It's an area of Amberford where the supernatural and human worlds overlap," Didi explained. "There are businesses there that cater to both communities."

"It's the perfect place to hide if you can change your appearance at will," Gavin acknowledged.

"There's no telling if he's really going to be at that address or not," Didi said thoughtfully. "We should carry out a surveillance operation." She paused. "Without repeating what happened last time."

I looked between them warily. "Do I want to know what happened last time?"

"No," Didi and Nigel said in unison.

"The fire department said most of the damage was superficial," Gavin protested.

This surveillance op was beginning to sound like a bad idea before it'd even started.

Didi wrinkled her brow. "We do this by the book." She focused on me. "Now's a good time to tell you about the protocols we have to follow during supernatural surveillance."

I spent the next couple of hours learning about said protocols and helping Didi and Gavin plan the surveillance operation. Bo assisted with surprisingly useful suggestions he'd gleaned from watching one too many true crime shows.

"So, that's what we'll do," Didi finished. "Any questions?"

"Yes." Bo wagged his tail with a hopeful expression. "Can we get those earpiece things, you know, like in the spy movies?"

Nigel brightened. "I have some in IT storage—"

"No," Didi and I said firmly.

The conference door opened. Samuel walked in.

My inner wolf stood up straight.

The Hawthorne alpha looked drop-dead gorgeous in a three-piece suit and was carrying takeout bags stamped with a logo that said The Notorious P.I.G. My stomach growled embarrassingly loud at the amazing smells coming from them and him.

His smile made my heart stutter. "Are you ready for lunch?"

I was ready to jump him. I hadn't realized how badly I'd missed the man until I saw him just now. Also,

I wasn't sure what it was about his scent today, but it was doing weird things to my pulse.

Samuel arched an eyebrow. "Wanna join me in my office?"

I chewed my lip. His office was dangerous territory. We'd be alone and I could definitely see myself doing something that would give the Hawthorne & Associates employees gossip material for at least a decade.

Didi made a mildly disgusted expression and waved vaguely at the sexual tension thickening the air. Nigel looked like he wanted to take notes. Gavin was focused on his fire extinguishers and not paying attention.

"How about the break room?" I suggested reluctantly.

"Okay," Samuel said.

The way his shoulders trembled told me he'd totally guessed the filthy direction my thoughts had taken and was enjoying the hell out of this.

Lunch was a surprisingly enjoyable affair despite the attraction sparking between us. I learned that The Notorious P.I.G. was a sought-after sandwich place and delicatessen in downtown Amberford and that it catered almost exclusively to the supernatural clientele working in the business district. Samuel had gotten the luncheon special for everyone on the fifth floor.

We'd just finished eating and were having coffee when Victoria swept into the break room with Pearl. The atmosphere grew decidedly chilly as Hawthorne & Associates's top management considered their boss's mother warily.

"I'm glad to see you disabled DEFCON 3 for my visits," Victoria told Samuel with a sniff.

Pearl ruined the effect she was going for by greeting the room with a nonchalant, "Yo, you lowly peasants."

Victoria's expression glazed over a little. The rest of us stared at Pearl like she'd grown another head.

Pearl looked at Bo. "Did I say that right?"

"Maybe lose the 'lowly peasants' next time," Bo huffed.

I cut my eyes to my dog.

"We decided she should practice some commoner slang," Bo said innocently.

"Oh God," Samuel mumbled. He recovered his composure and addressed Victoria with a frown. "Why are you here, Mother?"

"I'm sorry to interrupt," the Hawthorne matriarch said, not looking sorry at all, "but I need to borrow Abby. The Council of Elders wants to see her this afternoon."

My stomach sank. I'd almost forgotten about that.

"I have meetings for the rest of the day, so I won't be able to attend," Samuel said curtly. "Get them to reschedule."

"No one said you had to be there," Victoria declared dismissively.

"But I want to be there," Samuel growled.

I intervened before Nigel started digging a hole in the break room so he could escape. Judging from the way Didi was scowling and gripping her coffee cup, she was busy contemplating whether to turn everyone into a frog.

"I'll be okay." I placed a hand on Samuel's arm. "Besides, Victoria and Pearl will be there."

"No worries, homie," Pearl said with regal dignity. "We'll make sure you don't look sus in front of the squad."

The rest of us narrowed our eyes at Bo.

He wagged his tail. "What?"

HOW TO MAKE ENEMIES AND INFLUENCE WEREWOLVES

THE DEN OCCUPIED A LIMESTONE MANSION IN TEMPLE Heights that made the Hawthorne residence look modest in comparison. Victoria's Mercedes purred to a stop in front of wrought-iron gates bearing the club's insignia: a crescent moon wrapped around a martini glass.

"Remember what we discussed," Victoria said as the gates opened.

"Try not to start any blood feuds," I recited dutifully.

Victoria's expression grew pinched.

"I'm sorry, but the 'speak only when spoken to' stipulation that preceded that instruction does not sit well with me," I said adamantly.

"It's for your own good." Victoria rolled onto a driveway lined with topiary bushes shaped like various supernatural creatures. "The people we're about to meet are vultures. The minute they sense any weakness from you, they'll pounce."

"Can I pounce back?" I asked innocently.

Bo wheezed on the rear seat. Victoria's left eye started twitching.

I sighed. "Alright, I'll be on my best behavior. I promise."

Victoria parked in a lot full of gleaming, expensive vehicles that would probably make Wheeler green with envy. I followed her up stone steps to a pair of ornate wooden doors guarded by a man in an impeccable tailored suit.

I could tell from his scent that he was a werewolf.

"Good afternoon, Mrs. Hawthorne." He bowed. "The Council is expecting you in the Moonlight Room."

Someone needed to come up with more original names for these places.

"Yo, my guy," Pearl greeted the werewolf imperiously. "Looking fresh today."

The werewolf's eyes bulged slightly. Victoria pretended to be fascinated by a nearby topiary. Bo wagged his tail and grinned.

To his credit, the doorman recovered his aplomb swiftly. He was reaching for the door when his gaze landed on me. He froze, his eyes widening all over again.

A strange feeling came over me then. One that sent an eerie chill down my spine.

I could practically taste the werewolf's apprehension as he gazed at me. And not just his apprehension. I could sense his quickening heartbeat and almost decipher his racing thoughts.

I looked him calmly in the eye.

He blinked, his expression growing slightly glazed. Then we were past him and inside the club's foyer.

"What was that?" Victoria asked quietly as we gave our coats to a cloakroom attendant projecting distinct pixie vibes.

"What was what?"

Victoria shot me a guarded glance as we proceeded down a hallway lined with wood-paneled walls displaying portraits of people who did not look completely human.

"The thing you did to that man," she elaborated. "Like a silent command."

I arched an eyebrow. "What kind of silent command?"

"I could practically hear the word 'heel' in your gaze."

I frowned. It had not been a conscious act.

"Maybe it's your white luna powers manifesting themselves," Bo suggested. "You know, like that spider dude."

Pearl flicked her tail curiously. "Who's that?"

"A guy who gets bitten by a radioactive spider and turns into a superhero," Bo explained with the enthusiasm of a secret fan.

Pearl curled a lip. "That's totally unrealistic."

"I could say the same thing about you, furball," Bo huffed in a tone surprisingly devoid of animosity.

"Don't make me come over there and scratch your eyes out, mutt," Pearl said equally good-naturedly.

Victoria and I exchanged a look. Having our pets

bond was not turning out to be the heartwarming, kumbaya experience it was supposed to be. Although "pet" was hardly the right word to describe Pearl.

We passed through a lounge where waiters in formal attire were serving drinks to a well-dressed supernatural clientele lounging in leather armchairs and playing billiards and cards. The noise level dropped noticeably as our passage attracted inquisitive stares.

"This place is pretty swanky," Bo observed.

"Indeed," Pearl said. "It has rich vibes, no cap."

"Pearl?" Victoria groaned as a vampire in a three-piece suit nearly dropped his bloody martini.

"Yes, Victoria?"

"How about you lose the slang?"

Pearl blinked. "But I am rather enjoying the language of the peasant populace."

Victoria looked accusingly at Bo. My dog avoided her eyes.

"Remember," the Hawthorne matriarch said as we approached a sweeping staircase, "you should—"

"I know," I muttered. "Keep my mouth shut as much as possible."

Victoria didn't look convinced by my promise as we climbed the stairs to the second floor.

I had a feeling this was going to be a very long afternoon.

She led the way into a west-facing corridor, the thick carpet swallowing our footsteps. I eyed the display cases we passed warily. They held strange-looking items that were making my newly awakened wolf senses tingle.

"Those are magical artifacts," Victoria explained at my expression. "They were used during the Shadow War."

"What's the Shadow War?" I asked curiously. "You mentioned it last night."

"It was a supernatural conflict that coincided with the American Civil War," Victoria said curtly. "Thousands of our kind lost their lives during the battles that took place across the country."

She stopped in front of a set of mahogany doors carved with phases of the moon before I could ask more questions. I could hear voices coming from behind them.

Victoria straightened her already perfect bearing. "Ready?"

"No," I admitted.

Bo gulped beside me. He looked nervous for the first time since we'd arrived at the private club.

"Chill," Pearl said with dignified poise. "We'll make sure you two don't fumble the vibe."

Victoria sagged a little. She sighed and reached for the handle.

The door opened onto a large, tenebrous room. Bo and I headed inside after Victoria and Pearl. My scalp prickled at the supernatural power that washed across my skin.

Shadowy figures appeared in the gloom. I squinted.

Bo swished his tail hesitantly. "Well, that was anticlimactic."

A group of werewolves who looked well past their prime sat drinking tea around a long table. Half of them looked like they'd stepped out of a historical novel, complete with lace cuffs, walking sticks, and nineteenth-century sensibilities. Though they appeared innocuous at first glance, they radiated the kind of authority that only came with age and status.

"Welcome to the Moonlight Room," a voice boomed mournfully behind us.

Bo yelped and jumped an inch in the air. I clutched my chest and winced as a sudden bout of acid reflux hit the back of my throat.

Several of the elderly werewolves spilled their tea.

"For crying out loud, Camilla." Victoria frowned at the figure behind the door.

It was a middle-aged woman with mousy hair and watery eyes. Her nostrils flared when she spotted me. She gave me a cautious look.

"Yeah, what was that for?" an elderly werewolf with a wrinkled face that made her look like a desiccated prune asked with a heavy scowl.

Someone equally wrinkly shook their walking stick at Camilla. "We told you to stop doing that, dammit. I nearly peed myself. And I'm wearing my best undies and everything, in honor of meeting the new luna."

I wasn't sure what to make of this and decided diplomatic silence was the best solution under the circumstances.

"But it's tradition," Camilla protested. "As the Council's secretary, it's my duty to announce—"

"So you're the white wolf everyone's been talking about," a voice interrupted coolly to my left.

My gaze found the woman who'd spoken. Her chestnut hair was sprinkled with an elegant dash of gray and her clothes looked even more expensive than the outfits Victoria had bought for me from Moonlight Couture. She was around fifteen years younger than the rest of her peers and carried herself with the same elegance and grace as Victoria.

I got instant Karen vibes from her.

Sparks sizzled between Victoria and the werewolf.

"Helen," Victoria said frostily.

"Victoria," the woman greeted with equal iciness.

"That's Helen Sheridan," Pearl murmured with an annoyed flick of her tail.

Seemed I was right about her being a Karen. I was dying to know what the story was between those two but was conscious I was attracting curious stares. The elderly werewolves were studying me with varying degrees of interest.

"Well?" Helen demanded haughtily. "Is she going to say anything?"

She was looking at me like I was dirt under her Jimmy Choos. I narrowed my eyes a fraction.

Bo stamped his paws indignantly. "I don't like her."

Helen's gaze shifted. She stared down her nose at my dog.

"Who is this flea-infested creature?"

Pearl spoke before I could tell the Karen wannabe where she could shove that question.

"The canine is under my protection," she stated, her

voice dripping with scorn. "He is an honorary member of our pack. Any disrespect toward him will be construed as a challenge to the Hawthornes."

"Furball," Bo keened gratefully. He attempted to lick Pearl and got booped on the nose. "Ouch."

Helen decided to pretend she hadn't just insulted my dog.

"Is your new luna mute, Victoria?" she said irritably. "Or is she just stupid?"

The thin thread of my patience snapped with a sound I suspected the others heard. I felt my nails lengthen as I lowered my brows at the werewolf socialite.

"How about you and I step outside—"

Victoria cut off my low growl.

"Is this how our Council treats a new luna?" she said in a steely voice. "And one belonging to the most powerful pack in Amberford, no less?"

Helen bristled. "Who said the Hawthornes are the most power—"

"Helen," a voice said quietly.

SMOKE AND MIRRORS

My head snapped to the right. A woman with dark eyes and silver-speckled dark hair was watching me with an unreadable expression, her teacup poised perfectly in her manicured hands.

I hadn't noticed her when I'd walked into the room. From the way Bo's ears flattened briefly, neither had he. Which was odd, considering the subtle hostility I could feel radiating off her.

Helen backed down grudgingly at the stranger's tone.

Victoria addressed the dark-haired woman in a polite voice. "Priscilla, I'm glad to see your health has improved enough for you to attend the Council meetings again."

"Thank you," Priscilla said with a smile that didn't quite reach her eyes. "I'm pleased to see you too, old friend."

Her emphasis on the word "friend" wasn't lost on

anyone. Several of the elderly werewolves exchanged troubled glances.

I now understood what Victoria had meant when she'd said the Council was a flock of vultures.

Victoria ignored the tension in the room and addressed her peers. "Everyone, I would like to formally introduce the Hawthorne luna. This is Abigail West, Samuel's mate. And this is her dog, Bo."

"Hi," I said guardedly.

"Sup," Bo greeted with a hesitant wag of his tail.

The Council welcomed us with a series of curious hellos and a few judgmental nods.

"Why don't you sit down and have some tea?" Camilla Lynch said timidly once introductions were complete.

"Do you have anything stronger?" I said bluntly.

A few of the elderly werewolves swallowed snorts. Some wrinkled their brows disapprovingly. The color rising in Helen's cheeks indicated she was about to blow.

Priscilla Holt's expression remained inscrutable.

"It was a joke," I muttered.

Victoria shot me a warning look and guided me to a chair. I pulled it back. The top rail shattered in my grip. My stomach dropped.

A hush fell over the room. Victoria paled a little. Pearl sighed.

"That's one way to make an impression," Bo said brightly.

"You know, I don't think that dog's a familiar,"

Martha Claymore, the elder with the fresh undies, hissed to a wrinkly counterpart.

"I think you're right," Felicity Newfield grunted.

I realized half the Council was studying me like I was one hot second away from turning rabid on them.

I swallowed. "Is this an antique?"

"Yes," Helen snapped.

"No," Victoria groaned at the same time.

I looked at Pearl.

"It costs as much as your clothes did," the cat said.

My eyes glazed over a little.

Victoria wordlessly indicated the next chair, her movements stiff. I recalled my training with Samuel and handled it gingerly as I sat in it.

There was a knock at the door.

"Come in," Camilla said in a brittle voice.

A waiter walked in with a pot of tea and a cake stand packed with sandwiches, cakes, and cookies.

"So," Priscilla said politely once we all had fresh cups and had helped ourselves to something to nibble on. "Tell us about yourself."

I watched her guardedly. According to Victoria, the Council of Elders had no official leader and all decisions were taken by a majority vote. Yet it seemed Priscilla had appointed herself the de facto head of the assembled werewolves. From the uncomfortable glances some of the other Council members were exchanging, not everyone was on board with her behavior.

"Yes," Camilla added eagerly, trying to break the fraught silence. "We want to know everything."

"Especially about that first pack run," Isobel Lynton said coolly. "I heard it was quite spectacular."

"Isobel," Victoria warned in a low voice.

"What?" Isobel looked unrepentant. "It's not every day the Hawthornes get a new luna, Victoria. Even if she is a human who was bitten by your wayward son."

Victoria stiffened.

"And we all know why he turned out that way," Helen added in a syrupy voice.

The temperature in the room dropped several degrees.

I couldn't tell if Victoria's rigid expression was from Helen's words or the general reference to Hugh.

"Now, now," Priscilla said smoothly. "Let's not dwell on the past." She focused on me. "How are you finding life as a werewolf, Abigail?"

There was something about her perfectly pleasant tone that made my inner wolf uneasy. Judging from the way Bo was watching her, my dog felt the same.

Since Victoria had decided to ignore the thinly veiled insults directed at the Hawthornes, I elected to do the same.

"It's been interesting," I said calmly.

"Interesting?" Helen scoffed. "Is that all you have to say?"

I arched an eyebrow. "Would you prefer I describe my first transformation in detail?"

"Abby," Victoria pleaded softly.

I ignored her. I knew I was playing right into the Council's hands, but the way they were treating Victoria was getting on my nerves.

"The pain hit me like a brick wall." I bared my teeth in what I hoped passed for a smile but judging from the way a few eyes widened probably came across as a threatening smirk. "Luckily, my alpha decided to dull my agony by kissing me. It was hot. And heavy. Tongue was involved—"

Martha and Felicity choked on their teas.

Several of the elderly werewolves sucked in air behind their cups, their expressions a mix of shock and horrified interest.

"No need to be crude, dear," Priscilla said with a tight smile.

Martha steered the conversation in a less confrontational direction.

"I must say, you seem to have adapted remarkably well for someone so newly turned," the elderly werewolf said affably.

"Indeed," Isobel said in a disapproving voice, steering it right back in the danger zone. "The pixies say you're faster than any werewolf they've ever seen."

My shoulders knotted. I could see where this was going and I didn't like it one bit. Judging from the way Pearl's eyes shrank to slits and Victoria's knuckles whitened on her cup, neither did they.

"The pixies need to mind their own business," Victoria said sharply.

"But it's true, isn't it?" Isobel arched an eyebrow. "Your new luna outran the entire pack during her first run."

I shifted uncomfortably as all eyes locked onto me.

"I wouldn't say the entire pack."

"I was told even the proud Hawthorne alpha couldn't keep up with you." Isobel's expression turned calculating. "When was the last time we had a white wolf in Amberford?"

"Not since my great-great-grandmother's time," Victoria replied reluctantly in the fraught silence.

"Hmm." Isobel sipped her tea. "Fascinating how these things skip generations, isn't it?"

I suppressed the growl working up my throat. Bo pressed against my leg, equally tense. Surprise jolted me when Pearl jumped from Victoria's lap onto mine.

I could tell from the cat's body language that she was telling me to stay calm.

"Speaking of fascinating things," Helen said in an oily voice. "I notice Samuel isn't here today. You would have thought he would have wanted to come, considering it's the first time his luna is being introduced to our community."

"He had meetings," Victoria said coolly. "We weren't exactly given a lot of notice."

"Really?" Helen's lips curved. "Or maybe he's avoiding his responsibilities, like his father."

Victoria's teacup cracked. Some of the elders traded troubled looks. Even I could tell Helen had crossed a line.

Pearl hissed and arched her back. "How dare you mention Alexander!"

Bo thumped the floor irritably with his tail. "Should I rough her up?!"

I narrowed my eyes at Helen. "You seem awfully

interested in the Hawthornes's private business, Karen."

The werewolf was oblivious to my deadly tone.

"My name is Helen!" she snapped, her face reddening.

"Oh, is it?" I cocked an eyebrow. "I would call you that if you stopped sticking your nose where it doesn't belong."

"How dare you—" Helen snarled.

"Now, now," Priscilla intervened in a voice laced with a steely warning. "We're all friends here."

"Yeah, I don't think so," I said coldly. I glanced at Victoria and decided I'd had enough of the Council's attitude toward us. "You know, I'm not sure why you put up with this behavior. Maybe it's because I wasn't born a werewolf, but if humans acted this way, they'd get slammed against the wall and punched in the throat."

Bo grinned. Pearl smirked. Victoria blinked.

Admiration glittered in Martha's eyes. She leaned toward Felicity and hissed, "I like her!"

Camilla was staring at me in wide-eyed awe. Helen spluttered incoherently beside her.

I crossed my arms, leaned back in the chair, and scanned the Council. "Why don't you people get to the point? It's clear you have something you want to say."

For once, Victoria seemed grateful for my intervention. I could tell the mention of her husband had rattled her.

"Perhaps we should move on to official business,"

Camilla suggested. She glanced hesitantly around the table.

Priscilla fixed me with a piercing stare. "We are here to discuss your position as luna."

Victoria stilled.

"What about it?" I said in a chilly tone.

"The Council has certain expectations," Helen said with the expression of someone who'd been made to swallow a raw lemon.

"Such as?" I asked dangerously.

"Such as proper decorum and behavior," Isobel replied. "Oh, and suitable associations." Her gaze dropped meaningfully to Bo.

Pearl's tail bristled. "Excuse me?!"

"What Helen and Isobel mean," Priscilla said smoothly, "is that we want to ensure you understand the gravity of your position." She paused and fixed me with an unreadable stare. "Especially given your unique abilities."

I didn't like the way she said *unique*.

"The Council would like to monitor your development," Camilla concluded in a sickly tone. The secretary looked like she wanted to sink into the ground.

"Monitor?" I repeated flatly.

"For your own good, of course." Priscilla said. Her smile made her look like a shark. "We wouldn't want anything unfortunate to happen because you don't understand your role."

I saw Victoria's fingers curl into fists on her lap.

It was clear the Council intended to put a leash on

me. Whether this was because they feared the Hawthornes gaining even more power and influence than they already had, or because they didn't know how to cope with the sudden appearance of a white wolf, only time would tell.

"Is it my imagination, or is there a threat buried in those words?"

Priscilla's smile widened in the tense silence. "Oh, we would never dare threaten a luna. We only wish to help."

THE SINS OF THE FATHER

VICTORIA'S STUDY LOOKED NOTHING LIKE WHAT I'D expected from the Hawthorne matriarch. Instead of the antique furniture and oil paintings that characterized the rest of the mansion, the room was decorated in rich vintage tones, with comfortable modern sofas and art. The only traditional touches were the Persian rug and the grandfather clock ticking away in the corner.

Victoria indicated an armchair by the fireplace and went straight to a cabinet.

I sat down, Pearl in my arms.

The cat had unilaterally adopted me after the Council of Elders meeting ended on a chilly note. Bo didn't seem to mind.

Victoria returned with a crystal decanter and a pair of glasses. "I think we both need this." She poured two generous measures of amber liquid and passed me a glass.

I sniffed it cautiously. It smelled expensive.

"Twenty-five-year-old Macallan," Victoria said

dismissively. She settled in the armchair opposite me and took a fortifying sip. "A gift from Alexander."

My ears pricked at the mention of Samuel and Hugh's father.

"Where is he?" I asked carefully.

"Your guess is as good as mine." Victoria's mouth curved slightly, her face carrying a wealth of resignation. "I last saw him three months ago. He showed up out of the blue at two a.m., wearing a poncho and carrying a crate of rare tequila. Said he'd won it off a warlock in a poker game in Mexico."

I was not expecting that.

Victoria's expression grew wistful. "He stayed for breakfast, told the most outrageous stories about his adventures, then disappeared again." She swirled the whiskey in her glass. "That's Alexander for you. Like a summer storm. Here one minute, gone the next."

"He sounds like an interesting guy," Bo panted.

Pearl licked a paw. "That's one way of putting it."

"How did you meet?" I said curiously.

It was clear Victoria was in the mood to chat. Now was as good a time as any to find answers to all the questions I still had about the Hawthornes.

Victoria's eyes grew distant. "At a pack gathering. My family was hosting a summer ball." Her lips curved. "He crashed it."

I blinked. "Crashed it?"

"Literally. He flew his plane into our topiary garden." Victoria's smile widened at my shocked expression. "He claimed he had engine trouble, but I found out later he'd done it on purpose. He said it was the only way to get past my family's security."

I could see where Hugh got his dramatic flair from.

"Your family didn't approve?"

"The Rochesters are old money." Victoria's tone turned sardonic. "Very old money. Though the Hawthornes are equally wealthy, they have a reputation for being unconventional."

"Batshit crazy is more accurate," Pearl contributed acerbically. "Alexander's grandfather once tried to start a werewolf circus."

I choked on my drink.

Bo wagged his tail enthusiastically. "That's so cool!"

"He said it was for the supernatural appreciation of the arts." Victoria's eyes sparkled with humor. "It didn't end well. Especially after someone let the tigers out."

"Those tigers had it coming," Pearl muttered darkly.

I was beginning to suspect there was more to Pearl's history with the Hawthornes than met the eye.

"So what happened?" I asked. "With you and Alexander?"

Victoria's face softened. "We fell in love. Much to everyone's horror." She took another sip of whiskey. "My father threatened to disown me. Alexander's family on the other hand was thrilled to have me. They thought I might be able to tame him." Her smile faded. "They were wrong about that, in the end."

I decided to shift the conversation slightly. "What's the beef between you and Helen?"

"She was Victoria's love rival," Pearl said with a sneer.

Victoria grimaced. "She tried to seduce Alexander several times before our marriage. He rejected her emphatically."

"That crazy werewolf turned up in his room one night in a see-through negligee," Pearl muttered in disgust.

We all shuddered.

The grandfather clock in the corner ticked quietly in the silence that followed.

"The first few years of our marriage were wonderful," Victoria finally said. "Alexander was charming, brilliant, full of wild ideas. But he was also kind. He doted on the boys and treated his role as the pack alpha seriously." Her voice caught. "Then the attempts on his life started."

My scalp prickled. I suddenly recalled how Aunt Lucille had lost her teeth. "There was more than one attempt?"

"Yes. Someone wanted the Hawthornes gone. We never found out who it was." Victoria's knuckles whitened on her glass. "The attacks grew worse. More frequent. Alexander..." She paused and swallowed. "He changed. Started disappearing for longer and longer periods. He said he was trying to protect us by staying away."

Though I could guess the answer, I still asked the question. "Did it work?"

"No." Victoria's voice turned bitter. "The attempts just shifted to the rest of us. Samuel was fifteen when he had to fight off an assassin who'd broken into the mansion. Hugh was twelve at the time." She closed her eyes. "That's when Alexander left for good."

I was still digesting this shocking revelation when the study door opened.

Samuel stood in the doorway, his expression dark behind his glasses. "I see you're telling Abby about Father." His hair was all messed up, like he'd been running his hands through it all afternoon.

I resisted the urge to go over and smooth his wild locks down.

Boy did I have it bad.

Victoria's face tightened. "She deserves to know."

Samuel avoided my gaze and crossed the floor to grab a glass from the drinks cabinet. He poured himself a generous measure of whiskey from the decanter and headed over to a window overlooking the gardens.

"Did you tell her how he sends postcards? From Tibet, Hawaii, wherever the hell he is?" His voice grew hard. "How he thinks gifts and stories make up for not being here when we needed him?"

"Samuel—" Victoria started.

"Or how about how his absence affected Hugh?" Samuel knocked back his drink. "After all, watching our father run away from his responsibilities taught him it was okay to do the same."

His bitter words rang in the silence. Bo whimpered.

My chest tightened. Even though I'd known Samuel and Victoria for less than a week, I found myself wanting to erase the pain in their eyes. I guessed that made me a member of the Hawthorne pack in every sense of the word now.

Victoria sighed and set her glass down with a quiet clink. "I should have known the Council would try something like this."

Samuel's head snapped around. "Why?" His expression turned dangerous. "What did they do?"

Victoria hesitated. "They want to monitor Abby."

The mate bond hummed with a sudden burst of rage that made me draw a sharp breath.

Samuel noticed and inhaled raggedly, his knuckles white on his glass.

The fury I felt from him abated to a dull, red thrum.

"Because she's a white wolf?" he said between gritted teeth.

"Yes. Or at least, that's the excuse some are using to try and put a leash on her."

"They have no right—" Samuel growled.

"They're scared, Samuel." Victoria's voice turned weary. "They're terrified of the power that a white wolf, especially a white luna, can wield. There hasn't been one in generations. Not since Elizabeth."

My pulse quickened at the name. "Was Elizabeth your great-great-grandmother? The one who united the New England packs during the Shadow War?"

"Yes," Victoria replied.

Samuel placed his glass on Victoria's desk with more force than necessary. "The Council is overstepping. They have no authority over pack matters."

"We do when it comes to white wolves," Victoria said quietly. "The power to influence other packs is not one to be taken lightly. It's an unwritten rule we have to abide by, whether we like it or not. After all, it's what Elizabeth herself wanted."

A chill ran down my spine. "What?"

Victoria pinched the bridge of her nose. "Elizabeth didn't just unite the New England packs during the Shadow War. She worked with other supernatural species to establish towns like Amberford, where we could live in open secrecy among humans."

"She also helped create many of our modern supernatural political structures and the organizations that maintain law and order among our kind," Samuel added grudgingly. He hesitated. "Making sure a white wolf didn't abuse their power is something she would have worried about." He prowled over and poured himself another drink.

I was tempted to ask him for a second one myself after everything I'd just learned.

Samuel sensed my stare and met my gaze. The amber fire that sparked in the depths of his eyes made me shiver.

"The Council can go to Hell," he growled. "Abby is under our protection."

I heard the hidden *mine* in his sentence and flushed.

"I agree," Victoria said, surprising me all over again.

I stared at her. "You do? But you just said we had to—"

"It doesn't mean we have to dance to their tune. There are ways to interpret what they say and want." Victoria exchanged a meaningful look with Pearl.

The cat smirked.

I could see why those two got on so well.

"There is something that worries me." Victoria wrinkled her brow. "Priscilla seemed particularly interested in Abby's abilities."

Samuel's eyes narrowed behind his glasses. "Priscilla Holt has always been ambitious."

"She gives me the creeps," Bo contributed. "And not in a good way."

Samuel gave my dog a dubious look. "There's a good way to get the creeps?"

"Yeah," Bo huffed. "Like when you watch true crime shows."

We all rolled our eyes, Pearl included.

"Priscilla's son Marcus is about to come of age," Victoria said thoughtfully. "He'll need to prove himself as an alpha soon."

Samuel's expression hardened. "If she thinks she can use this situation to gain more influence—"

"She wouldn't dare." Victoria stared into her drink with a frown. "Not after what happened with her husband."

Bo's ears pricked. So did mine.

"Why, what happened to him?"

Victoria and Samuel exchanged a loaded look.

"Arthur Holt disappeared under mysterious circumstances ten years ago," Victoria finally said.

I decided I really didn't want to know what that meant. Learning about the dark side of the supernatural community and werewolf assassinations was bad enough.

"Marcus is weak." Samuel lowered his brows. "It's

not the kid's fault, but I doubt he'll ever make a proper alpha. He needs somebody strong at his side."

The grandfather clock chimed the hour.

"I should go," I said reluctantly. "Ellie will be wondering where I am."

"I'll drive you," Samuel said.

Victoria watched us head for the door. "Abby?"

I stopped and turned.

"Thank you." A tired smile curved Victoria's lips. "For standing up for me at the Council meeting."

I shrugged. "That's what family does, right?"

Victoria's expression softened.

Samuel squeezed my hand as we left his mother's study.

"I'm sorry I couldn't be there. It sounds like you had a rough time."

I grimaced. "Not really. I flipped and told those stuffy werewolves where to stick it. You should have seen their faces."

"They looked like Ellie when she has marmite," Bo added helpfully.

Samuel chuckled. His gaze dropped to my mouth. His eyes grew heated.

"Wanna go check out my room before I drop you off?" he drawled seductively.

My mouth went dry. Darn, this man could really flip my wolf's switch with his voice and his come-hither eyes. I swallowed convulsively.

"How about we save that for another day?"

He laughed at my strangled voice.

ON THE TRAIL

"THIS IS BORING," BO COMPLAINED FROM THE BACK OF the van.

"Real-life surveillance usually is," Didi said from the driver's seat.

"What happened to car chases and explosions?" Bo huffed.

"I wouldn't be doing this job if it involved car chases and explosions," the witch muttered.

"Ditto," Gavin said distractedly.

He was peering through the lens of a high-powered camera at an apartment building down the road. The dragon newt was surprisingly focused on our surveillance operation, his nostrils occasionally sparking as he concentrated.

"At least a hot dog cart going past would be nice," Bo grumbled.

I couldn't exactly disagree with him.

We'd been watching Wheeler's registered address all morning. So far, the only exciting thing that had happened was a kid dropping an ice-cream cone on the sidewalk and two seagulls fighting over it like it was the Holy Grail.

The Crossroads was aptly named. Supernatural and human businesses operated side by side, though the humans remained oblivious to their otherworldly neighbors. A vampire-run coffee shop going by Bloody Good Coffee sat next to a normal bakery. A pixie flower shop was doing business alongside a convenience store.

"So," Didi said, shooting an overly casual glance my way, "how did the Council meeting go?"

Gavin's horns perked up.

I swallowed a groan. It was clear both of them were dying to know what had happened yesterday afternoon.

"It was…" I faltered for a beat. "Interesting."

"That bad, huh?"

I grimaced. It seemed I was going to have to tell them about it whether I liked it or not.

"Let's just say I may have threatened to punch several Council members in the throat."

Gavin choked on his energy drink.

"Let me guess?" Didi rolled her eyes. "Helen Sheridan?"

"Bingo."

"It's a miracle no one's turned that woman into a newt yet. No offense, Gavin."

"None taken."

I hesitated. "What do you guys know about Priscilla Holt?"

Didi and Gavin traded a cautious look.

"She comes from a very old werewolf family," the witch said carefully. "Rumor is her ancestors were in New England before the Hawthornes arrived from the Old Continent."

I digested this information with a frown. Was that the reason Priscilla disliked the Hawthornes being referred to as the most powerful pack in Amberford?

"Do you know anything about her husband's disappearance?"

Didi drummed her fingers on the steering wheel.

"The supernatural task force did a thorough investigation into the incident. I remember because it was all over the papers and on TV. They concluded he was the victim of a deal gone wrong." The witch shrugged at my puzzled stare. "The Holt pack owns a third of the businesses in Amberford."

The more I learned about the supernatural community I now belonged to, the more uneasy I became. Life as a human seemed like a picnic compared to the perils of my new werewolf existence.

I thought back to last night's conversation. "What about Priscilla's son?"

"You mean Marcus Holt?" Didi said.

"Yeah."

"He's the quiet, bookish type," Gavin said. "Rarely speaks, mostly because of his stutter. Kind kid, if a little gullible. Wouldn't hurt a newt."

Didi and I stared at him.

"I went to school with him," Gavin admitted.

Didi wrinkled her brow. "Didn't he go to that ritzy private school the next valley over?"

"He did." The dragon newt squirmed when our stares turned piercing. "My family is rich."

"Is it because of all the hoarding?" Bo asked innocently.

Smoke curled from Gavin's nostrils.

Didi hastily redirected the conversation back to our surveillance op. "Nigel's still got eyes on the back entrance?"

The boogeyman was assisting in our stakeout from his closet at Hawthorne & Associates.

"Yeah," Gavin confirmed. "He's monitoring the street cameras."

"Someone just came out," Bo panted.

We peered through the van's tinted windows. A woman had emerged from Wheeler's building.

"That's not him," Didi muttered.

Gavin sighed. "This is going to be a long day. How about one of us grabs some lunch?"

Bo wagged his tail enthusiastically. "I like that idea."

I listened with half an ear. The woman from Wheeler's building was crossing the road. She was wrapped in a thick coat and scarf and wore a beanie hat that covered her long, blonde hair.

Something about the way she walked had me staring.

"Abby?" Didi said, puzzled.

The blonde walked into Bloody Good Coffee.

"Why don't I get us some lunch from there?"

I opened the van door and stepped outside before Didi or Gavin could protest.

Bo hopped down after me. "I could murder a cheese sandwich."

The coffee shop boasted a Victorian-style storefront with a black-and-crimson awning and gold-leaf Gothic lettering on the windows. The exterior menu board advertised Type-O Lattes and Plasma Punch, although the names flickered to more traditional human coffee names even as I watched.

The door jingled when we stepped inside. The smell of freshly ground coffee, blood, and otherworldly creatures filled my nostrils. I looked around.

The interior was all dark-wood paneling, exposed brick walls, and plush velvet booths in deep burgundy. Antique brass light fixtures cast a warm light over comfortable armchairs and strategically placed mirrors.

Vampire baristas were working vintage coffee grinders and serving food behind a counter made of polished black marble with red veining. The blonde from Wheeler's building stood in the queue in front of it. She was talking in a low voice on her phone.

I was wondering if I had been imagining things when a stringent voice spoke behind me.

"Abigail?"

I turned and swallowed a groan. It was Helen.

I spotted Priscilla sitting in a booth past her shoulder. The werewolf matriarch's face displayed surprise before she schooled her features into a neutral expression.

Bo stepped closer to me. "What are they doing here?"

Helen heard him. Her mouth pressed to a thin line. "I could say the same about you two. Aren't you supposed to be working?"

I frowned. "Last time I checked, I didn't need the Council's permission to buy a coffee."

Helen bristled. "How impertinent!" She crossed her arms and scowled. "Then again, I guess I shouldn't expect anything better from the Hawthorne luna."

My hackles rose at her contemptuous tone.

The noise level in the coffee shop dropped as we became the focus of attention.

Priscilla had risen from their booth and was approaching. "Helen, lower your voice. This is not the place to be discussing—" She froze, her gaze locking on something behind me. Confusion flared in her eyes.

A scent I had never smelled before danced across my nostrils. Bo's ears flattened.

I whirled around, my inner wolf on alert.

The blonde I'd followed into the coffee shop had put her phone away and was staring at us over her shoulder.

"Holy Moly!" Bo mumbled.

The woman's features literally changed as we watched. Her height, build, even her clothes rippled and morphed into an entirely different figure. One I recognized instantly.

It was Clayton Wheeler.

RUN, WOLF, RUN!

HE MOVED BEFORE I COULD REACT AND VAULTED OVER the counter. The baristas cried out in alarm as he pushed past them and made a run for the kitchen.

Instinct kicked in. I bolted after him and cleared the counter in a single jump.

Thank God the dress code for surveillance was civilian clothes instead of a suit.

Bo scooted under the serving bar and followed me. By the time we burst out into the alleyway behind the coffee shop, Wheeler was nowhere in sight.

"He went that way!" Bo turned left.

My inner wolf caught the mimic's scent as I started after my dog.

I overtook Bo, half-skidded around a corner, and caught a glimpse of our suspect as he disappeared over a wall. I yanked my cell out of my pocket and dialed Didi's number as I picked up speed again.

She answered on the first ring. "What's up? You short on cash? Didn't Janet give you a business—"

"The blonde who came out of the apartment building was Wheeler!" I barked. "I'm chasing after him! Head north! Bo will catch up and guide you!"

I reached the wall Wheeler had climbed, crouched, and leapt.

I was on top of it in the blink of an eye.

"Find Didi and Gavin!" I told Bo as he slid to a halt beneath me.

He backed away and fidgeted and whined uncertainly before taking off toward the main road.

I dropped down into a narrow lane that backed onto several businesses and emerged onto a side street one block over. I stopped and looked around wildly, the noise of the traffic rumbling past and the smells around me blinding my senses for a moment.

Movement captured my gaze. Wheeler was in the park across the road, his coat flapping around his legs as he made a run for it.

The surveillance van screeched into view to my left as I sprinted across the street.

"See if you can cut him off on the other side!" I yelled at Didi.

She nodded, spun the wheel around, and headed for the side road circling the park.

I accelerated, my feet eating up the distance to Wheeler and the wind whistling in my ears. I was surprised I wasn't out of breath—especially since it seemed I was nearly half as fast at running in my human form as I was in my wolf form.

The temptation to transform and chase down Wheeler was almost too hard to resist. The only things that stopped me was the fact that I wasn't wearing shift-friendly clothes and that Victoria and the Council of Elders would probably have a coronary if rumors of a white wolf running through the streets of Amberford made headlines tomorrow. I had no doubt Samuel would have something to say about that too, in a brooding, sexy way.

My sensitive hearing picked up an unusual buzz of activity ahead.

Wheeler darted into some bushes and headed in that direction.

Branches scraped my exposed skin as I bolted into the vegetation where he'd disappeared. One of the park's exits lay beyond. I shot through it, lurched to a halt on the sidewalk, and cursed.

A busy outdoor market filled the cobbled streets on that side of the park. One the doppelgänger could easily lose himself in.

A stream of smells assaulted my nostrils. Humans, werewolves, witches, vampires, pixies, dragon newts, and otherworldly creatures I couldn't yet identify.

I closed my eyes and focused, my heartbeat loud in my ears.

My wolf picked up Wheeler's scent. It was faint and fading fast.

I opened my eyes and followed it.

Wheeler soon came into view. The mimic was darting through the crowd, his body changing appearance every few seconds as he jostled passersby in his rush to escape. He looked over his shoulder and glared when he spotted me closing in on him.

He accelerated, willfully knocking over displays to block my path.

I swore under my breath as I dodged flying fruit, cream cakes, and ornaments.

Didi's shout came from somewhere behind me. I heard Bo's low bark.

I ground my teeth. Wheeler was going to get away.

I felt my wolf slip under my human skin as I drew on her speed. I shot through the crowd like a bullet and quickly gained on Wheeler. I was reaching out to grab his collar when something slammed into me from the side.

My breath got knocked out of me.

I went down hard and rolled across the cobblestones, the world spinning around dizzyingly. I came to rest on my front, my heart pounding violently against my ribs and my elbows and knees stinging from fresh scrapes.

"Oh my goodness! Are you—are you okay?!" someone stammered in a flustered voice.

Camilla was standing over me.

I looked to the left and cursed. Wheeler had long disappeared into the crowd.

Didi, Gavin, and Bo arrived just as I was climbing to my feet, the Council's secretary helping me up with a cautious expression.

Didi scanned me from head to toe. "Are you hurt anywhere?!"

"The only thing hurt is my dignity," I muttered.

Bo whined and jumped up on me, pink tongue licking at my chin.

Camilla's gaze danced between us. "I'm sorry, Abby. I didn't mean to bump into you." Her voice quavered.

"It's okay." I winced and looked at my knuckles. I'd scraped them raw.

"Marcus?" Gavin was staring at the figure hovering behind Camilla.

It was a timid-looking young man with dark hair and eyes. He gave off a werewolf scent not dissimilar to Priscilla's. His shoulders hunched at my stare.

"H-hi, Gavin," he stammered, avoiding my eyes.

Camilla glanced at her companion in surprise. "Do you know each other?"

Marcus nodded hesitantly. "We w-went to school together."

"Oh." Camilla recovered her composure and gave us a chagrined look. "I'm sorry, we have to be somewhere." She glanced at me uneasily before guiding Marcus into the crowd.

Didi scowled. "Dammit. We almost had Wheeler."

"How did you know that woman was him?" Gavin asked me curiously.

"The way she walked. It reminded me of the footage from Moonlight Couture." I clocked the dragon newt's awkward stare and the strange glances I was receiving from some of the human passersby. "What is it?"

"You might want to rein in your inner wolf," Didi advised. "Your eyes are glowing and you've gone all—" She waved a hand vaguely.

I touched my face gingerly and groaned at the facial fuzz that had sprouted during the chase. No wonder Camilla had given me a weird look.

Bo plopped down on his haunches and watched me with shiny eyes, his tail thumping the cobblestones.

"You were so cool! Like a superhero. But a hairy one, with anger-management issues."

Trust my dog to ruin my brief moment of glory.

28

FIRST AID, WITH A TOUCH OF ROMANCE

"Yikes." Fred stared as we trudged into Hawthorne & Associates half an hour later. "You look like you went ten rounds with a brick wall."

"She face-planted in front of half of Amberford," Bo said helpfully.

I swallowed a sigh. My knees and elbows still stung from my encounter with the cobblestones, though the scrapes were already starting to feel better.

The Hawthornes had told me werewolves had accelerated healing powers.

"Did one of your surveillance ops go awry again?" Charlene asked sympathetically. The banshee shot a worried look at Gavin. "Wait. He didn't set fire to something again, did he?"

"I did not." Gavin huffed indignantly and almost set a lobby plant ablaze.

We left Charlene and Fred hastily patting down smoking vegetation and took the express elevator to the fifth floor.

Barney looked up from his typewriter when we emerged in the open office area. "I smell blood."

Hugh stared at me where he was leaning a hip against the vampire's desk. "You look terrible."

"Thanks for those useless observations," Didi muttered.

"What are you doing here?" I asked Hugh.

He shrugged. "Mother and Samuel decided I could return to work."

"He's our social media manager," Barney explained.

Somehow, social media manager suited Hugh to a T.

Janet came out of her office and rocked to a stop at my disheveled state. "What the heck happened to you?"

"Our surveillance op kinda failed."

Janet eyed Gavin warily. "He didn't set fire to something again, did he?"

The dragon newt stormed toward his desk, tail popping out and swinging irritably.

Nigel poked his head out of a corridor. "Did you guys get any footage of Wheeler?" Several tentacles manifested in his agitation.

"No." Didi made a face. "But you might be able to find something from the cameras in Bloody Good Coffee."

Nigel adjusted his glasses nervously. "I'll see what I can do." He headed back toward his lair.

Mindy materialized through the break room wall.

"I've color-coded the incident reports you guys need to fill in," she said briskly. She paused at my sight and wisely elected not to comment. "They're on your desk." She perked up when she spotted the boogeyman's retreating form. "Want me to help with anything, Nigel? I've got some free time."

A strangled sound escaped the boogeyman. It was followed by a rushed "I—I would like that very much!"

The rest of us watched Mindy disappear after Nigel.

"Ten bucks says he manifests all his tentacles at once," Didi muttered.

"Do you think Mindy knows he has the hots for her?" Janet asked warily.

We all exchanged a glance.

"Nah," we muttered at the same time, Bo and Hugh included.

"By the way," Hugh asked curiously. "What *exactly* happened during your surveillance op? Abby looks like she's been rolling around in dirt."

I was saved from having to explain by Samuel's arrival. He took one look at my scraped hands and torn clothes and lowered his brows in a way that chilled the air.

"My office. Now."

"Uh-oh," Hugh murmured. "Someone's in trouble."

Samuel cut his eyes to his brother. Hugh blinked innocently.

Bo gave me a cautious look. "Want me to come with you?" His ears flattened a little at Samuel's expression. "I'll go check out the muffins in the break room," he added hastily.

"You do that," Samuel said coolly.

I plodded reluctantly after the Hawthorne alpha as

he headed for his office, conscious of the stares burning into my back.

Samuel closed the door and indicated the couch, his jaw tight. "Sit. I'll get the first-aid kit."

"I'm fine," I protested. "Werewolf healing, remember?"

His eyes flashed amber behind his glasses. "Sit. Down."

I scurried over to the couch.

Samuel went to a cabinet and returned with the kit. He crouched in front of me and carefully took my hand. The mate bond sang at his touch.

I swallowed, suddenly conscious that we were alone.

"These need cleaning," he said quietly.

"They're already half healed."

"They'll heal faster if they're clean." He opened an antiseptic wipe. "This might sting a little."

I tried not to focus on how good he smelled or how his fingers were sending little sparks of electricity up my arm as he took care of my wounds. The last thing I needed was to jump him in his office. Although that desk did look sturdy—

I cut that thought off hastily when his nostrils flared at the sudden burst of lust thrumming through our bond. Damn werewolf senses.

"So," he said as he dabbed at my knuckles. "Want to tell me what happened?"

I reluctantly explained how I'd followed Wheeler into the coffee shop and the ensuing chase.

"Helen and Priscilla were in the coffee shop?" Samuel's voice held a dangerous edge.

"Yes." I clocked his expression. "Wait. You don't think they have something to do with this case, do you?"

"It's just strange that they'd be there."

I wrinkled my brow. Amberford wasn't exactly a metropolis. Priscilla and Helen being in that coffee shop may have been pure coincidence.

"I was more surprised to see Marcus Holt with Camilla," I admitted reluctantly.

Samuel blinked, nonplussed. "Priscilla's son was with Camilla?"

"Yeah. That's how I lost Wheeler. Camilla accidentally bumped into me."

"Interesting." He finished cleaning my hands and indicated my elbows. "Those need attention too. So do your knees."

I tried to pull away. "They're fine."

His expression darkened. "Stop being stubborn."

"I'm not being stubborn. I'm being practical." I gestured at my clothes. "Unless you want me to take these off in your office?"

It was the wrong thing to say.

Samuel's pupils dilated. The mate bond sparked with sudden heat.

Desire coiled through my veins. My breath caught when he cradled my face and leaned in to kiss me.

Someone knocked on the door.

Samuel closed his eyes and cursed under his breath before reluctantly letting go of me.

"Come in," he growled.

Hugh stuck his head in. "Am I interrupting?" he asked innocently.

"Yes," Samuel snapped.

"No," I said self-consciously. I flushed at Hugh's small, knowing smile.

"What is it?" Samuel said impatiently.

"Barney says the investors' meeting is starting soon."

Samuel glanced at his watch. "Dammit." He studied me with a frown, his eyes dark with concern. "Do you think you can get home okay?"

I nodded, a little disappointed that our moment had been interrupted.

"Good." Samuel surprised both Hugh and me by kissing my brow tenderly. "I'll be in touch this weekend. Make sure you get some rest."

I went out into the main office and tried to not get distracted by the lingering effects of my close encounter with Samuel while I filled out the incident report.

As bonded mates, the attraction between us was undeniable. I was painfully conscious we were both avoiding the inevitable. After all, we'd met each other less than a week ago and hadn't spoken much. Yet the more time I spent with Samuel, the more I felt like I had known him my whole life.

Which was weird.

"You'll have to be more careful from now on," Didi warned as I handed over the paperwork. "The Council of Elders will be watching your every move after what happened today."

Gavin nodded. I did my best not to grimace.

Doing my job under a magnifying glass sounded like my idea of Hell.

By the time Bo and I got home, I was more than ready for the weekend. A pang of guilt shot through me as I slipped the BMW's key in my bag.

Ethel was still in the Hawthornes's garage.

"I'll give the new car back eventually," I told Bo as we rode the elevator.

"I didn't say anything." He gave me an innocent look and swung his tail like a snake oil salesman pitching a miracle elixir. "That BMW's AC is gonna be sweet come summer though."

My dog knew how to make a convincing argument.

We walked through the front door of our apartment and found it smelling of coffee beans and something distinctly otherworldly.

"Is that—?" Bo sniffed the air cautiously.

"Vampire," I confirmed warily.

Ellie was in the kitchen. She was surrounded by coffee-making paraphernalia and practically vibrating with excitement.

"You'll never guess what happened," she blurted.

"You got a job at Bean Me Up?" I hazarded.

Ellie deflated slightly. "How did you know?"

It was scary how accurate my wolf's nose was getting.

"Lucky guess." I decided not to mention that she reeked of Virgil's scent. "When do you start?"

"Monday." She beamed. "The manager said I have a natural talent for customer service."

Bo and I exchanged a look as she went back to practicing her coffee making.

"You should stop her," Bo whispered stealthily. "She'll probably poison someone!"

"You don't know that!" I whispered back.

The doorbell rang before my dog could come up with a clever repartee.

I left the kitchen to go answer it and stiffened when I picked up on a pair of familiar scents coming from the hallway. Bo followed me with a look of hesitant hope.

Victoria was on our doorstep, Pearl in her arms.

"Good evening," the Hawthorne matriarch said.

"Yo, fam," Pearl said regally.

"Furball!" Bo wagged his tail so fast I was worried he would achieve vertical lift off.

I let them inside. "I didn't know you were coming over."

"I'm sorry I didn't call first." Victoria swept past me, her gaze taking in our apartment with barely concealed curiosity. "I was in the neighborhood and thought it best to tell you this face-to-face."

I narrowed my eyes. Judging from recent experience, I was pretty convinced I wasn't going to like what she said. Victoria pretended not to notice my suspicious stare.

Ellie popped her head out of the kitchen. "Oh. It's nice to see you again, Mrs. Hawthorne." She hesitated. "Would you like some coffee?"

Victoria's mouth curved in a small smile. "I would like that very much."

"The coffee might be poisoned," Bo warned Pearl in a low voice.

I hushed him. Victoria pretended not to notice as I escorted her into the living room.

"So this is how the other half lives." Pearl jumped down from Victoria's arms and looked around. "This place is smaller than my litter box." For once, her voice didn't drip with its usual degree of contempt.

"Not everyone can afford a million-dollar mansion," I muttered.

"Try ten million," Pearl said.

I choked on air while she navigated the floor gingerly with her delicate paws.

"Wanna see my pad?" Bo asked excitedly.

"You have a pad?" Pearl asked doubtfully.

"Okay, it's a basket, but it's still nice."

Victoria and I watched them leave.

"It's good to see Pearl getting along with your dog," Victoria murmured. "She doesn't have many friends."

I hesitated. "You know that's because she acts like a prima donna, right?"

Victoria sighed. "Rumor has it the first thing she said to her mother after she was born was 'How dare you present me with such a filthy litter of siblings.'"

I could totally see that.

Ellie brought our coffee over and joined us. To my surprise, it was delicious.

"So what is it you needed to tell me?" I asked Victoria guardedly.

I could tell she was trying to avoid the subject.

Victoria put her cup down and visibly steeled herself. "There's a regular social function at Château Montmartre we need to attend."

Yeah, I pretty much hated every word she'd just said.

"Château Montmartre?!" Ellie gasped. "You mean that posh place where they serve tea in gold-rimmed cups?"

I chewed my lip. Château Montmartre was one of the most high-end hotels on the East Coast. It boasted luxurious suites that catered to celebrities and royalty, two Michelin-star restaurants, and an afternoon tea salon with a one-year wait list.

It was not the kind of place that ever featured on my bucket list.

"I'm sorry, Abby," Victoria said apologetically at my accusing expression. "It completely escaped my mind after what happened with the Council. All the important supernatural families in Amberford will be there. I intend for it to be your official introduction to our supernatural society."

"When is this thing?" I asked wearily.

"Tomorrow afternoon."

My mouth pressed to a thin line.

My weekend of R&R was doomed before it even began.

29

HIGH TEA AND HIGHER STAKES

A GOTHIC CASTLE LOOMED OUT OF THE MIST CURLING off the waters of a lake, a few miles outside Amberford. I studied the gray stone walls and dark slate turrets of Château Montmartre as it rose in the distance.

The place looked like something out of a dark fairy tale under the grim winter sky.

"Charming, isn't it?" Caroline murmured.

The pack enforcer was tagging along for the tea party.

From Ellie's research last night, Château Montmartre was built in the late 1800s by a French count with more money than sense, ergo a vampire. The castle had fallen into a state of disrepair after its original occupants returned to mainland Europe in the mid-1900s. It was eventually bought by a business conglomerate and turned into a luxury hotel that quickly became known as a prime destination for the wealthy to enjoy all the great things the East Coast had to offer.

To their credit, the architects in charge of the restoration had kept the castle's original features, including the weathered-faced gargoyles watching the surrounding forest with eternal vigilance from their perches along its crenellated parapets.

Victoria drove through gates bearing bats on their supporting pillars and headed up a winding driveway that meandered through the forest before opening onto a large, graveled forecourt. A parking lot discretely hidden by carefully manicured hedges sat to one side.

Victoria turned into it and parked her Mercedes between a Rolls Royce and a Bentley.

"This place is fancier than your litter box," Bo told Pearl.

"Please." Pearl sniffed imperiously. "It wishes it were as nice as my litter box."

"She's right," Caroline murmured as we climbed out of the car. "Her litter box expenses are exorbitant. Not that she does anything to earn her keep in this household." She gave the cat a pointed look.

Pearl hopped into Victoria's arms and blinked slowly. "But I'm pretty."

Bo grinned and thumped his tail on the ground.

Tension tightened my belly when I looked up at the castle's imposing facade.

Pointed Gothic arches framed its tall, mullioned windows, the leaded glass gleaming in the weak winter sunlight. Flying buttresses ran along the walls and supported a roof adorned with elaborate copper finials that had long since turned green. Wisps of smoke curled from the stone chimney stacks rising like sentinels between the steep gables.

The hairs on my nape rose when I sensed traces of magic in the air.

My gaze found the keystones above the windows and doors.

Victoria noticed my stare. "The count had protective runes carved into the building."

"Why would a vampire's castle need protective runes?"

"Maybe to fend off villagers with pitchforks and flame torches?" Bo panted.

"That sounds unlikely," I muttered.

"Bo's right," Caroline said.

I blinked. "He is?"

Caroline shrugged. "Yeah."

I wondered once more if my dog was some kind of savant. He ruined the moment by sniffing a bush and cocking his leg against it.

"*Noooo!*" Victoria and I hissed in simultaneous horror.

Bo lowered his leg at our glares. "Sheesh."

Pearl narrowed her eyes. "I see I have my work cut out for me. I shall make a gentleman out of you yet, mutt."

Bo wagged his tail hesitantly. "Do gentlemen get to roll around in mud?"

"Only if they're savages."

Victoria ignored their conversation and directed a stern look at me as we crossed the forecourt. "Do you remember what I said?"

My shoulders slumped.

"Try not to embarrass the family name or start an interspecies war," I replied morosely.

"And?" Victoria prompted.

I allowed myself a dramatic sigh. "And absolutely no punching anyone in the throat."

"Even if they deserve it," Victoria added with a sniff.

"Jesus, what happened at the Council of Elders?" Caroline muttered.

This was going to be another long afternoon.

"How come Samuel doesn't have to attend these functions?" I complained as we neared the entrance.

"Because a roomful of werewolf alphas and the heads of vampire clans is bound to end in bloodshed," Victoria said curtly.

"Victoria is right," Pearl said. "They tried it once."

I grimaced. "What happened?"

"Look up the Amberford Fire of 1872," Caroline said.

A handsome doorman in a tailcoat bowed and opened the door as we approached, his scent marking him as fae.

We stepped inside a grand foyer with a checkered marble floor, crystal chandeliers, and gilt-framed mirrors. Uniformed staff stood behind an ancient, solid oak counter to the left, their voices quiet as they spoke on phones and to the smartly dressed guests checking in. Soft, classical music drifted from somewhere.

The air was thick with the scents of supernatural creatures, money, and expensive perfume.

A concierge with sharp canines came over, his face

wreathed in a smile. "Mrs. Hawthorne, Caroline, it's a pleasure to see you both." He pressed his lips to the back of Victoria's hand and air-kissed Caroline before beaming at Pearl. "You look spectacular."

Pearl nodded regally. "Jean-Pierre."

The vampire's curious gaze landed on me. "I don't believe I've had the pleasure of meeting your companion."

Victoria made introductions. "This is Abigail West. She is the new Hawthorne luna and my future daughter-in-law."

Caroline's eyes widened fractionally. I nearly swallowed my tongue.

It was the first time Victoria had referred to me as her daughter-in-law.

Ears pricked around the foyer.

Curious fascination lit up the vampire's eyes. It faded a little when he spotted Bo.

"And who's this charming dog?" Jean-Pierre asked politely.

Pearl's tail swung lazily. "This is Bo, a new member of the Hawthorne pack. He's my protégé."

Bo stood up proudly so he could show off his bow tie.

To his credit, the vampire's smile didn't crack. "I shall show you to the afternoon tea salon."

We followed him down a corridor lined with suits of armor to a vast room with floor-to-ceiling windows overlooking the hotel's manicured grounds and the lake. Tables set with fine bone china and silver tea services occupied strategic positions across the floor. A bevy of supernatural creatures in designer clothes sat talking in low voices around them. Most were women but there were men here and there.

The noise level dropped when the socialites clocked our entrance. I became the focus of dozens of cool stares.

Helen was holding court at one of the tables. Her lip curled at the sight of me. She whispered to one of her companions.

"Wonderful," Caroline muttered.

"You said it," I murmured.

"Be nice, both of you," Victoria warned under her breath.

Jean-Pierre handed us over to a waiter who guided us to a table by the window. Martha Claymore and Felicity Newfield were already seated at it. They wore matching floral dresses that brightened the room.

"Hello, Abby," Martha said in a friendly voice. Felicity nodded warmly.

"Hi, Martha, Felicity." I sat down gingerly while Victoria and Caroline exchanged greetings with the elderly werewolves, conscious of the stares we were attracting.

I was glad Victoria had chosen my outfit for the function.

The dark silk pantsuit I wore was cut perfectly and molded to my curves in flattering lines. The silk blouse underneath was a shade of cream that matched my complexion. Even my usually unruly hair had cooperated with Caroline's painstaking ministrations that afternoon and fell in soft, enchanting waves around my face.

"At least you don't look like you rolled in dirt today," Pearl had commented after Caroline's makeover.

Coming from her, that had been high praise indeed.

Martha leaned over presently.

"Rumor has it you were involved in a nefarious incident in the Crossroads yesterday," she hissed conspiratorially.

I grimaced. "Did Camilla tattle?"

Martha gave me a blank look. "Camilla?"

"Yeah, she was there yesterday."

Martha and Felicity exchanged a puzzled glance.

"Remember," Pearl told Bo as she settled on a chair with a special cushion that brought her to the height of the table. "One does not lap from the saucer."

"What about the cup?" Bo asked hopefully.

"Absolutely not."

I was busy pretending to study the menu and ignoring the stares burning into my face when Victoria straightened beside me. I followed her gaze to the middle-aged vampire couple who had just entered the salon. Their clothes looked like they cost more than my rent.

"That's Gregory and Constantia Tremaine," Victoria explained quietly. "They own most of the properties in the East End."

"And half the banks in Amberford," Caroline murmured. "They're the top vampire clan in town," she added at my curious look.

The Tremaines headed toward a table hosting a group of vampires. Gregory's nostrils flared slightly as they passed us. He inclined his head politely.

"Victoria."

"Gregory."

Crimson gleamed briefly in Constantia's cool eyes as her gaze skimmed over me.

I spotted more Council members arriving. Priscilla and Isobel were among them, both wearing dark outfits. They acknowledged us with curt nods and crossed the room to their seats three tables over.

"The witches are fashionably late as usual," Felicity observed as three women in couture outfits materialized near the entrance.

"The Lincoln sisters," Victoria said for my benefit. "They control the supernatural clinics in and around Amberford. Oh, and that's Portia O'Keefe. She's the head of the Amberford banshees."

"They're not the biggest clan, but what they lack in numbers they make up for in volume," Martha said. She winked and nudged me in the ribs. "Get it?"

"The floor got it, Martha," Felicity groaned.

More socialites arrived, their names soon a blur. I was wishing Mindy had come along to organize some kind of visual map of the who's who of the Amberford supernatural society when Camilla walked in.

"She doesn't look well," Caroline observed with a faint frown.

The Council secretary was pale and appeared a little flustered, like she hadn't been sleeping well.

I wondered if this had to do with her nervous

disposition or the fact that she regularly dealt with Council members who acted like vipers. I was about to ask the question when I felt Victoria and Caroline tense.

A middle-aged werewolf with graying red hair piled up in a chignon had swept into the salon after Camilla. She was dressed in an elegant outfit and was accompanied by two women who looked and smelled like her daughters.

I stared.

The sisters were tall and built along the same lean lines as Caroline.

"What are they doing here?" Martha muttered.

"Who are they?" I asked curiously.

Caroline shot a worried glance at Victoria. "The Luptons."

Ah. More drama.

30

THE LUPTONS

My shoulders knotted as I watched the three werewolves approach.

"Wasn't one of them supposed to become Samuel's fiancée?" Bo asked in a stage-loud whisper.

"The discussions never progressed that far," Caroline murmured.

The Luptons stopped at our table.

Victoria addressed the middle-aged werewolf with a stiff nod. "Danielle. I wasn't expecting to see you here."

"Victoria." Danielle Lupton's smile was razor-sharp. "We were in the neighborhood." Her gaze shifted briefly to the other side of the salon. "Priscilla invited us."

Her daughters exchanged amused glances at her tone.

Danielle's gaze landed on me, her expression inscrutable. "I take it you are the famous new luna we've been hearing rumors about."

I held her eyes unflinchingly. "Hi, I'm Abigail West." I paused. "Everyone calls me Abby." I offered her my hand impulsively.

Caroline drew a sharp breath.

The noise level in the salon dropped to an expectant hush.

Surprise flared briefly in Danielle's eyes. She recovered her composure and graciously shook my hand. "It's nice to meet you…Abby."

"Don't mind Mother," one of the Lupton sisters said with a smile. "It takes a while for her to warm to new people. I can already tell she likes you."

Danielle cut her eyes to her daughter.

The latter shrugged. "What? It's true. Everyone in our pack calls you the Fluffy Rottweiler."

Martha choked on her tea. Caroline muffled a snort into her napkin.

Danielle sighed, not at all unfazed by the revelation of her unflattering nickname. "These are my daughters, Lauren and Beatrice."

Lauren was the one who'd spoken and looked to be the older sister. She was dressed entirely in black and had purple streaks in her hair. Multiple silver rings adorned her fingers and a skull pendant hung around her neck.

She looked like she belonged at a heavy metal concert rather than a fancy tea party.

Beatrice was her complete opposite. The younger sister wore a designer outfit in pastel pink and had started filming the salon with her phone.

"This is going to get so many likes," she enthused. "My followers love supernatural tea drama."

"Bea," Lauren drawled. "Put the phone away before Mother has an aneurysm."

A vein had started throbbing in Danielle's temple. Victoria gave her a sympathetic look.

"But my fans—" Beatrice protested.

"Can wait." Lauren's dark lips curved as she observed me. "I gotta say, you're not at all what I anticipated."

"I'm not?" I asked warily.

"Nope. I always thought Samuel's mate would be as stuck up as he is. After all, the guy acts like he permanently has a stick up his ass."

Victoria and Caroline narrowed their eyes slightly.

"I'm trying my best to remove it," I said bluntly.

Victoria and Caroline gasped and gave me hurt looks.

I crossed my arms defiantly. "You both know it's true."

Lauren burst out laughing, the sound echoing around the salon. Bea and Danielle seemed shocked at the sight.

"I like you," Lauren chortled, wiping her eyes. "Mind if Bea and I sit here?" She dropped into an empty chair without waiting for a reply, her sister following suit. "Mother's going to catch up with her old friends." Her grin widened. "And by catch up, I mean engage in passive-aggressive warfare."

I found myself smiling back.

"Lauren!" Danielle said sharply.

"What?" Lauren's expression turned innocent. "I'm just stating facts."

Danielle lowered her brows. "You do know I'm the luna of our pack, right?"

Lauren shrugged. "And I'm your top enforcer. Now, why don't you be a dear and go over to Priscilla's table? Isobel looks like she's about to fall out of her chair with curiosity."

Danielle's shoulders slumped. She addressed the table. "I apologize in advance if my daughters say anything to upset you."

"I'm sure they won't," Victoria said diplomatically.

Danielle excused herself and left.

"By the way, I heard what you said to Helen the other day," Lauren said as a waiter poured her and her sister tea. "That woman needed someone to take her down a peg or ten."

The rumor mill in Amberford was a scary thing.

"Is it true you threatened to punch her in the throat?" Beatrice asked carefully.

"It was a manner of speech," I half protested.

"No, it wasn't," Bo said.

Lauren and Beatrice stared at my dog.

Lauren arched an eyebrow. "He talks?"

"I'm Abby's dog." Bo preened a little. "And Pearl's friend."

Pearl flicked her tail in a pleased manner at this.

I grimaced. "We think he might have werewolf blood in his ancestry."

"Which part?" Bea asked warily.

I noticed a pair of vampires rise and start to make

their way to our table. A witch followed at a leisurely pace. I straightened, Caroline and Victoria growing similarly alert beside me.

They'd warned me that this would happen. No one could ignore a new luna, let alone a white wolf. As such, the leaders of the various supernatural factions in Amberford were bound to pay their respect to me.

The afternoon progressed with most of the assembled socialites coming over to officially meet me. Though I sensed wariness and hostility from some, the majority seemed merely curious.

Everyone having finally done their duty, the subtle tension in the salon gradually abated. I started to relax.

"You did well," Victoria said quietly.

"Yeah." Lauren grinned. "Shame no one did anything that warranted a punch in the throat."

Caroline chuckled.

Beatrice looked disappointed at the lack of social-media-worthy drama.

I sighed, gave Bo a muffin, and decided I might as well enjoy the rest of the tea party.

I was in the middle of explaining to Lauren and Beatrice how I'd ended up as a werewolf when my skin prickled with awareness. A hush fell over the salon.

My breath caught when I looked toward the entrance.

Samuel cut an arresting figure as he crossed the floor to our table, his dark suit molded to his muscular physique in a way that made my inner wolf stand to attention and pant.

He stopped at our table and leaned down to kiss my

cheek, his eyes smoldering behind his designer specs. "You look beautiful."

I managed a strangled greeting.

Victoria stared at her son as he took a seat. "I thought you had somewhere to be."

"I rescheduled." His gaze found mine, the mate bond humming between us. "I love what you've done with your hair."

My cheeks grew warm. "Thanks. Caroline helped."

I wasn't going to admit to him that she'd used products from the Moon Shine: Extra Glossy Coat range to tame my locks.

Samuel's expression cooled as he gazed at the Lupton sisters. "I'm surprised to see you two here."

Lauren's smile turned sharp. "Why, if it isn't my favorite stick-in-the-mud."

Beatrice sighed at the hostile sparks between Samuel and Lauren. Caroline bit into a sandwich, her avid gaze swinging between the pair like she was at a tennis match.

"So Lauren is the chick he was originally supposed to get engaged to?" Bo whispered to Pearl.

"Yes." Pearl wrinkled her nose. "Although I doubt they would have made it down the aisle without killing each other or burning the church down."

Samuel and Lauren pretended not to hear her.

"Still working too hard?" Lauren asked sweetly.

"Still terrorizing innocent civilians?" Samuel countered.

"Only the ones who deserve it."

"Here we go again," Beatrice muttered.

Caroline grinned.

"Abby here was just telling me she was trying her best to remove the stick permanently wedged up your ass," Lauren told Samuel silkily.

"Unlike you, Abby can do whatever she wants to my ass," he retorted smoothly.

I choked on a macaron. Martha and Felicity sucked in air with shocked delight. Victoria looked like she was contemplating fainting. Caroline wheezed behind her napkin, eyes crunched up and shoulders trembling.

Bo looked at me cautiously. "I wonder if Ellie knows you're into butt-play."

Caroline's wheezing got worse.

I groaned and pushed away from the table. "Excuse me, I need to use the restroom." I was halfway across the salon when I realized my dog was following me. "Where are you going?"

"I'm your bodyguard, remember?" Bo said.

I'd forgotten Victoria and Caroline had assigned him the role with strict instructions to howl like a banshee if I got into any trouble at today's tea party.

A waiter guided us to the closest facilities.

The place was exactly what I'd expect from the luxury hotel. The walls were covered in deep burgundy silk damask wallpaper and decorated with gilt-framed mirrors. The marble floor had been laid in an intricate pattern of black and white diamonds. Crystal wall sconces cast a warm light over the gleaming antique fixtures.

Even the toilet stalls were fancy, their brass hardware polished to a mirror shine.

"This bathroom is nicer than our apartment," Bo commented, his paws clicking on the marble floor.

"You're not planning to follow me into a stall, are you?" I asked suspiciously.

"What and watch you poop?" Bo huffed indignantly.

I was eyeing a discrete sign requesting that werewolf guests please refrain from marking territory when Helen emerged from one of the stalls. She paused at the sight of me, her mouth pressing to a thin line.

"This is the ladies' room," she said pointedly, glaring at Bo.

"Luckily he identifies as a service dog," I said sweetly.

Bo embraced the blatant lie and straightened proudly. "I'm here to make sure Abby doesn't suffer from constipation."

Helen made a disgusted sound and went over to a sink. I waited until she'd washed her hands and left before using the facilities.

"Did you poop okay?" Bo asked when I came out of the stall.

I swallowed a sigh and hoped Pearl's etiquette lessons cured my dog of his sassiness.

We'd just stepped out of the restroom when a scent danced under my nostrils. I stiffened, instantly recognizing it.

"Bo, can you smell that?" I said tensely.

My dog was staring at a door opposite where we stood. "It's coming from over there!"

We bolted through the door and found ourselves on the castle grounds.

The scent grew stronger. With it came a tang of magic that raised goosebumps on my skin. We moved swiftly along a stone path, our breaths misting in the cold air as we followed Wheeler's trail. It wound through manicured gardens dotted with stone benches and ornate fountains and led us toward the forest backing the castle grounds.

We lost Wheeler's scent at the tree line.

"He was definitely here," Bo said, nose to the ground. He looked up and whined in frustration.

I stroked his head, equally annoyed. My skin prickled uncomfortably.

That strange magic I'd felt earlier was stronger out here.

"Let's head back," I said reluctantly.

We took a different route and emerged in a rose garden. We'd just come in view of a door when movement caught my eye. Bo stiffened beside me, ears pricking.

A figure was rushing around the side of the castle, her back to us.

It was a woman wearing a dark dress. My pulse quickened as I tracked the direction she was running from.

She'd come from the forest.

The woman disappeared before we could go after her.

"Wasn't that—" Bo started.

"Come on!"

We hurried back inside the castle and made for the salon. I scanned the room as we entered it, my pulse racing. Priscilla and Isobel sat at their table, deep in conversation with Danielle Lupton.

I headed over to where Samuel and Lauren were still trading barbs.

"Did Priscilla or Isobel leave the salon at all?"

They both looked up, startled by my urgent tone.

"No," Lauren said. "They've been here the whole time, talking to Mother." She raised an eyebrow. "Why?"

Samuel's expression sharpened at my troubled look. "What's wrong?"

I hesitated. "Nothing. I thought I saw one of them outside just now. I must have been mistaken."

His frown told me he wasn't buying my answer. I avoided his eyes and focused on my cooling tea.

There was no point raising alarm bells until I had proof.

CONNECTING THE DOTS

"So let me get this straight." Didi arched an eyebrow and steepled her hands under her chin. "You think Wheeler was at Château Montmartre this weekend?"

"Yes. And I think he was there to meet with Priscilla Holt or Isobel Lynton."

I described how Bo and I had caught Wheeler's scent and followed it to the forest.

"The woman Bo and I saw when we returned to the hotel was wearing an outfit similar to Priscilla's and Isobel's," I finished quietly.

Gavin's nostrils sparked slightly. "That's a serious accusation." He exchanged a troubled glance with Nigel. "Not only do they come from prestigious families, they're both highly regarded in the supernatural community."

Nigel nodded in agreement.

I sighed. "That's why I wanted to talk to you guys before I said anything to Samuel."

It was Monday morning. Two days had passed since the tea party at Château Montmartre. I'd spent most of Sunday dodging Samuel's questions about what had happened in the castle gardens.

"Was there anything else?" Didi furrowed her brow. "Any clue that might help figure out what he was doing there?"

I hesitated. "There was some kind of magic lingering with his scent. It was…weird."

"It creeped us out," Bo elaborated.

Didi's expression turned thoughtful in the hush that followed.

"Could the magic you sensed have come from the crystal skull?"

I blinked, my pulse quickening. I hadn't thought of that.

The cursed artifact was reputed to carry dark magic. Maybe that's why it felt different from the magic I'd detected from the artifacts in the Den and even the runes carved into the keystones of Château Montmartre.

"I think you might be right," I mumbled.

"I have new information on Wheeler." Nigel tapped a couple of keys on his laptop and turned it around so we could see the screen. "One of my contacts in the criminal underground got back to me this morning. Rumor has it Wheeler recently met with some rather unsavory characters."

We studied the murky pictures on the screen. It showed a group of some twenty people.

"Who are they?" I asked warily.

"Vampire mercenaries," Nigel said nervously. "And a couple of rogue witches."

Bo's ears flattened.

Dread knotted my stomach. This case was starting to take a dangerous turn. The kind that usually ended up in one of the true crime shows my dog liked to watch, with dead investigators buried in shallow graves.

"We should keep an eye on Priscilla and Isobel," Didi said grimly. "See if either of them makes contact with Wheeler."

"Agreed," Gavin said.

I nodded.

The next few days passed in a blur of surveillance at the same time we doubled our efforts to track down Wheeler and the crystal skull. To my chagrin, neither Priscilla nor Isobel did anything suspicious. They went about their daily activities and attended meetings and social functions like nothing was wrong.

I was starting to wonder if we were on the wrong track when Nigel called us into his office late Friday afternoon, after we'd returned from investigating yet another dead end.

The boogeyman manifested several tentacles distractedly where he sat behind his main computer. "I've gone through the security footage from Château Montmartre. I didn't see Wheeler or anyone who looks like Priscilla or Isobel in the gardens."

We watched the accelerated recordings playing on the monitor. The time stamps were from the time the tea party had started to when it'd ended.

"Could they have avoided the cameras?" Gavin asked after the playbacks ended.

"Possibly." Nigel adjusted his glasses nervously. "The hotel's security system is state-of-the-art, but there are blind spots."

Didi frowned. "Was that everything you had for us?"

"From Château Montmartre?" Nigel said. "Yes." His eyes gleamed in the gloom. "It's a good idea I decided to keep monitoring Bloody Good Coffee."

"Oh," Bo huffed. "I smell a clue!"

The boogeyman typed on his keyboard. "I just went over the latest recording. This is from two p.m. today."

Footage from the coffee shop's security camera filled the screen.

Gavin paled. Didi drew a sharp breath.

I grew deathly still.

Marcus Holt sat drinking coffee at a table near the window, a stack of books beside him. A blonde woman in an expensive coat entered the shop and headed straight for him.

I leaned forward sharply, startling Nigel. "That's the woman I chased in the Crossroads!"

"Keep watching," the boogeyman said once he'd dimmed his glow. "It gets more interesting."

Marcus looked up as the woman approached. His face lit up with recognition.

"He knows Wheeler," Didi breathed.

Bo wagged his tail. "That's what you call a smoking gun in crime jargon."

The footage showed Wheeler sitting down. The two

talked for several minutes before Wheeler passed Marcus a black bag.

"Can you enhance that?" I said tensely.

Nigel hit a key. The image zoomed in. We stared at the grainy shot.

"Someone please tell me that bag isn't bulging in a way that suggests it contains a crystal skull?" Didi asked leadenly.

A ripple shook Bo's fur. "Yeesh. I feel like someone just walked over my grave."

I knew what he meant. The hairs were lifting on the back of my neck.

"We need to talk to Marcus." I turned to Gavin. "You're the best person for the job. He trusts you."

The dragon newt's horns and tail popped out. He hesitated before dipping his head, visibly upset.

Didi lowered her brows. "I think we should watch him first to be on the safe side." She glanced at me. "There's no point exposing ourselves to danger."

I heard the witch's unspoken warning. The crystal skull was a powerful artifact. If Marcus had it on him when we intercepted him, there was a chance he could use it against us.

Nigel promised to get us more information so we could plan our next surveillance operation.

"I still can't believe Marcus is involved in this," Gavin muttered as we left the boogeyman's closet.

"People change, Gavin," Didi said in a hard voice.

Gavin's shoulders slumped.

Despite the evidence I had just seen, I couldn't help but feel we were missing something. Something that would explain why Marcus had met with Wheeler.

The chance to talk with Priscilla's son ended up coming much sooner than I'd expected and from the most unlikely source.

Mindy floated toward me when we entered the open office.

"Samuel's looking for you."

I was still thinking about Nigel's recent finding when I knocked and walked into Samuel's office.

"You wanted to see—" I stopped and stared.

Victoria was sitting on the couch. "Hi, Abby."

Hugh was perched beside her.

Unease danced through me at their troubled expressions. Now what?

I looked over to where Samuel was making coffee for everyone while Bo trotted over to greet Pearl.

"What's wrong?" I asked warily.

"I'll let Mother explain." Samuel indicated the couch.

Victoria waited until I took the seat opposite her before removing a cream envelope that had been sealed with dark red wax from her handbag. The seal was engraved with a family crest I didn't recognize. She placed it on the table and pushed it toward me.

I stared at the envelope like it might bite. "What's this?"

"Priscilla's hosting a ball this weekend. The representatives of every supernatural race as well as the leaders of all werewolf packs, vampire clans, and covens in Amberford are invited."

A chill ran down my spine. This couldn't be a coincidence.

I wasn't sure if my dark sense of foreboding was coming from human Abby or werewolf Abby. I hesitated before reaching for the envelope and taking out the thick, gilded card inside.

The ball was taking place tomorrow night at seven p.m., at the Holt mansion.

I looked up into the Hawthornes's perturbed faces. "Isn't this a bit short notice?"

"It is." Victoria's face tightened. "But that's not what concerns us." She traded a worried glance with her sons. "It's exceedingly rare for all the heads of the supernatural races in Amberford to be under one roof. The people who attended the function at Château Montmartre were carefully selected to represent their race and the prominent supernatural families among them. Even then, not every family was invited. Only those who hold the most power in Amberford get an invitation to the tea party."

My stomach churned. I suspected I knew the answer to my next question, but I asked it anyway.

"What would happen if everyone important was under one roof?"

Pearl jumped on the table. "It would be the perfect scenario to spring an ambush."

My knuckles whitened on my lap.

"Has that happened before?" I asked Samuel.

He nodded reluctantly. "In the past. But that's only part of the problem."

It sounded plenty enough to me.

"What else aren't you telling me?" I said in a hard voice.

Samuel rubbed the back of his neck, his expression awkward. "The last time the Holts held a ball, Arthur Holt disappeared."

My mouth went dry.

The situation had just officially gone from bad to diabolically bad.

"Let's not forget the ley lines," Hugh said darkly.

I stared between them, confused. "What ley lines?"

"After Arthur disappeared, a witch in the supernatural task force charged with investigating the case discovered that the Holts' ancestral home was built on a convergence of magical ley lines." Samuel frowned. "Apparently, the head of the pack at the time the mansion was erected wasn't aware of this."

I could tell he didn't believe this.

Victoria furrowed her brow. "Some people in the supernatural community wondered whether Arthur was researching ways to tap into that power before he went missing."

I swallowed. "Why would a werewolf want to access ley lines? We can't use magic."

A fraught hush filled the office.

"No," Samuel said quietly. "But that magic could be used to make dangerous artifacts."

My shoulders knotted. "Like that crystal skull?"

Samuel dipped his head.

"Arthur was interested in the occult," Victoria explained. "He was fascinated with the stuff ever since he was a child. I know Priscilla feels guilty for encouraging him to pursue his interests after they got married."

I exchanged a glance with Bo in the tense hush.

"You should tell them," he quavered, tail tucked between his legs.

Samuel's puzzled gaze swung between us. "Tell us what?"

THE BALL

THE BENTLEY'S HEADLIGHTS WASHED ACROSS ANCIENT oaks and towering pines as Samuel drove up a winding private drive, the gnarled branches of the dense forest reaching toward the dark winter sky like skeletal fingers. The trees parted briefly to reveal a sprawling Gothic residence when we rounded a bend.

I stared.

The Holt mansion's gray limestone walls and black slate towers rose from the forested slopes like the fortress of some demented, medieval tyrant. Elaborate flying buttresses stretched between the towers like the ribs of some prehistoric beast who'd met his unfortunate demise atop the building. Gargoyles perched along every cornice and gable, their stony faces watching the line of expensive cars snaking up the torch-lit driveway.

Château Montmartre looked practically quaint in comparison.

"This place gives me the heebie-jeebies," Bo mumbled from the back seat of Samuel's Bentley.

Hugh shuddered beside him. "You're not the only one."

I shot a sideways glance at Samuel. His jaw was clenched and his knuckles white on the steering wheel, his tension filtering through our mate bond and setting my own teeth on edge.

"Remember what we discussed," Victoria warned from the back seat as we approached the mansion. "Act natural."

Pearl sniffed from her perch on Victoria's lap. "That's going to be a problem for a certain someone."

"But I've been practicing my fancy manners," Bo protested.

"I didn't mean you, mutt." Pearl side-eyed Hugh. "I meant the werewolf-nip-addicted nutjob in the family."

"You're hurting my feelings," Hugh groaned. "And I'm over my addiction."

"Really?" Victoria asked sharply. "Because we've heard that line before."

"I'm truly over it this time." Hugh's gaze found mine in the rearview mirror. "After all, I wouldn't want to turn another human into a wolf," he finished guiltily.

An awkward silence followed. I scratched the tip of my nose.

"You know, being turned isn't the complete disaster I thought it would be. If anything, I kinda like my new life." I glanced around the car. "I wouldn't have met all of you if it hadn't happened. And I wouldn't have been able to talk to Bo."

Even though some days I wish he would shut up, but I refrained from saying that out loud.

Samuel watched me intently. "Do you mean that?"

I smiled. "Yes, I do."

Bo grinned and wagged his tail.

Hugh sniffed and wiped his eyes with the back of his hand. Victoria sighed and passed him a hanky.

Samuel negotiated the final curve of the driveway, rolled into a paved courtyard, and pulled up in front of the entrance. Caroline and Kent's BMW rolled to a stop behind the Bentley. The Hawthorne pack enforcers had decided to act as backup after we'd told them our plans last night.

A pair of valets took the car keys.

I exited the Bentley and studied the foreboding mansion rising before us before tapping the discreet earpiece hidden behind my hair.

"Can you guys hear me?"

"Loud and clear," Didi said over the comm.

She was in a surveillance van stationed in the woods behind the mansion with Gavin and Nigel. Samuel had tasked them with monitoring events at the ball via the tiny cameras pinned to our clothes. If things went south, they were to call for backup.

"Why is Nigel gurgling in the background?" I asked warily.

"Mindy just messaged to wish him good luck on our mission," Didi muttered.

I grimaced. "Mindy has a cell phone?"

"There's a supernatural electronics store in the Crossroads," Gavin said. "They sell all kinds of stuff."

I made a mental note never to reveal this to Ellie.

Samuel offered me his arm. "Shall we?"

I nodded and steeled myself as I took it.

Tonight's assignment was simple: recover the crystal skull and survive whatever—

"By the way, have I told you how beautiful you look tonight?" Samuel's gaze had grown heated.

Trust my alpha to completely wreck my train of thought.

To be fair, I looked pretty darn gorgeous. The sparkling, midnight-blue dress Claudette had chosen for the ball clung to my curves like a second skin and rippled sensuously with my movements.

I flushed. "You don't look so bad yourself."

That was an understatement. His tuxedo should have come with a health warning. Had it not been for more pressing matters, I would have dragged him into the bushes and let my wolf loose.

"Can you two stop eye-banging each other?" Hugh grumbled. "We have a job to do."

Victoria sighed. Pearl rolled her eyes. Caroline and Kent exchanged a knowing smile.

"Yeah, look at you two flirting," Didi said in a syrupy voice.

I looked down to find Bo panting at me with a grin.

"Bet you want to take your alpha for a ride right about now, huh?" my dog sassed.

Samuel's shoulders trembled.

"Can you please not," I told Bo coolly.

Gavin's voice crackled in our earpieces as we headed for the entrance.

"Three of the valets are vampire mercenaries," the dragon newt warned. "Nigel just ran their faces through his databases."

Caroline and Kent tensed. Samuel's expression darkened.

I focused on the scents swarming the air. It didn't take long to clock the vampires. They weaved a thin red trail of nervous adrenaline that stood out among the chaotic bouquet rising from the supernatural creatures arriving for the ball.

"I see them," I murmured.

The Hawthornes followed my gaze discreetly.

"They smell like trouble and cologne," Bo huffed.

"Cheap cologne," Pearl added acerbically.

The grand foyer was already full of figures in evening wear.

I observed our surroundings curiously as we followed them through the mansion. Though the decor was fancy, there was something off about the place. Maybe it was the way the shadows seemed deeper than they should be. Or maybe it was the magic I could feel deep beneath my feet.

Bo moved closer to me. "I don't like this place."

"Indeed." Pearl flicked her tail irritably. "The ley lines are making my fur stand on end."

I looked at the cat, surprised. "You can feel them too?"

Pearl blinked, tail freezing for a moment. "I'm more surprised that you can."

"It's probably because you're a white wolf," Victoria

murmured uneasily. "I believe Elizabeth was similarly sensitive to magic."

I sobered at that.

We emerged into a vast ballroom with a domed ceiling that offered a beautiful view of the night sky. Elaborate flower arrangements dotted the long tables brimming with appetizers and champagne towers along the walls. Waiters circulated across the floor, silver trays full of sparkling flutes and canapés. A string quartet played on a raised dais at the head of the room.

"They really went all out, huh?" Caroline murmured.

"The Holts had a reputation for holding the best balls in our community," Victoria observed. "Before the incident with Arthur, that is."

I recognized many of the guests from the tea party at Château Montmartre. The Tremaines were deep in conversation with the Lincoln sisters across the way. Helen held court near a massive fireplace, the usual crowd of sycophants around her.

Pearl sniffed the air. "I smell caviar." Her tail swayed happily.

"Want to go check out the menu?" Bo huffed.

Pearl hopped onto my dog's back. "Take it away, maestro."

We watched the pair disappear toward a catering table, the assembled guests startling and moving out of the way when they clocked their presence.

Hugh grimaced. "Anyone else thing they make a freaky couple?"

"Yes," we replied as one.

"Are they going to be okay?" Kent asked worriedly.

"Between the two of them, I'm pretty sure they'll browbeat anyone who gets in their way," Caroline said drily.

I scanned the ballroom. "I don't see our hosts."

"It's standard protocol to wait until all the guests are gathered before making an entrance," Samuel explained.

A familiar voice rose behind us.

"I'm glad you came."

TRAP

I turned to find Lauren and Beatrice approaching with their mother. Lauren wore a black dress that would have looked more appropriate at a heavy metal concert. Beatrice was in a pink taffeta confection and filming everything with her phone.

Victoria stared, surprised. "You're still in town?"

"We were planning to leave yesterday, but Priscilla insisted we stay for the ball," Danielle explained. Her mouth pressed to a thin line as she studied her youngest. "Beatrice, what did we discuss?"

"But, Mother, my followers will love this!" Beatrice protested.

Danielle scowled. "Give me the phone."

Beatrice reluctantly handed over her cell.

Hugh's face had glazed over at the sight of Beatrice in her dress. Samuel elbowed him sharply in the ribs.

Before I could decipher what that was about, I spotted the Council of Elders entering the ballroom.

Martha and Felicity detached themselves from the group and came over.

"Has anyone seen Camilla?" Martha asked curiously.

Victoria shook her head. "We just got here."

"Did you know the Holts were planning to hold a ball?" Caroline asked Martha and Felicity.

The pair exchanged a guarded look.

"It was news to us," Felicity admitted quietly.

"Judging from the rest of the Holt pack, it was news to them too," Martha said shrewdly.

I followed her gaze to a group of werewolves standing near the dais. Several were talking in low voices, their expressions strangely tense. The rest forced diplomatic smiles on their faces as they greeted guests.

Didi's voice suddenly crackled in my ear. "Your three o'clock. Those four waiters behind that ficus. They're mercenaries."

I picked a couple of champagne flutes from a passing server and turned to hand one to Samuel. The suspects appeared in my line of sight.

"You see them?" Samuel murmured, taking a leisurely sip of his drink.

"Yes."

"Is there something going on?" Lauren's puzzled gaze swung between us.

I hesitated and looked at the Hawthornes.

"It wouldn't hurt to have more allies if things go south," Caroline said with a shrug.

Kent nodded beside her.

"You can trust these ladies," Victoria stated confidently.

"I hate to admit it, but we could do with having Lauren and Beatrice on our side," Samuel said reluctantly.

"Wait," Didi exclaimed in my ear. "You're not seriously thinking of bringing civilians in on this assignment, are you?!"

"That's a bad idea," Gavin mumbled.

Lauren narrowed her eyes, oblivious to the arguments taking place over my earpiece. "Now I'm positively dying of curiosity."

My gaze swept our surroundings. "Let's move this conversation somewhere the walls don't have ears."

We found a quiet spot on a terrace outside the ballroom. Caroline and Kent kept a lookout while Samuel and I briefly explained the situation to Martha, Felicity, and the Luptons.

"Holy shit," Beatrice said leadenly.

Danielle had gone pale. "*That* crystal skull went missing?"

I nodded reluctantly and glanced at Lauren's scowling face. She seemed terribly upset for some reason.

"You really think Priscilla and Marcus are going to use it at this ball?" Martha asked uncertainly.

Felicity clutched her walking stick. "I know Priscilla can be unpleasant at times. Arthur's disappearance really affected her, after all." She frowned. "Still, I can't believe she would do something so dangerous."

Caroline came over. "We should head back. It looks like our hosts will be making an appearance soon."

Bo padded toward us when we entered the ballroom. "Where'd you go?"

"We were on the terrace," I explained. I tensed at his agitated look. "What's wrong?"

"I got a close whiff of one of the bad guys," Bo whined. "They've got something strange on them."

Pearl's eyes shrank to slits. "I hope I'm wrong, but I think it's wolfsbane and silver."

Caroline swore. Kent scowled. Lauren looked like she wanted to say something.

A muscle jumped in Samuel's jawline.

My stomach sank. I'd forgotten to ask the Hawthornes about werewolves' weaknesses.

"What happens if we come in contact with those?" I asked nervously.

Samuel opened his mouth to answer when a commotion at the head of the ballroom drew our gazes. Our hosts had appeared.

Priscilla looked resplendent in an emerald gown. Diamonds glittered in her ears and at her throat.

Lauren stiffened at the sight of Marcus shuffling nervously beside his mother in a black tuxedo.

The rest of the Holts gathered around them as Priscilla accepted the champagne flute a waiter handed her.

An expectant hush fell over the ballroom.

"Welcome everyone," Priscilla said with a smile. "It has been some time since the Holts last held a ball." Her expression turned misty. "Although I still miss my dear

Arthur, my son Marcus convinced me I should let go of the past. It was his idea to host this ball and I am truly pleased that he will be soon be the alpha of the Holt pack."

Marcus paled at little at her words. He put on a brave smile as a round of applause echoed across the ballroom.

My pulse quickened. I exchanged a startled look with Samuel.

"The ball was Marcus's idea?!"

"Looks like Priscilla may not behind whatever is going on here," he said in a hard voice.

Didi's voice came urgently over my earpiece. "The woman in the red dress at your nine o'clock is one of the witches Wheeler contacted. And Nigel just identified four more mercenaries among the waitstaff."

My wolf stirred. The vampires I'd spotted before had been joined by more of their associates and were spreading out across the ballroom. Surprise jolted me in the next instant.

Something had just surged deep beneath the ground under my feet.

Pearl's fur rose on end.

"Guys," Didi said stiffly. "Nigel's picking up some strange energy readings. He thinks the ley lines are becoming active."

I clenched my jaw. "I can feel them."

That's when I picked up the troubling magic I'd sensed at Château Montmartre. It was stronger than it had been outside the forest where I'd chased Wheeler.

My head snapped around, my wolf scenting the trail. Bo's hackles rose.

We both stared at Marcus as he made swiftly for a corridor to the right.

The magic scent was coming from him.

Marcus looked nervously over his shoulder. I followed his anxious gaze. Before I could figure out why he'd glanced at Lauren before staring at one of the vampire mercenaries, he faced forward again and quickened his steps as if the hounds of Hell were on his tail.

I turned to Samuel, my heart slamming against my ribs. "I need to check something out."

His eyes narrowed behind his glasses. "I'm coming with you."

"No." I squeezed his arm. "Stay here and keep an eye on things. Bo and I will be careful."

He didn't look happy but nodded nonetheless.

"Don't do anything stupid," Pearl warned.

Caroline, Kent, and Lauren watched us leave with faint frowns.

I slipped through the crowd and escaped the ballroom with Bo.

"Where are you going?" Didi asked suspiciously.

"Following Marcus," I said quietly. "You were right about that magic I smelled at Château Montmartre. I'm pretty sure it's coming from the crystal skull. And Marcus reeks of it."

We moved silently, following the growing trail of eerie magic laced with Marcus's scent. It led us up a sweeping staircase to the first floor.

Bo sniffed the ground and looked up. "It's coming from there."

I narrowed my eyes at the double doors at the end of a shadowy corridor to my left.

The only light illuminating the hallway was a ray of moonlight that had escaped the overnight sky and pierced the tall windows overlooking the front courtyard.

We crept closer to the doors.

One of them was ajar. A sliver of brightness escaped from the room beyond.

Voices drifted through the gap as Bo and I pressed against the wall.

"Who—who are the people you brought with you tonight?" Marcus stammered agitatedly. "I just smelled wolfsbane and silver on one of them!"

"I'm surprised you managed to detect that with your weak nose."

A chill danced down my spine. I exchanged a shocked look with Bo.

It was Camilla, but not the Camilla we knew.

The woman who'd just spoken had ice in her voice and sounded infinitely more dangerous.

I clenched my jaw. Was this the real Camilla?

The loaded silence coming from my earpiece indicated Didi, Gavin, and Nigel were listening in on the conversation.

A choked sound escaped Marcus. "What—what do you mean by that?"

Camilla sighed. "This is getting boring. Grab him."

I tensed as Marcus's protests got lost in the sounds

of a scuffle. Bo tucked his tail between his legs and shifted closer to me.

"What is the meaning of—of this?!" Marcus shouted angrily. "I did everything you asked of me! I got you that crystal skull and convinced Mother to host this ball." His voice broke abjectly. "You said you would bring my father back! Damn you—"

The rest of Marcus's words got cut off. He grunted and wheezed like he'd been hit in the gut.

My blood ran cold. If Camilla had tricked Marcus into working with her by making a false promise, then the only thing he was guilty of was being gullible.

"Make sure he stays quiet," Camilla said coldly. "I've always hated the sound of that idiot's voice." She paused. "Well, well." The Council secretary's voice hardened. "It seems we have visitors. How about the two of you reveal yourselves? I can smell you rats outside."

HOW TO RUIN A BALL IN THREE EASY STEPS

THE DOORS FLEW OPEN.

My heart slammed against my ribs as I stared at the scene before me.

Things had just gone way south.

Two vampire mercenaries had Marcus pinned against a wall inside a library. A third vampire held a silver knife to the terrified Holt heir's throat.

A woman in a purple dress stood beside them, her hands glowing with a sickening light. From the way she was glaring at me, I guessed it was her magic that had caused the doors to open.

My gaze found Camilla.

She watched Bo and me with an amused expression from her perch on the edge of an antique table, the crystal skull resting on a velvet cloth beside her. She looked nothing like the mousy, nervous secretary I'd met at the Council meeting. Her hair was styled in an elegant chignon, her makeup was flawless, and her black dress was cut to kill.

"I was wondering when you'd figure it out." Her smile was cold. "Though I must admit, you're much sharper than I gave you credit for. It must be because you're a white wolf."

I cursed myself for overlooking what had been staring at me in the face all along.

"It was you I saw at Château Montmartre, wasn't it?" I said accusingly. "You were also wearing a dark dress."

"Yes." Camilla's eyes glittered dangerously. "I was there to collect the skull from Wheeler, but things didn't go as planned." She glanced at Marcus. "This moron interfered."

My hands curled into fists. The sinister magic radiating from the skull was making my nails lengthen and my jaw ache. My wolf slipped under my skin when she sensed the danger I was in.

"That day at the Crossroads. You deliberately bumped into me to help Wheeler escape." I could hear Nigel calling the cops in my earpiece.

"Guilty as charged." Camilla's expression turned mocking. "I must say, having you and your crew chase Wheeler around town has been most entertaining."

Bo stamped his paws. "You're not very nice, lady!"

Camilla's eyes shrank to slits. "Nice doesn't always pay in this world, mutt. I played nice for years and look where that got me."

The moonlight washing through the corridor behind me made my body itch and my bones tremble as my wolf clawed to get out. I kept her at bay by a sheer act of will and glanced at Marcus.

"Let him go. You don't have any further use for him."

"That's where you're wrong." Camilla picked up the skull and cradled it lovingly in her hands. "You see, I still need him." Her smile widened. "Just like I need everyone downstairs to be good and stay put."

The pieces of the puzzle clicked into place like death knolls inside my head. Dread churned my stomach.

"You're going to use the skull to control the supernatural creatures at tonight's ball, aren't you?"

Didi and Gavin gasped in my ear.

"Finally caught up, have you?" Camilla's voice dripped with contempt. "I am done pandering to stuck-up werewolves and their antiquated Council. Done bowing and scraping to vampire aristocrats who think they're better than everyone else." Her eyes blazed. "It's time Amberford had a new leadership."

"You're—you're insane!" Marcus choked out. He was glaring at Camilla with glowing amber eyes, his wolf on show.

"Shut up." Camilla glowered at him. "You're just as weak as your damn father. He would still be alive if only he'd listened to me!"

I froze, my eyes rounding. Bo whined.

Marcus paled. "What—what are you talking about?"

"Arthur discovered what I was planning to do with the skull. He stole it and left it at that witch's shop." Camilla's face twisted. "It took me ten years to find the damn thing. Unfortunately, Arthur had to die for his mistake."

Horror dawned on Marcus's face. "You—you killed my father?!"

"Someone had to." Camilla shrugged. "He was going to expose my plans to the Council."

Yup, Camilla was batshit crazy.

"You're a monster," I growled.

Camilla gave me a callous look. "Aren't we all?" She signaled silently to her henchmen.

The witch raised her hands. Magic crackled between her fingers. It grew into a dazzling ball of light that made the hairs rise on the back of my neck.

"Don't let that hit you!" Didi yelled in my ear.

The third vampire launched himself at me, silver knife glinting.

I ducked under his swing, grabbed his arm, and used his momentum to throw him into a wall. He hit it with a satisfying crunch that dented the plaster.

Bo snarled and went for the witch's ankles just as she cast her magic at me. She shrieked and stumbled, her attack ruffling my hair as it whizzed past my head before obliterating the door behind me.

The vampires holding Marcus threw him aside and advanced on me, fangs gleaming.

My wolf bared her teeth back as she pressed against my skin.

The vampires hesitated.

A yelp had my head snapping to the left. The witch had kicked Bo and sent him flying into the antique desk. Marcus grabbed her around the waist as she attempted to stamp on Bo's head.

Rage burned through my veins.

Camilla was skirting the room toward the exit, the crystal skull in hand.

The vampires attacked.

I stopped a punch to my head with my fist, crushed the first vampire's hand, and narrowly missed a magic blast as I elbowed the second vampire lunging for my throat viciously in the face.

The first vampire kicked me in my flank and sent me staggering sideways.

It was enough for the witch to fire off another energy blast while she struggled against Marcus. I gasped as it slammed into my left shoulder and sent me flying into a bookcase. I landed on the floor with a thud, Didi's shout echoing in my ear.

That did not go as planned.

Bo rose shakily and limped toward me, anxious whimpers working up his throat.

I groaned and rolled to my feet. "I'm okay."

Though the magic stung something fierce, it hadn't broken through skin or bone.

I lifted my head and glared at the witch and the vampires blocking my path while Camilla made her escape. Marcus was on the floor, all but knocked out.

"Didi, we're moving to Plan B!" I snapped. "Let Samuel know what's happening!"

Camilla laughed from the doorway. "Your precious alpha and his friends downstairs won't be able to hear you. Not with the magic my witch cast. And they're about to get very busy."

A loud rumble shook the mansion. Distant screams

erupted from the direction of the ballroom. Fear squeezed my heart.

"What did you do?!" I snarled.

"Let's just say the party just got interesting." Camilla's eyes glowed with malevolent glee. "Get rid of her and bring Marcus to the ballroom. I want to see Priscilla's face when I kill her precious son in front of her." She vanished into the corridor.

The vampires and witch advanced on me, their expressions murderous.

"Any last words?" the witch sneered.

"Yeah." I gave them a dark smile as I finally let the beast inside me loose. "You should have brought more backup."

My wolf surged forward, the dress Claudette had chosen for tonight shimmering and changing with me as I transformed.

Like the Hawthornes had promised, this time shifting was as easy as breathing.

The vampires and witch froze, their faces turning ashen at the sight of my white wolf.

"Holy shit," one of them breathed.

Bo's hackles rose.

I launched myself at the nearest vampire, my jaws snapping. He screamed when my teeth sank into his shoulder. I used my momentum to throw him into his companion. The witch cast another energy blast. I dodged it and pounced, my claws raking her arms as she tried to shield herself.

The third vampire came at me with his silver knife. I twisted away from his swing and clamped my jaws around his wrist while Bo bit his calf. He howled as bones crunched and flesh gave way.

The knife clattered to the floor.

Footsteps thundered in the corridor. A pair of figures skidded into view in the library doorway.

"Duck!" Didi yelled.

I dropped as a fireball whooshed over my head and struck the witch square in the belly right as she'd been preparing to launch another attack. She flew backward and hit the wall with a sickening sound.

Gavin's horns and nostrils smoked as he and Didi rushed in.

The vampires lunged at them.

Didi blasted one away with magic and cast her broomstick straight into the jaw of a second vampire, knocking him out. Gavin sent the third vampire flying into the fireplace with a powerful strike from his tail.

I transformed back into my human form, my dress rippling with the change.

"Are you guys okay?" Didi asked anxiously as she helped a groaning Marcus to his feet.

"We're fine." I grimaced at Bo's limp. "Though Bo might need to see a vet."

"I do not!" my dog protested. "It's just a scratch."

"You're bleeding."

"We've got bigger problems," Gavin said grimly. "We can't get into the ballroom. There's some kind of magical barrier stopping anyone from going in or out."

Like things couldn't get any worse.

I scowled. "What about Samuel and the others?"

"We lost contact with them a few minutes ago," Didi

said darkly. "Nigel's coordinating with the supernatural task force, but it will take a while before help gets here. From what we could see through the windows of the ballroom before the barrier went up, it's chaos in there. Those vampire mercenaries are using silver-tipped and wolfsbane-coated weapons to fight the werewolves. The witch in the red dress is overpowering the other guests with magic."

Another tremor shook the mansion. The sounds of fighting echoed from below.

"Let's go." I headed for the door, my wolf prowling restlessly under my skin. "And someone grab that knife. We might need it."

Didi scooped up the silver weapon. "What about him?" She jerked her head at Marcus.

The Holt heir's face had hardened. "I'm coming with you. Camilla killed my father." His stutter was gone, fury making his eyes burn amber.

"Fine." I gave him a stern look. "But you do exactly what we say."

Marcus nodded.

We ran for the stairs and followed the sounds of supernatural warfare to the ballroom.

WHITE WOLF

I FELT THE WALL OF MAGIC BEFORE I SAW IT. ALL THE hairs rose on my body.

Judging from the others' reactions, they felt it too.

We turned a corner and came in sight of the hallway leading to the ballroom. Pale light crackled eerily at the end. Blood pounded in my veins as we bolted toward it

My stomach plummeted when I reached the barrier. The scene beyond was pure bedlam.

Werewolves and vampires fought each other viciously across the floor, their formal wear in tatters and their faces twisted with rage. Other supernatural creatures clashed between them, banshees lashing out at fae and pixies while dwarves and dragon newts went at each other with axes—which had materialized from somewhere unknown—and fireballs. The witches were hurling spells at anyone who got in their way and seemed oblivious to the friendly fire they were incurring.

I swallowed. It had already begun.

"What—what's going on?!" Marcus said numbly.

"Camilla activated the curse," I said grimly, scanning the ballroom.

"There!" Didi pointed.

Camilla stood on the dais previously occupied by the string quartet, the crystal skull glowing ominously in her hands. The witch in the red dress was beside her, along with more vampire mercenaries. Camilla laughed cruelly as she watched the supernatural elite of Amberford tear each other apart.

Dread knotted my shoulders when I caught a glimpse of Samuel and Gregory Tremaine lunging at each other's throats in the melee.

"Snap out of it, dammit!" Samuel roared at Gregory.

I blinked. Samuel sounded like he was in control of his senses.

Gregory opened his mouth in a wide snarl, his eyes glassy and his claws ripping Samuel's tuxedo to shreds. The Hawthorne alpha slammed his shoulder into the vampire's chest and sent him crashing into a pillar.

Relief made me weak when my gaze found the rest of the Hawthornes and the Luptons. They were defending themselves against vampire mercenaries and other supernatural creatures while protecting a group next to the terrace doors, the elderly Council members and Priscilla among them.

Kent picked up a vampire and slammed him into the marble floor, his eyes watering from wolfsbane exposure. Caroline kneed a werewolf in the balls and sent a group of pixies slamming into the barrier. Hugh was punching fae and witches in the throat. Lauren and Beatrice had transformed and were snapping their jaws at the dragon newts trying to attack.

I was wondering why the curse had not affected their minds when I spotted Pearl. The cat stood close to Victoria, her eyes glowing with a mystical light that made my pulse quicken. I knew instinctively she was the reason why Samuel and the others had not fallen under the influence of the curse.

"How are they keeping this barrier up?" Didi asked tensely, bringing my focus back to our most immediate problem. She touched the wall gingerly and winced when static burned her fingers. "This thing contains an insane amount of magic!"

"Camilla's using the ley lines under the mansion," Marcus said in a hard voice. "Look at her feet."

A strange light pulsed through the marble floor beneath the Council secretary. The witch in the red dress had jabbed a weird-looking object into the dais next to her.

"Dammit!" Didi cursed. "That's an artifact. They must be using it to tap into the magic beneath this place!"

I fisted my hands. "We need to get in there." An idea came to me then. One born of my wolf's instincts. I looked at the knife in Didi's hand. "Give me that."

"What?" Didi's eyes rounded. "But—it will burn you!"

"I don't think it will." At least, I hoped it didn't.
Didi hesitated.
I met the witch's eyes steadily. "Trust me."

An anxious whine escaped Bo as Didi carefully handed me the weapon.

I steeled myself and took it. The knife felt cool in my hand.

I swallowed. It seemed my suspicions were correct.

I was immune to silver and wolfsbane.

I listened to my wolf, jammed the knife in the base of the magic barrier, and carved an opening in the wall.

The others gasped.

"How the hell did you do that?!" Didi mumbled.

"Silver. And probably because I'm a white wolf." I eyed them hesitantly. "I'm pretty sure I'll be able to resist the spell, but there's a chance you'll fall under it the minute you step inside that ballroom."

"We're coming with you," Marcus said adamantly. He glanced at Priscilla. "I have to protect Mother."

"What he said," Didi muttered while Gavin nodded.

I looked at Bo.

"You're not leaving me out here," my dog said mutinously.

"Alright. Just don't blame me if I end up knocking you guys out."

I grabbed the edges of the opening and stretched it so we could pass through.

The witch on the dais startled when she felt the break in the barrier. She looked over, narrowed her eyes, and said something to Camilla.

Camilla's gaze found mine.

I bared my teeth, pointed at her and me, and made a deliberate throat-slicing motion with my thumb.

"Remind me never to piss you off," Didi muttered.

Camilla barked an order to the vampire mercenaries. Half the group jumped off the dais and headed toward us.

I cracked my knuckles. "Time to get this show started."

The curse washed over me like a wave when I stepped inside the ballroom. Bar tickling my skin, it did nothing to me.

I checked the others carefully as they joined me. Everyone seemed surprisingly okay. I furrowed my brow.

Was it the effect of being close to a white wolf?

There was no more time to think as the first wave of vampire mercenaries reached us.

I grabbed one of the men by the throat, spun, and hurled him into a wall. "Bo, head over to Pearl and the others!"

Bo fidgeted before making his way across the room with a slight limp.

Didi and Gavin engaged the mercenaries alongside me. Marcus transformed into a black wolf and lunged at his attackers with an angry snarl.

Priscilla's eyes widened across the way when she saw her son. "*Marcus!*"

Lauren's wolf snapped her head around. Relief brightened her eyes at the sight of Marcus.

A fireball struck the ground next to Didi's left foot before I could make sense of what I was seeing.

"Hey, watch it!" the witch snapped as she blasted a mercenary in the face with her magic.

"Sorry!" Gavin said while merrily setting fire to a vampire's clothes.

I was beginning to suspect the reason his and Didi's last surveillance job had gone wrong was because the dragon newt was actually a pyromaniac.

"Can you guys handle the rest of the mercs?" I asked them.

"Leave it to us." Didi's broomstick hummed eagerly as she used it to assault a vampire somewhere no vampire should ever get assaulted.

Marcus's wolf whimpered and looked at me beseechingly.

I punched another vampire's lights out and sighed. "Alright, you can come with me."

We made our way across the ballroom, Marcus staying in his wolf form to help me keep the other supernatural creatures at bay. Despite baring their teeth at us and growling, no one tried to attack.

I was wondering why when it dawned on me then that the eerie sensation I'd experienced at the Den was back. I hesitated before focusing on the feeling and staring the creatures we passed in the eye. Their glazed looks faded. Some of the werewolves shook their heads and looked around, confused.

My mouth went dry. Was my presence acting like an antidote to the skull's curse?!

We finally came in sight of Samuel. I scowled, dragged the dragon newt attacking him away by the tail, and sent him flying into a champagne tower.

"Hands off my alpha, you damn lizard!"

Samuel gaped before recovering his composure and engulfing me in a bear hug. He pulled back and scanned me worriedly, his touch making my wolf whine.

"Are you okay?!"

I nodded then noticed the faint burns on his hands and face. They were already healing. Still, the fact that he'd gotten hurt set my rage level to the max.

"Marcus, go protect your mother," I ground out. "Samuel and I will finish off that shrew."

EVERYONE GETS A TIME OUT

WE WATCHED MARCUS SCAMPER OVER TOWARD Priscilla before we began clearing a path to the dais, the mate bond humming between us helping to coordinate our movements.

"You know," Samuel said as he threw a vampire casually over his shoulder without breaking a sweat, "this isn't exactly how I planned our first date to go."

I grabbed a lunging fae by the throat, tossed her across the ballroom, and arched an eyebrow. "This was supposed to be our first date?"

"Yeah."

I ducked under a witch's spell, kicked her legs out from under her, and winced when I heard bone crunch. "If this is standard courtship in werewolf society, maybe we should revisit the rules."

Samuel grinned. A werewolf jumped on him and took him to the ground.

I peeled the offending figure off and booted him

across the ballroom with a snarled, "Excuse me, we're having a conversation here!"

I helped Samuel up and scanned our surroundings. "We have to stop this infighting before the supernatural elite of Amberford rip each other to pieces."

Samuel's tone turned steely. "There is only one way to do that."

Our narrow-eyed gazes found Camilla.

My voice deepened to a growl as I let my beast slip under my skin. "Shall we finish this?"

Samuel's eyes flashed amber. "Yes."

We transformed and bounded toward the dais, our wolves knocking adversaries out of the way with ease.

Camilla's eyes blazed as she spotted us approaching. The witch in red did something with her artifact. Magic surged through the ley lines, making the floor vibrate.

The crystal skull's glow intensified.

Samuel's wolf spoke in my head. *We need to get that artifact away from that witch.*

We could do with a distraction.

Did someone say distraction? Hugh appeared beside us in his wolf form. He was grinning manically and his pupils were slightly dilated.

Samuel groaned. *Please tell me you didn't just take werewolf nip?!*

I did not. Hugh's wolf whined. *Where the hell would I get my hands on werewolf nip around here?!*

I studied him warily. *Then why do you look stoned?*

Hugh's wolf had the grace to look abashed. *I think*

the werewolf nip still in my system is reacting with the curse and making me hyper.

That explained his earlier enthusiastic throat punching.

I looked at Samuel and did the wolf version of a shrug. *There's no better distraction than a werewolf high on drugs.*

Samuel's wolf sagged. *I never thought the day would come when I said this.* He straightened and commanded Hugh. *Go over there and do something crazy.*

Hugh beamed and charged the dais with a demented howl.

"Kill them!" Camilla screamed at her remaining mercenaries.

The vampires hesitated, clearly thrown by the unexpected assault tactic that was a crazed werewolf.

I used their confusion to circle around while Samuel engaged them head-on.

Hugh waited until I reached the back of the dais before snarling and lunging menacingly at the witch. She startled and turned to blast him with her magic.

I pounced in a flash, grabbed the artifact with my jaws, and yanked it free.

The magic it contained stung my tongue. I held on fast and crunched down viciously.

The ley lines' power cut off abruptly. The witch staggered, her magic flickering. She spun around, horror widening her eyes as I spat out the remains.

"*No!*"

The barrier fell.

Camilla raised the skull, her expression defiant. "You're too late! The curse is already active!"

My heart sank as I looked at the ballroom. She was right. Though some of the supernatural creatures had broken free of the spell, most were still fighting.

My wolf stilled when I spotted Gregory and Constantia cornering Victoria and Pearl.

"They're all going to tear each other apart!" Camilla laughed maniacally. "And then I'll be the only one left to rule Amberford!"

I ground my teeth. As Pearl would put it, the woman was officially batshit crazy.

I shifted to human Abby and strode toward Camilla.

"You know what your problem is?" I snarled. "You talk too much!"

I put the full power of my wolf behind me and lunged. Camilla grunted as I tackled her to the ground in a tangle of limbs and evening wear. The skull slipped from her hands and flew in the air.

"*No!*" she screamed.

We both dove for it as it started its inevitable descent.

Unfortunately for Camilla, I was faster.

I backkicked her viciously in the stomach, pushed up, and jumped, my fingers clawing like I was trying to catch a lacrosse ball. The skull hit the wall of air in front of my hand and rolled gently into my grasp.

Magic surged through me when the cool crystal kissed my skin. I gasped.

It was old and powerful and dark.

"*Give it back!*" Camilla screeched like a banshee.

She stumbled to her feet and pounced.

Samuel hit her from the side and sent her sliding off the dais.

My jaw tightened as I gripped the skull in both hands and fought to control the ancient magic inside it. I was seriously wishing my werewolf lessons had included a session on how to undo curses when my wolf slipped under my skin and whispered in my ear.

I blinked and looked to the ballroom. I knew exactly what I had to do to end the spell. The hairs rose on the back of my neck as I tapped into the skull's power instead of fighting it.

"Everyone STOP FIGHTING and SIT THE HELL DOWN!"

The effect was instantaneous. Every supernatural creature sat down with a thump, Samuel included. A champagne tower collapsed with an embarrassed tinkle in the fraught hush that swept across the ballroom like a tidal wave.

I became the focus of a sea of mortified stares.

Well shit. Who knew the command would be so humiliatingly effective?

"This is worse than obedience school," Bo commented awkwardly from his sitting position.

Several werewolves whined in agreement.

"I totally meant to do that," Pearl sniffed, somehow maintaining her dignity despite having plopped down in the middle of clawing Gregory's face.

Victoria was squatting on the vampire, her expression stringent.

"Can you get off me now?" Gregory groaned.

"Does it look like I can get off you?!" Victoria snapped. "Just shut up and stay put until whatever the hell this is wears off."

Constantia looked murderous where she sat obediently a few feet away.

Beatrice shifted back into her human form and began filming with the phone she'd somehow managed to recover from her mother. "This is totally going viral!"

Danielle's eyes rounded at the sight of the device. She patted her purse urgently before squinting at her daughter. "Beatrice, put that darn thing away *right now!*"

"What and miss the cream of Amberford society making complete fools of themselves?!" Beatrice protested.

"Hey, you're infringing on our supernatural rights!" a witch complained.

A group of dwarves and dragon newts groused in agreement.

Lauren smirked at Samuel's wolf where she was sitting seiza style next to her sister. "Not so high and mighty now, are you?"

Samuel's wolf scowled.

My gaze found Camilla. She had her butt firmly planted on the ground and was glaring daggers at me. I was about to say something sharp and pithy when the ground shook violently beneath my feet.

Now what?!

Dazzling light flashed through the crack the witch's artifact had made in the dais. It grew until it blinded the entire ballroom, me included. I grunted when something heavy fell on top of me.

I landed on my front with a curse and barely managed to keep hold of the skull. It took a moment to blink away the black spots swarming my vision.

The ballroom came into view. Everyone was gaping at me.

"Holy crap," someone mumbled.

I squeezed my eyes shut briefly and prayed Camilla's evil scheme hadn't just dragged some kind of demon from the depths of Hell before cautiously turning my head.

A man with long hair and an unkempt beard was blinking at me. He smelled like a werewolf and looked bewildered.

He was also very naked.

My wolf went *Uh-oh* as the mate bond heated up.

Samuel changed into his human form and glared at the stranger.

"*Get off Abby, you lout!*"

"Fa-Father?!" Marcus stammered in a trembling voice.

Priscilla gasped and pressed her fingers to her mouth, her face crumbling. "*Arthur!*"

I did not see that one coming.

AFTERMATH (WITH EXTRA AWKWARD)

"MA'AM?"

I turned to find a sergeant from the supernatural task force hovering nervously next to me where I stood on the terrace outside the ballroom of the Holt mansion. He was one of the few officers who'd arrived with Nigel after I'd used the crystal skull's power and therefore wasn't currently stuck on his butt, unlike many of his unfortunate and very embarrassed colleagues.

"Yes?"

"It's been two hours." Sergeant Holmes grimaced. "Detective Johnson is getting tired of being under Officer Brigham. Also, half the guests are complaining about numbness in their nether regions." He hesitated. "Any idea when this command of yours might wear off?"

I peered inside the ballroom. Most of the supernatural creatures were indeed still firmly planted on their backsides, their expressions ranging from mortified to possibly murderous. The Lincoln sisters had started a game of cards with Didi and Gavin. Helen was sulking in a corner. Gregory was attempting to maintain his dignity while Victoria used him as an ottoman and discussed pack matters with Caroline and Kent. The dragon newts and the dwarves were hurling insults at the vampire mercenaries and witch who'd assisted Camilla, the Council of Elders assisting with elegantly pointed barbs. The fae and the pixies were having some kind of lighting competition, which meant the place now looked like a chic club with a glitzy disco ball.

As for the officers who'd managed to get inside when the barrier fell, they were looking distinctively uncomfortable at being in such close proximity with Amberford's supernatural elite.

"I'm sorry, I have no idea." I made a face. "Using an ancient cursed artifact wasn't top of my to-do list tonight, believe it or not."

Samuel had broken free of the skull's effect and was drinking a coffee beside me. Hugh had also emerged from the spell early, a fact we were attributing to the werewolf nip.

Sergeant Holmes sighed. "Right."

"Look on the bright side." Bo wagged his tail. "At least no one's trying to kill each other anymore."

"Word," Pearl said stoically beside him.

Sergeant Holmes studied them warily. News of the pair had already circulated among the officers, not least because Pearl had spent a good part of an hour criticizing Amberford's socialites about their unseeming behavior.

Pearl having extricated herself early from the humiliating spell I could put down to the fact that she wasn't an ordinary cat. Plus there was that weird light she'd projected from her eyes to protect the Hawthornes and the Luptons from the skull's curse.

As for Bo, the jury was still out on how he'd managed the feat.

Sergeant Holmes took off his hat and sighed. "Arresting the perpetrators is going to be interesting. We've cuffed the ones we found in the library." He glanced at where Camilla sat scowling. "We'll have to wait until the spell wears off before we can move any of them." He scratched the back of his head. "Maybe we should order takeout."

One of his colleagues overheard him.

"I want pizza," the officer called out where he squatted atop a vampire mercenary. "And someone better expense this!"

The mercenary raised a hand shyly. "Could I have a type-O, garlic-free, pepperoni pizza?"

"May I remind everyone that I'm still in charge of this operation?" Detective Johnson said indignantly from under Officer Brigham. He waited until his officers stopped grousing before addressing Holmes as haughtily as a man who was being squatted on could. "Hawaiian for me, please."

The whole ballroom quickly dissolved into an argument about why pineapple on pizza was the epitome of the devil's work.

My gaze found the Holts. Someone had given Arthur clothes. He sat with his arms around Priscilla and Marcus, waiting for the spell to wear off. Priscilla looked like a different woman after their tearful reunion, her expression speaking volumes about her adoration for her husband.

Samuel and I went to check on the crystal skull after Sergeant Holmes left. It looked deceptively harmless where it sat in a velvet-lined box in the back of the forensics team van.

I was not fooled.

The magic it emitted still made my skin crawl.

"What will happen to it now?" I asked warily.

"The supernatural task force will take it to a secure facility. After that, we have to decide what to do with it."

"We?"

Samuel's face tightened. "The Amberford Alliance. I intend to take you to the next meeting."

I liked the sound of that about as much as I liked the idea of waxing my boobs.

He sighed at my crestfallen expression. "It can't be helped." He pressed a kiss to my brow that made my skin tingle. "You did good tonight."

"Thanks." I leaned against him and tried not to think too hard about the fact that his torn clothes exposed parts of his anatomy my wolf and I very much wanted to explore. "Though I could have done without Arthur Holt emerging from the ley lines stark naked."

The bond between us hummed with his irritation.

"Everyone could have done without that."

❄

IT WAS WELL AFTER MIDNIGHT WHEN WE ARRIVED AT THE Hawthorne mansion with the Holts, tired and disheveled. Caroline and Kent had gone home to check on their kids. Since Lauren had insisted on accompanying the Holts, the Luptons tagged along. Despite the hour, Bernard arranged beverages and snacks for everyone in the formal sitting room.

"I still can't believe you were trapped in the ley lines all this time." Priscilla clutched Arthur's hand where they sat on a couch.

Marcus had fetched his father's old clothes before we'd left the Holt mansion. Despite his hair and beard, Arthur looked remarkably well for someone who'd spent ten years in magical limbo.

"It was my own fault." Arthur grimaced. "I'd forgotten I was carrying a magical artifact in my pocket when I returned from leaving the crystal skull at Mystical Moments that night."

"Why did Camilla claim she'd killed you?" I asked where I sat beside Samuel.

Marcus pressed close to his father at the question, his face turning ashen again as he no doubt recalled the awful revelation Camilla had made in the library.

"I have no idea." Arthur gently squeezed his son's shoulders. "That woman is crazy. Who knows what goes on inside her head?"

He had a point. Camilla had looked decidedly unhinged while she'd been wielding the crystal skull.

"Only a werewolf would forget about a magical

artifact in his pocket," Pearl scoffed. "This is why proper supernatural creatures use designer handbags."

Victoria and Danielle nodded wisely. Priscilla sighed.

"What exactly happened the night you disappeared?" Samuel asked curiously.

Arthur's expression darkened. "I'd discovered Camilla's plans for the crystal skull the week before I got sucked into the ley lines. As you probably know, I've always been fascinated by the occult. When Camilla originally approached me and expressed an interest in similar matters, I presumed her enthusiasm was benign. She was the one who convinced me to track down the crystal skull at an auction and buy it." A muscle jumped in his cheek. "We were at a luncheon organized by a society with a special interest in occult arts to discuss the artifact I'd purchased when I overheard Camilla talking to a witch about how to access the ley lines beneath our mansion. I confronted her about it later that afternoon. She got upset and let it slip that she was obsessed with the idea of controlling supernatural creatures." He hesitated and looked at Victoria. "There's something else. Before I disappeared, I found evidence suggesting she might have been behind the attempts on Alexander's life."

Victoria paled. Samuel exchanged a frown with Hugh.

"It's just a theory," Arthur added hastily in the fraught silence.

Pearl's eyes shrank to slits. "It would explain many

things. Though I still think the attempts behind Alexander's life originated from several sources."

Samuel's jaw tightened. "We may never know the full truth."

"And I doubt Camilla will cooperate with the supernatural task force's interrogation," Victoria murmured, her knuckles white where she clasped her cup.

"By the way, why exactly did you want to be here?" Hugh asked Lauren.

Lauren arched an eyebrow at Marcus. "It's now or never."

I stared between them, puzzled.

Marcus cleared his throat in the expectant hush. "Father, Mother, there's something I need to tell you."

Priscilla wrinkled her brow at her son's nervous tone. "What is it?"

"Lauren and I are—are together."

Priscilla froze. Bernard's monocle fell out of his eye.

Danielle choked on her tea. "What?!"

"Oh boy," Beatrice muttered.

Pearl swished her tail languidly, her eyes sparkling with fascination. "What an unlikely pairing."

"Not that unlikely." Lauren sauntered over to Marcus and pulled him to his feet. "We're perfect for each other."

Marcus's ears reddened.

This explained a lot of things.

"So Samuel really isn't your type?" I hazarded.

Samuel scowled at me. "How could you think that?!"

Lauren grimaced. "Please. Like I want to bed that beast. I like my men soft and pliable." She gazed fondly at Marcus. "It makes it easier to tie them up and—"

Marcus hastily pressed a hand to her mouth, his face bright red. He yelped when Lauren bit his palm.

"Now, now, Pookie Bear, there's no need to be shy," Lauren crooned.

Beatrice and Hugh made identical gagging noises before exchanging a startled glance. They both looked away and blushed.

I stared. I'd evidently completely misread that situation too.

Danielle looked beseechingly at the ceiling and muttered under her breath. Victoria leaned over and patted her gently on the shoulder.

Arthur was trying to calm a spluttering Priscilla.

"But—but, you can't!" Priscilla blurted out. "Marcus is going to be the next alpha of our pack! He can't possibly marry into the Luptons!"

"I'm not intending him to marry into the Luptons," Lauren drawled. "I will be marrying into the Holts and I'll support Marcus in his role as the next alpha." She shrugged nonchalantly. "After all, I'm the strongest enforcer in Connecticut."

Arthur watched this unfold with surprising equanimity. "Well, at least the Holt pack will be in good hands."

Danielle frowned at her eldest daughter. "Aren't you forgetting your own pack?"

Lauren pointed at her younger sister. "You just have to have Beatrice marry Hugh."

"What?!" Beatrice squealed.

"I don't know what you mean!" Hugh protested.

Bo wagged his tail. "You've both gone beetroot red."

"Oh God," Victoria mumbled. "Bernard, can you pour some whiskey into my coffee?"

"You're drinking tea, ma'am."

"Then give it to me neat!" Victoria snapped.

I wished I could take up drinking too, but the last time I did that, I ended up becoming a werewolf.

It was at this point that Lauren dipped Marcus dramatically and proceeded to kiss him princess style. The whole room sucked in air, Bernard almost dropping the whiskey decanter.

I recovered first and stole a look at the couch where the Holts sat.

"Quick, Priscilla is foaming at the mouth!"

38

EPILOGUE - THE THING ABOUT ALPHAS

It was another hour before the Holts and the Luptons finally left.

Victoria and Hugh said goodnight and climbed the stairs to their rooms.

Samuel sighed where he and I stood in the foyer.

"It's late. Why don't you just stay the night?"

I chewed my lip. There were many questions that still needed answers. What was Pearl's power? How had my wolf known how to use the crystal skull? Where the hell had the dwarves hidden the axes they'd wielded in the ballroom and what was their beef with dragon newts?

I decided that those could all wait until later.

"Are you asking me to check out your bedroom?" I raised an eyebrow full of hope.

Samuel blinked, surprised. His eyes darkened behind his glasses, the flash of amber in their depths making my pulse quicken. "You sure you're ready for what will happen if you do?"

His voice had dropped to an octave that made my wolf stand to attention and wag her tail.

"I think so," I managed in a strangled voice. "How about you lead the way and we go find out?"

A chuckle left him. He offered me his hand. I took it, his touch scalding my skin.

We started for the stairs.

I realized Bo was following us.

"Go away," I told my dog firmly.

Bo blinked innocently. "I promise I'll be quiet as a—"

Samuel pointed imperiously in the direction of Victoria's study. "Why don't you use this opportunity to spend some time with your bosom buddy Pearl?"

"I don't think her basket is gonna be big enough for the two of us."

"There's a Persian rug in Victoria's office," I pointed out.

This piqued my dog's interest. "I've never slept on one of those before." He wagged his tail and disappeared in the direction of the study.

"Do you think he knows?" Samuel asked quietly.

"That he's a supernatural creature?" I wrinkled my nose. "I don't think so."

It was the only explanation as to why Bo had fallen under the skull's spell when I'd issued the command that had ended the battle.

Samuel and I climbed the stairs, the mate bond a live wire that made my nerves sing with anticipation. He stiffened when we reached his bedroom door, his expression that of a man who'd just recalled something vitally important.

"Er, give me a minute."

He slipped inside his bedroom. I grinned when I heard frantic rustling and the sound of things being shoved into drawers. Samuel returned and opened the door, slightly breathless.

"Come in."

I looked around curiously as I walked past him.

His quarters occupied the west wing of the mansion's second floor. Like his office at Hawthorne & Associates, it was a perfect blend of old money and modern comfort. Antique furniture mixed with contemporary pieces, including a California king bed with an elaborately carved headboard that probably cost more than my new car. Floor-to-ceiling windows offered a view of the gardens and forest beyond, while built-in bookcases crammed with everything from ancient texts to modern business magazines lined one wall.

I spied a door leading to a walk-in closet that would make Claudette weep with joy and another opening into a private bathroom that looked like it belonged in a luxury spa. Everything was meticulously organized, though I caught glimpses of hastily hidden chaos in the closet where Samuel had done his emergency clean-up.

"Nice place," I said, trying not to focus on the bed.

"Thanks." Samuel adjusted his glasses a little self-consciously. "Though Mother keeps telling me to hire an interior decora—"

I turned and twisted the lock with a decisive click.

"Er, Abby, why are you locking the door?" Samuel asked nervously.

I flashed him a predatory smile over my shoulder.

He gulped.

A LOUD THUD WOKE ME THE NEXT MORNING.

I opened my eyes, squinted at the bright sunlight streaming through the windows, and stretched languorously on luxurious Egyptian cotton sheets. I rolled over and found Samuel on his knees on the floor next to the bed, gloriously naked and groaning.

I licked my lips as I admired the teeth marks decorating his rather spectacular behind.

He sensed my stare and stiffened.

"What's the matter?" I asked nonchalantly.

"I was trying to go to the bathroom," he mumbled. "My back seized up." He scowled at my heated look. "No, we're not going for another around!"

"Why not?"

"Because apparently the famed Hawthorne stamina pales in comparison to a white wolf's!" he snapped.

I had the decency to blush a little. It had indeed been a night of hitherto undiscovered delights. I doubted any luna had ever ridden her alpha like a bronco before.

I was trying to convince him another round might cure his back when a knock came at the door.

"Your morning coffee and paper, sir," Bernard called out dutifully.

Samuel's eyes widened in horror.

Bernard tried the handle in vain. A key turned in the lock from the outside. I threw a blanket on Samuel and yanked the bed sheet up to my neck just as the door opened.

Bernard stepped inside the room, froze, and mutely dropped the tray in his hands. It crashed at his feet and sent a newspaper skittering across the floor.

It hit Samuel's ankle.

"Oh God." My alpha buried his face in one hand.

The blanket slid off his back a little, exposing a buttock adorned with teeth marks.

"What was that?!" Hugh shouted in the distance.

Footsteps thundered in the corridor.

Hugh burst into view. He was closely followed by Victoria, Bo, and Pearl.

It was clear everyone was still nervous after last night's events and revelations.

They all froze at the sight of Samuel kneeling naked on the floor.

I held the sheet to my chest and beamed at them from the bed. "Morning."

Victoria's face glazed over. "Oh. Hi, Abby."

"What happened to Samuel?" Hugh asked warily.

Pearl wrinkled her nose. "It seems his stamina needs work. I must say I'm disappointed, Samuel. A proper alpha should be able to last more than one night."

"Kill me now," Samuel mumbled.

A strangled sound finally left Bernard.

Victoria patted the butler's shoulder with a "There, there, why don't I make you a drink?"

The blanket fell off Samuel.

Bo cocked his head. His eyes bulged. "Wow! Look at the size of his ding-a—"

I threw a pillow at him before he could finish that sentence.

THE END

Abby and Bo's adventures continue in How to Stake a Vampire.

Make sure to sign up to my store newsletter for special deals on my books and new release alerts. Or you can sign up to my author newsletter to get upcoming release notifications, sneak peeks, and giveaways.

ACKNOWLEDGMENTS

To my friends and family. I couldn't do this without you.

To my readers. Thank you for reading It All Started with a Bite. I hope this crazy new series full of wacky, unforgettable characters had you howling out aloud! If you enjoyed my book, please consider leaving a review on Goodreads or on the store where you purchased it. Reviews help readers like you find my books and I truly appreciate your honest opinions about my stories.

BOOKS BY A.D. STARRLING

SEVENTEEN NOVELS

Hunted

Warrior

Empire

Legacy

Origins

Destiny

SEVENTEEN SHORT STORIES

First Death

Dancing Blades

The Meeting

The Warrior Monk

The Hunger

The Bank Job

LEGION

Blood and Bones

Fire and Earth

Awakening

Forsaken

Hallowed Ground

Heir

Legion

WITCH QUEEN

The Darkest Night

Rites of Passage

Of Flames and Crows

Midnight Witch

A Fury of Shadows

Witch Queen

The Incubus and The Bodyguard

SEVENTEEN UNIVERSE

The Party

DIARY OF A RELUCTANT WEREWOLF

It All Started With A Bite

DIVISION EIGHT

Mission:Black

Mission: Armor

Mission:Anaconda

MISCELLANEOUS

Void - A Sci-fi Horror Short Story

The Other Side of the Wall - A Horror Short Story

ABOUT A.D. STARRLING

Visit Shop AD Starrling and buy all of AD's ebooks, paperbacks, hardbacks, audiobooks, and exclusive special edition print books direct.

Want to know about AD Starrling's upcoming releases? Sign up to her author newsletter for new release alerts, sneak peeks, giveaways, and more.

Join AD's reader group on Facebook The Seventeen Club.

Check out this link to find out more about A.D. Starrling Linktr.ee/AD_Starrling.